der ——————————————— u
for ——————————————
It's what he's asking for, George. Pay the constable to do it, if you're too softhearted yourself."

Doctor Carter shook his head. "That's hardly called for, James."

He turned back toward Michael. "You need to get over your grudge and think clearly, Michael. You can't lay blame now for what's happened in the past. Slavery's been with us a long time. Mista Harrison and I aren't responsible for it. You can't deny you've been well treated all your life, either. If I hadn't bought your mother and you at the slave auction someone else would have, who might have been a lot harder on you."

Only the last sentence registered. Michael felt frozen where he stood. When he spoke, it was with icy control. "You didn't buy my mother and me, Doctor Carter. You bought Mama, all right, but you got me for free. And got your pleasure out of my mama too!"

Mista Harrison recovered first, his face red

ing with anger. "I'd take a rawhide to yo

for your insolence, boy. If I were your master

AS FAR AS BLOOD GOES

a novel by
Rochelle H. Schwab

An Original Holloway House Edition
HOLLOWAY HOUSE PUBLISHING CO.
LOS ANGELES, CALIFORNIA

Rochelle H. Schwab was born in New York City in 1941, and grew up in New York and New Jersey. She graduated from Antioch College and earned a master's degree in sociology at Howard University. Her articles have appeared in newspapers and magazines. She has two grown daughters and lives in Alexandria, Virginia with her husband Dick, a researcher with the Federal Highway Administration.

Published by
HOLLOWAY HOUSE PUBLISHING COMPANY
8060 Melrose Avenue, Los Angeles, CA 90046
International Standard Book Number 0-87067-837-X
Printed in the United States of America
Cover illustration by Glen Tarnowski
Cover design by Jeff Renfro

To Tere Rios,
a mentor and a friend

Acknowledgements

Although I received advice and help in researching this book from many friends, colleagues and members of library staffs, the following individuals deserve special thanks: Charles Young for sharing his knowledge of early 19th century medical instruments and practices; Susan Ravdin, Assistant for Special Collections of the Bowdoin College Library for answering my questions so fully, and for supplying me with a copy of the 1835-36 catalog and regulations of the Medical School of Maine; and Alexandria Under Sheriff Richard Ruscak for showing me through the old Alexandria jail and supplying me with information on its construction. I owe thanks to Dr. Ronald Weiner for his critique of the manuscript sections dealing with microscopic research and for sharing his knowledge of cholera and microbiology; and to my nephew, William Schwab III, for taking time from his biomedical re search to review the manuscript for medical accuracy.

I found the historical study, *Black Bostonians*, by James Oliver Horton and Lois E. Horton an invaluable guide to issues and events in the ante-bellum Boston black community, and I would like to thank Dr. James Horton for his time in answering my further questions.

Any mistakes in medical or historical facts or interpretation are my own responsibility and not those of the individuals listed above.

I would also like to thank my neighbor and fellow writer, Charles A. Goodrum, for giving generously of his experience and advice; and fellow members of the Washington Independent Writers Arlington Fiction Group for their critiques and encouragement.

Finally, my husband, Dick Schwab, deserves my heartfelt thanks for his constant patience, love and support during the writing of this book.

Prologue

1815

The house was compact, as were most of the neighboring townhouses clustered along the square mile of cobblestone streets, running between the Potomac River and Shuter's Hill that formed Alexandria, Virginia, in 1815. In a shed-like room off the kitchen, a Negro woman lay on her pallet, worn by a long night of childbirth pains.

The doctor sitting at her side winced at the cries of the laboring female slave, which surely carried to the bedroom upstairs where his wife had lain in semi-invalid state since the birth of their son over a year ago. Now, as the head crowned at last, he helped ease the infant's shoulders through the birth canal. Holding the bawling newborn, he examined the boy carefully, barely admitting to himself that he looked less for well-formed limbs and clear breathing passages than to ascertain whether the child's appearance gave testimony to his half-white parentage.

The newborn's lusty cries echoed through the house as the next days passed, but they couldn't disturb Anne anymore. The ague that had kept her invalid through the winter had taken its final toll. She lay newly dead, one hand still stretched protectively toward her year old child in his cradle, her blond hair damp and heavy on the pillow.

The young doctor bowed his head, his eyes blinded by tears. He couldn't blot out the scene forever, though. He raised his head for a last look at his wife.

Annie's eyes were closed, her charm and gaiety vanished like a snuffed candle. Her brother knelt at her other side. The young man's handsome features were twisted with anguish, his hand lingering on his dead sister's.

The newborn's cries grew louder, intruding on the young man's grief. His eyes filled with anger as he looked his brother-in-law in the face. "She'd be alive now, if not for your adultery!"

The doctor shook his head in mute misery. "It was the ague took her, James. We have to accept the will of God. There was nothing else I could have done to save her."

The young man's anger grew. "Do you think Anne didn't know how you dishonored her house with your lust and rutting? No wonder she had no more will to live!"

"Anne never—" The doctor's voice broke. He looked down again, unable to meet the other man's eyes.

"You may fool yourself, George, but I know the truth of the matter. Anne was well aware of how you betrayed her while she was still laid low by her confinement!" He paused, lifting his nephew from his cradle. The one-year-old stared solemnly at his uncle, his small mouth closed around his thumb. His delicate features were a miniature of his mother's.

"Let me take Anne's son to raise. You know I'm well able to afford it, and you can rest assured I'll give him a decent,

10

Christian upbringing. Alice will welcome a child to care for at last, and you know I love David as if he were my own."

The doctor stared at him in shock. "You can't take my son from me, James! He's all I have left now that Anne is gone. You're welcome to see him as often as you like—"

The wails of the newborn infant interrupted the new widower's words. He took abrupt notice of the frightened slave woman hesitating in the doorway. "There's nothing you can do here, Hetty. For God's sake, go attend to your child."

His brother-in-law spoke again as the woman hurriedly withdrew. "No decent woman could have borne having her husband's nigger bastard born under her own roof. You didn't even have the decency to sell Hetty out of her sight. And now you're dishonoring Anne's memory by keeping the pair of them."

His handsome face hardened further. "It was Hetty having your bastard that killed her, George! You should have drowned him like a kitten the day he was born!"

Chapter 1

1822

"You ought to sell that boy!"

Michael backed away from the angrily raised voice, his bare brown feet noiseless on the pine boards as he sought the safety of the kitchen and his mother's presence. He'd never understood why Massa Carter's brother-in-law, Mista Harrison, disliked him so. But Mista Harrison never came to call without finding fault with something he'd done.

Today was no exception. Michael had set the tray on the front room table when David came home from school, pausing to greet his father and uncle.

"Your father tells me that you're reading in Murray's English Reader now." Mista Harrison smiled at David as he smoothed a stray lock of hair back from his nephew's forehead. "I'd like to hear you read a page of your lesson."

Michael edged closer to David as the older boy began reading aloud in a halting voice. How he wished he could understand the mysterious black markings! Suddenly he'd blurted out eagerly, "Can I learn to read too?"

What Massa Carter might have answered if he'd been alone, Michael didn't know. But Mista Harrison erupted as angrily as if Michael had deliberately sassed him. "I hope you've got better sense than that! Teach him his letters and you'll ruin him for good. He'll never be of use to anyone!"

"I assure you I had no thought of teaching him. I doubt it would be an easy task, anyway," Massa Carter replied.

Now Mista Harrison continued, "That boy doesn't know his place and it's your fault, George. I've told you for years you have no business raising him in your house! You ought to sell him!"

Massa Carter sighed. "I'm tired of your harping on the boy, James. He's a good playmate for David, and getting big enough to make himself useful as well. At any rate, I've promised Hetty never to sell him away from her, and her cooking suits me well enough not to make any changes."

Exhaling a held-in breath, Michael ran back to his mother. Hetty spoke in a low, harsh tone. "Boy, you gettin big enuf not to say everything comes into your head. Don't you never say nuthin to no white folks bout wantin to read. You hear me now?"

"Yes'm," Michael said. "But why can't I read? Bet I could learn good as David. What Mista Harrison mean bout it ruinin' me?"

Looking around, Hetty lowered her voice till Michael could barely hear her. "He mean readin a path to freedom for colred folks. Thass why they say it ain't allowed. Don't want no slave learnin how to run off to freedom."

Michael stared at his mother in surprise a long moment as her words sank in. He had never really thought of himself before as anything but a boy, no different than any other boy.

14

Now he said, equally softly, "I wanna be free when I growed."

"I pray it comes true," Hetty said. "But you watch your tongue in the meantime."

"I wish he *would* sell you," David told him a few minutes later. "You're just a pest following me around."

Michael shrugged. As his own sleeping place was a pallet laid at the foot of David's bed, it seemed to him he had a right to be in the bedroom too. Now he sat on the floor watching David. The older boy had opened his reader to the lesson assigned to be learned for the next day, but sat drawing with his quill pen on the back of an old copybook instead.

"And besides," David continued, "You never want to play what I do. You're my slave and you're supposed to do what I say. Uncle James says you're supposed to obey me."

"I ain't your slave. You don't own me," Michael retorted, though now he wasn't so sure.

"Well, Uncle James says I will when I'm grown, and anyway he says you should call me Master David, not just my name."

"Won't call you no massa."

"Well, you better. And you better stop always looking over my shoulder when I study my lesson, thinking you can learn how to read. Not that you could anyhow. You're nothin but a dumb nigger."

"I ain't dumb either," Michael said, stung.

Before either he or David could say anything else, Michael heard his mother calling him to come right away and fetch her a bucket of water from the corner water pump. For once, Michael was glad to be summoned from David's company.

The next few days passed no differently than the ones before. Michael helped his mother carry foodstuff home from the farmers' market, waited table at mealtimes and stole a few minutes to shoot marbles with other small boys whenever he was sent to fetch water. He and David still played with other boys, colored and white, in the back alleys and streets of the seaport town.

But inwardly, Michael felt different and confused. For one thing, David no longer wanted to play with him very often. And when he did, he acted bossy and mean. Mama said not to mind. David's own mama died when he was a baby, so no one had taught him good manners. Michael wished David hadn't learned so much meanness from his uncle, though. David was a lot less fun to play with than he used to be.

Then too, Michael realized that despite the hopes he'd had of starting school himself whenever he'd walked David to the red brick schoolhouse, he would never be allowed inside to learn reading and writing with the children there.

Worst of all, he would never grow up to be free like David would, and able to do what he wanted, but would always belong to him or someone else and have to do what they said.

Mama said reading could make you free, he thought. Right then, he made up his mind. He would learn to read. He could, too. He could shoot marbles as well as David, though at eight David was a year older, and find the others faster at hide-and-seek. There was no reason he couldn't learn to read as good as David. If he could just get someone to show him how.

Of course there were still plenty of other things to think about and do. Like Saturdays, when Massa Carter would sometimes ask David and him if they'd like to take a walk in the town. They always said yes. Their best walks ended at the wharves that stretched out into the Potomac River. There they could see sloops and schooners, their sails furled as noisily jostling men unloaded barrels of coffee, tea, sugar, salt and spices Michael didn't even know the names of, reloading the ships with salt herring and sturgeon from the Potomac, and bread and biscuits baked in the numerous Alexandria bakeries.

Even more than watching the ships being loaded and unloaded though, Michael was fascinated by Massa Carter's medical office. He never tired of marveling at the mysterious powdered medicines in their stoppered jars or the cabinet of pewter instruments, each with its own special purpose. He always asked what each was used for when he got a chance to visit, listening eagerly as Massa Carter smilingly paused to answer his questions.

It was only within the past few months that he had been allowed more than a brief peep inside the doctor's office, but now there were often small jobs that he could do there.

Massa Carter would as readily have welcomed David's help, Michael knew, but David avoided the surgery if he could. Just the sight of the lancet or bleeding basin made him turn pale and ask to be excused. Michael wasn't surprised at that. David even made him bait his hook when they went fishing.

A few days ago, Massa Carter had placed an advertisement in the Alexandria Gazette, a testimonial by one of his patients to the swift relief his treatment had given her.

"From a solemn sense of duty, I do hereby declare to the world, that I was afflicted with the dropsy for a long time, accompanied with a nervous weakness, indigestion and pain in my breast, for the removal of which disorders I used a variety of medicine, supposed calculated to effect this desirable end, but all to no purpose. In this hopeless condition, I applied to Dr. George Carter, about twelve months ago, and by the use and continuance of his medicine, a considerable quantity of water was in about three weeks discharged, and in about six weeks my complicated disorders became totally removed, when I found myself as well and as hearty as ever. Signed, Mary McDowell, Sworn before M.D. Tilden, August 10, 1822," he read aloud, when the notice appeared.

"And well situated to attract attention, at the top of the front page," he said to Mista Harrison, satisfaction in his voice. He hadn't yet been paid by Missus McDowell, Michael heard him add, but the increase in patients her testimonial might bring would be worth more than one fee.

This morning, saying his stock of medicines was scarcely adequate in case of need, he had sent Michael on an errand to the apothecary shop to get some calomel and emetic tartar.

Returning with the parcel, Michael stood quietly watching Massa Carter grind up medicines and store them in stoppered jars. "How you member which is which?" he wondered.

"When you've used them as long as I have you can tell them apart," Massa Carter said, smiling. "But of course, I also write the name of each medicine on a label and paste it on the jar to be certain."

"What the labels say?"

"Caolomel, jalap, emetic tartar." He pointed to each in turn.

"Could you teach me to read them?" Michael could have bitten his tongue when he saw the doctor frowning down at him, his good humor vanished.

"I thought it was clear, Michael, that you have no need to learn to read. I don't want to hear any more about it, do you understand?"

"Yassuh."

"Anyway," the doctor went on, in a kindlier tone, "you should be glad not to have to learn. Reading is hard work. Even David has trouble, and he's not a little colored boy."

This time, Michael knew enough to keep his thoughts to himself. If he was to learn to read, he would have to do so without asking anyone. Any grownup, at least.

The day he first began to learn though, Michael wasn't even thinking about reading. He'd promised Sammy, his favorite friend, to shoot marbles with him as soon as they finished

18

their work for the day. That evening he hurried to the water pump where the boys generally met in their free time. In addition to Sammy, who belonged to the owner of one of the numerous town taverns, Michael saw two other slave boys—Titus and Ned—and two white boys, Tom and Robert, about the same age as David. David had stayed at home, preferring to avoid the mosquitoes that also clustered around the pump.

A few feet off from the pump, where the weeds had been beaten down to bare earth, the boys had just finished digging the third hole for a game of nucks. Michael aimed his marble carefully when his turn to shoot came. Only once or twice had he succeeded in getting his marble into all three holes—spaced further apart than the length of his body—in one turn. But he sure didn't want to be last and have to grip his marble between his knuckles while the others shot at it.

This time, Ned knocked his marble away from the last hole with a well-aimed shot, but in turn had his own marble hit by Sammy and Tom. On his second try, Michael held his breath as he concentrated on shooting as hard as he could without losing his aim, then grinned happily as he made the third hole.

Sammy had to be back at the tavern in an hour to help clear the supper tables, and Titus and Ned said they'd walk that way with him. Michael was about to join them, when he had an idea. He picked up the pointed stick they'd dug out the holes with, and started scratching some lines in the packed dirt. "What're you doing?" Robert asked, as Michael had hoped he would.

"Writin my name with dis stick."

Both boys laughed. "That ain't writing, you dope. You don't know how to write at all."

"Bet you can't do no better."

"Course I can," Robert said. "I've been going to school two years."

"Les see you write Michael, then."

Robert took the stick from his hand and drew it up, down, up and down again. Then he stopped. "How do you spell Michael?" he demanded.

Michael had no idea, and neither, it seemed, did Tom. Luckily, Robert didn't wait for an answer. "Michael's too big for a runt like you, anyway. I'll write Mike, like David calls you."

"Okay."

"Well," Robert announced after scratching out three more letters, "there it is. M I K E. Just like I said."

Michael ran his fingers up and down the marks Robert had gouged in the ground, trying to fix them in his mind. "Yeah, you sure nuf can write," he said.

Whenever he saw writing in the next few weeks—in shop windows, street signs or the labels on bottles of medicine— Michael looked for the letters that spelled out his nickname. Soon he could spot them easily, but there seemed so many more letters to learn!

He didn't know if Robert or Tom would help him again, but there was no one else to ask.

"You know them letters in my name you showed me last month," he said to Robert one Saturday. "I can still member them all."

"Huh! that's nothing. I know all twenty-six."

"How 'bout showin me some more then," Michael said, trying to sound as if he didn't really care much.

"Nah, I better not. David says you're just trying to get above yourself, learning your letters."

"So what?" Michael managed to say. "I ain't gonna tell him! Anyway, you scared of David?"

"Course not! I tell you what—you give me that marble you been shooting with, and I'll show you another four letters."

Michael hesitated. His only other marble was too warped to ever shoot straight. But Robert was already starting to walk away. "Here," he said, handing it over.

All fall, Michael learned more letters whenever he could—from Robert or Tom, or other boys who hung around the water pump. By the time winter had come, and 1823 was underway, he knew all twenty-six letters of the alphabet. He could close his eyes and see their shapes clearly. But he still had no idea how to put them together to learn the mystery of reading.

He was discouraged, too, to overhear Massa Carter listening to David's lessons, and realize that David was still struggling with his reader, though he went to school every weekday. Maybe Massa Carter was right after all, and reading was just too hard for him to learn.

Massa Carter sounded out of patience, Michael thought, as he corrected David's mistakes. He was glad the doctor wasn't snapping at him like that, to "Sound it out, David! Don't you know how to sound out words at all by now?"

Suddenly Michael listened harder. Massa Carter was telling David how to puzzle out what the letters meant! Cautiously he drew closer, still filling the woodbasket with kindling as quietly and as slowly as he could.

"Think, son. You're not trying. Mmm. .arket. Can't you at least tell what sound the m makes? You can at least sound out that much."

The letters made sounds. That's what Massa Carter meant. That was the secret to reading.

M made an mm sound. M goes mmm to start market, Michael repeated to himself. And it goes mmm to start Michael, he suddenly realized! M I K E . . . Mmm . . . Mike.

Now that he, at last, knew the secret, Michael thought happily, all he had to do was learn the sounds other letters made and to put them together. Now he knew that he could learn to read!

It started practicing. "Dddd. David." It didn't sound right. Then he realized that in sounding the D his tongue began at the back of his two top teeth in front. But sounded it correctly to make it sound "David," required a different placement.

He would learn to read and do it correctly!

Chapter 2

1825

Michael ran into the kitchen, followed by Sammy. "Mama, can you fix us some bread'n drippings to take fishin?" he asked eagerly.

Hetty smiled. "Law, sech a hurry to go fishin. A body'd think the fish'd stop bitin fore you'uns got there."

Both boys laughed. They were in a hurry. Sunday was their one free day to spend as they chose. And Mama nearly always insisted that Michael go with her to prayer meeting Sunday mornings, when he'd much rather spend the whole day fishing!

It wasn't just the thought of delicious fried perch or shad that lured the two boys to the banks of the Potomac. Eleven years old to his ten, Sammy had been Michael's best friend as far back as he could remember. And Sunday was the one day they could spend in each other's company. As many Sunday afternoons as they could manage, from the time the sun first shone warmly in spring till autumn frosts again set in, the two slung their fishing poles over their shoulders and headed down to the river.

Michael liked most of the other boys and girls who made daily trips to the water pump—Titus, Ned, Ned's sister Cassie, even white boys like Tom and Robert—but he and Sammy were like brothers. There were no secrets they couldn't share. Sammy was the only person besides Mama whom Michael had told he could read—and even write a little.

Grownups—even Mama—often declared that he and Sammy made a funny pair. A head taller than Michael, Sammy's broad-nosed ebony face contrasted with Michael's light brown complexion and narrower features. Where Michael's face lit up with a ready smile, Sammy often wore a brooding expression that made him look fierce till he too finally smiled. Then his sweet nature showed through.

Thoughtful and slow to speak, Sammy's manner was also a contrast to Michael's eager speech and quick actions. Michael couldn't see what difference any of this made. They were friends, and that was what counted!

While waiting on Mama to fix their lunch, Michael glanced at David. Also back from Sunday services, David sat at one end of the trestle table eating a snack Hetty had fixed him.

"You wanna go with us, David?" Michael asked. He and Sammy couldn't really talk to each other if David came along, but it seemed rude not to ask him when he was sitting right there.

Michael thought David looked like he'd like to say yes for a minute, but he looked at them coldly, saying, "I'm too old to go fishing with niggers any more."

Michael shrugged, insulted and relieved at the same time. He saw Mama give him a warning glance, but he wasn't about to sass David back anyway. At ten, he knew enough to keep his face a polite blank in front of white folks. And Daivd was definitely into "white folks."

Finishing his food, David pulled out a scrap of paper and pencil and started drawing. His blond hair fell over his face as he leaned forward intently. Curious, Michael tried to look, but David quickly put his arm around his picture to keep it from being seen. Shrugging again, Michael said, "You ready to go Sammy? Thanks for the bread, Mama."

When they finally made their way out of the kitchen, he and Sammy didn't talk much till they'd passed the fish packing plants and rope factory and reached their favorite fishing spot a mile or so south of town. Lots of other people were fishing too, but they generally had this rocky slope to themselves.

"Can you stay all afternoon today?" Michael asked. Everyone knew Mista Hoffman, who'd bought Sammy to help in his tavern when Sammy was just six or seven, was a hard master to work for. Lots of times he didn't even give Sammy all of Sunday off, and though there was lots of food at the tavern, Sammy never got quite enough to fill his stomach, either.

"Nah, I gotta be back fore supper." Sammy stopped to bait his hook and toss his line out into the river. He gazed out at the flock of skiffs and sail boats that shared the flowing water with barges and ferries. "Sure wisht I could get on one a dose and go whereber I want."

"Me too. I'd liketa go on a big schooner with sails, see all the places that stuff they unload from em comes from."

"Where I'd liketa go," Sammy said, with a glance around them, "is somewhere I'd never see Massa Hoffman again. Somewhere no one ud be my massa." He gazed at the river awhile "Hear up North ain't no slavery."

"Hear the same thing."

"You smart. You know where that be?"

"Reckon it's that way," Michael answered, pointing upstream. "But sure don know how far."

Both boys gazed up the river awhile. Neither had ever been out of Alexandria, not even to the District of Columbia—the federal city that Alexandria was a part of.

Breaking the mood, Michael carefully opened the old newspaper in which Hetty had wrapped their food. They'd carry their catch back in it before she used it for kindling, but now Michael smoothed it carefully, glancing around himself to make sure no one saw, before starting to read the paper as best he could through the drippings.

Sammy watched him admiringly. Several times, Michael had offered to show him how to read, but Sammy always shook his head. "Nah, I'm too dumb. Anyway, where could I read that Massa Hoffman wouldn't catch me an whup me? And you can tell me what it say when we togedder."

Really, the paper didn't say too much that was interesting, Michael thought. The front page was all filled with advertisements for lottery tickets and music lessons and other things of interest to white folks. Suddenly he stopped, his finger on one of the advertisements.

"Cash to give for Slaves. The subscriber, who resides in Alexandria, D.C. wishes to purchase a few likely young Negroes, male and female, from 10 to 18 years of age. Persons having such property for sale, may find the subscriber living on Henry St. between King and Prince strts. Alexandria, near Mr. Swan's plaster mill in Mrs. Nutt's brick house.—John S. Hutcherson, June 1," he read aloud.

Both boys shuddered. It was one thing to dream of sailing away to freedom and strange sights, but to actually be sold— never see your home or friends or family again—was too horrible to think about.

The following day, Massa Carter told Michael he needed him in his office just as soon as he had fetched water for cook-

26

ing and emptied the chamber pots into the backyard privy.

Michael was delighted. He never tired of helping in the doctor's office. He knew Mama would just as soon have him work around the house. She worried about him being around sick people, especially when there was talk of cholera or yellow fever, but Michael never worried. And of course, if Massa Carter ordered him to help in his office, there was nothing Mama could say.

"I want you to wash these surgical instruments," Massa Carter said now. "They've gotten to need it. Be careful not to cut yourself," he added.

"Yassuh, I'll be careful," Michael said eagerly. He filled the bleeding basin with water and carefully dipped the instruments in one by one, before rubbing them with a soapy rag and dunking them once again to be rinsed.

Drying the pewter instruments, he laid them out again in their proper order. He knew what a number of them were used for, but two puzzled him. He turned them over, studying them.

"What you use these for, Massa Carter?"

Massa Carter picked up the oddly shaped hook and said, "That's to pull bad teeth. Just hook it around the tooth, give a good hard pull, and out it comes."

Michael nodded, glad his own teeth were sound.

"The other, that's a little harder to explain. It's called a trephine saw."

Michael stared at the small, circular instrument with sharp teeth all around one end. "Don look like no saw I ever seen before."

"I don't have call to use it often. But it's for a special type of head injury. Sometimes a blow to the head can make a person die because the blood vessels swell up in his head and damage the brain. There's no room for them to swell outward because the skull is too hard. With this saw, a doctor can cut into the skull bone and relieve the pressure."

"Then will they live?"

"Usually. It depends how quickly after the injury it's done," Massa Carter answered.

Suddenly there was a knock on the door and a small slave boy burst in. "Massa, my missus say run and ask the doctor ta come," he panted. "Mista Philip fell outa the tree he wuz climbin and his leg twisted all funny. Missus fraid ta tetch him, she say."

Massa Carter hurriedly picked out several splints and gave them to Michael to carry. "Come along, Michael. I'll probably need your help," he said.

In a few minutes they were down the street. Philip, a red headed boy Michael knew slightly, lay on the ground trying not to cry. His left leg was indeed twisted in an odd way.

"Is it badly broken?" his mother asked in an anxious voice, as Massa Carter knelt to examine Philip's injured leg.

Massa Carter spoke soothingly as he felt along Philip's leg with his thumbs. "Right here's the break. There's no cause for alarm. The bone is broken, right enough, but there's no break in the skin, so the flesh won't mortify.

"We can mend your leg with a splint and a little time. You'll just have to hobble around on crutches for a while," he added to Philip.

"If you can hold him down, Ma'am," he said to Philip's mother, "these boys and I will pull the broken ends of the bone apart so I can set it properly."

Philip's mother looked faint for a moment, but then followed the doctor's direction to hold her son still. After telling Michael and the smaller boy exactly where to grasp Philip's leg, Massa Carter and the two boys pulled strongly till the two ends of the broken bone were separated far enough for the doctor to fit them together properly again. Choosing the right size splint, he unfolded the leather and wood device, tying it firmly around the broken leg.

"Now stay out of trees till that heals," he said with mock sternness. Philip attempted a weak smile.

As they walked back to the office, Michael thought it must be fine to know all about healing folks like Massa Carter did, and to be able to make hurt people well again.

For a while after that, Massa Carter's practice grew busier, and he needed Michael more often. Sometimes Michael was sent to the apothecary shop twice in one week.

Hurrying there one afternoon, he heard the exciting clang of a fire engine a few streets off. He stopped, tempted to follow the crowd of men and small boys rushing to see which engine company would arrive first, but reluctantly remembered his errand and headed on towards the apothecary.

"Hey, ain'tcha gonna come see if the Star or Sun gets there first?" The two boys calling out to Michael—Charles and Henry—were brothers, children of one of the free colored families in town.

"Nah. I'm in a hurry. Gotta carry Massa Carter medicine from the apothecary."

"Won't take long to catch up with the engines," Henry said.

Michael shrugged. "Someone sick might come and Massa need the medicine."

"You sure eager to work for him," laughed Charles. "He payin you to run his errands?"

Without answering, Michael started to walk on.

"You too uppity to come with us," Henry called after him.

"Yeah, he uppity cause he half white," laughed Charles, the older of the two. "He workin for his daddy, thass why he so eager."

Michael whirled around. "I don know who my daddy is, and neither do you! Mos likely he dead, anyhow."

"You know who he is, all right, and he sure ain't dead,"

Charles called back as the two hurried after the engines again.

Michael tried not to care what Charles and Henry said, but he couldn't get their taunts out of his mind. Mama had never said anything about his daddy, but folks generally allowed he was a white man. And lots of times lately, other boys had called him uppity on account of it. Even Ned and Titus did when they were feeling evil. Sammy was the only one who never taunted him at all.

Most likely his daddy was white, Michael thought, but not Massa Carter! He couldn't imagine him and Mama together. But he couldn't keep the thought from bothering him.

Michael didn't want to say anything to Mama, but that evening as he was walking her to visit her friend, Aunt Sary, she asked him, "What troublin you, Michael? You mighty quiet this ebenin."

"What some boys say, Mama," he burst out. "You never tole me bout my daddy. They laugh at me cause they say he white. Say I'm uppity account of it."

"That ain't nothin to worry bout. Folks who call names ain't worth listenin to."

"But they say he Massa Carter," he said miserably.

"Who say that? People jes liketa go runnin they mouths off bout things they don know nothin bout."

Mama wouldn't say anything more on the way to Aunt Sary's, but Michael could tell she was troubled. Aunt Sary, an elderly woman who had been freed some years before, was Mama's closest friend. As soon as they reached her tiny house, Mama sent Michael outside to get more sticks for the fire. She really wanted to talk to Aunt Sary about him, he guessed, as he picked up the firewood.

"I been thinkin this be a good time to tell you bout your great granddaddy," Mama told him as he came back inside.

"My great granddaddy?" he asked, astonished.

"Thass right. My granddaddy. He born in Africa."

"Africa! You know him, Mama?"

"He dead fore I wuz born, but my mama tol me all bout him. he the smartes man in he village, and folks came ta him with all they worries. He know the bes time fer huntin and plantin crops, and plenny bout healin folks too. They make him chief when he still a young man. But he too restless ta stay put, so he go travelin all round, learnin other folks ways and teachin the bes of them to he own people. Had bad luck onna las trip and got laid up with a broke leg. Wuzn't for that, them white folks neva could've carried him inta slavery. He a right good fighter, too."

Michael looked up at Mama, hanging on her words. "What he name, Mama?"

"He call Mabaya."

Once Mama had started, she remembered lots more of her own mama's stories about her African granddaddy, and Michael never tired of hearing them.

Now if boys taunted him about having a white father, he thought, maybe so, but I got an African great granddaddy who was a real fine man. His great granddaddy Mabaya wouldn't have let foolish talk bother him, he told himself, and neither would he.

1826

Just before school started in the fall of 1826, Massa Carter announced that David would be attending a new school that year.

"I've been hearing very favorable reports about the academy opened the year before last by Benjamin Hallowell. I've already spoken to Mister Hallowell and enrolled you for this term," he told David at dinner.

The Quaker schoolmaster excelled in the teaching of natural philosophy, chemistry and mathematics, he added. "Those subjects will give you a fine background for admission to

31

medical school later on."

"Who wants to become a doctor?" David muttered, but under his breath, so that only Michael heard him as he cleared David's plate.

"I would," Michael thought. He'd give anything if he had David's chances. How he wished he could go to school and study to be a doctor himself!

Massa Carter was saying that he hoped David would do better in his new school. "I don't mind saying, son, that I've been disappointed with your rate of progress so far. I hope this transfer will spur you to do the work I'm sure you're capable of."

"Yes, sir," David mumbled, staring down at the tablecloth.

David's new school books did look more interesting, Michael thought. He wished he could sit down and read through them all. There wasn't much chance to sneak a look at them, though. Now that colder weather was here, David spent most of the time he wasn't in school in his room, drawing pictures he rarely showed anyone, except once in a while to his Uncle James.

With David there, Michael was glad to get out of the house anyway. The weather was too cold for fishing now, and he and Sammy spent Sunday afternoons sitting around with other friends. Generally, they crowded around the fireplace at Ned's house. Ned was really lucky, Sammy always said, that even though he was a slave just like them, he lived with his mama and daddy both, as well as his sister, in their own tiny cabin. Ned's father was a carpenter, and in his spare time he had filled the cabin with bedsteads, a table and benches and even a rocking chair.

This winter, for the first time, the boys were joined by some of the girls—Cassie, a year older than her brother Ned, and her best friend, Marnetta. Sammy was sweet on Marnetta, everyone teased him. Sammy grinned bashfully, and didn't deny it.

The talk this time of year was mostly about the upcoming Christmas holidays, though. It was the best time of year, no doubt about it. Everyone had time off from work and looked forward to good food and partying.

"Mama's making me a new dress to wear for Christmas," Cassie announced. Michael thought she looked fine even in her old one. Slender and mahogany colored like her brother, though not so tall, Cassie held her head high under its crown of intricately woven plaits. Michael thought she was just about the finest looking girl he'd seen. Not that he was about to let on to her, though!

He doubted she'd give him a second glance even if he did. The shortest of the boys, Michael still looked like a youngster, he knew, though he'd be twelve in January. Sammy, who reckoned he was just about thirteen, was already nearly as tall and strong as a grown man. Sometimes Michael despaired of ever catching up to his friends.

Sammy was talking excitedly of the trip he would make over Christmas to visit his mama in Prince William County. Since he'd been bought by Mista Hoffman, he'd only been able to visit her at Christmas and Easter. Sometimes she would declare she scarcely recognized him from one visit to the next, he said. Now he was wondering what he could bring her for Christmas, not to mention his baby sister and brothers.

Michael wished he could buy Mama a new dress, but that would cost a lot more than the eight cents he'd managed to earn running errands for the dockworkers in his free time. Maybe he could buy her a new hanky to carry to prayer meeting. He'd already decided to get Sammy some licorice candy, a treat he rarely saw, and give it to him before he left for his Christmas visit.

On Christmas Day, Michael himself received licorice and

a shiny penny from Massa Carter. Mama surprised him with a shirt she'd sewn for him, working secretly after he'd gone to sleep. It was the first piece of clothing he'd owned that hadn't been David's first, and he felt proud wearing it to prayer meeting.

He was glad he'd been able to get her the hanky. Mama looked pretty proud herself, and showed it off twice to Aunt Sary as they ate Christmas dinner together.

After dinner, Mama excused Michael to meet with his friends at Ned's house. Ned's mama had pushed the furniture back against the walls, and his daddy played the fiddle for the young people to dance to. When they grew tired, they drank hot cider and sang till way after dark. And as if that wasn't enough, Cassie gave a special smile he was sure was meant just for him, when it grew time to finally say their thanks and go home.

If only Christmas could last all year!

After New Year's of course, the holidays were over, and things were back to normal for another year. Michael didn't mind working, though, as long as he was helping Massa Carter in his medical office. Nearly every day there was something new he could learn there.

"Why you bleed people, Massa Carter?" he asked a few afternoons later, after emptying the basin full of warm blood the doctor had drawn from his last patient.

"To bring about relief from fever."

Michael hesitated. The doctor's answer didn't really tell him everything he wanted to know. Massa Carter might think it was uppity to question him any more, but he blurted out anyway, "How you know, suh?"

"How do I know what?"

"How you know what bleedin does?"

It seemed to Michael that Massa Carter looked at him strangely a moment, as if seeing him for the first time.

34

"Michael, you ask more questions than anyone I know."

"I jes like to learn much as I can, suh. I wisht I knew all about medicine."

"I see. Well, the doctor I learned medicine from taught me what remedies to use for various illnesses, and well-trained doctors always bleed for fever. You could see for yourself that Mister Mercer broke out in perspiration, and his skin grew cool to the touch after I bled him."

Turning away from Michael he muttered, "I wish David took half as much interest in learning."

Michael didn't answer. He was sure he wasn't meant to overhear the last remark.

Chapter 3

1827

"Hey, wake up Mike!"

David's excited voice pierced through his sleep. In a second he was wide awake. He'd never heard such a clanging of bells! Now he heard the night watchman calling, "Fire! Fire! Bring your water buckets!" Looking out the window, he saw flames rising across town.

He pulled his clothes on fast as he could. David's old shoes pinched his feet, but never mind that now. The whole town was on fire!

Running downstairs at David's heels, he was surprised to see Massa Carter also rushing toward the door, and Mama throwing on her shawl and grabbing up the kitchen buckets as she ran.

Everyone in town was running through the streets, Michael realized. Men, women, boys and girls together. Most carried buckets, or failing that, some kind of cooking utensil. A few had even grabbed up china nightpots in their hurry to help quench the flames.

The whole town wasn't burning, he saw now, but entire block seemed to be in flames. Fairfax, King, Prince and Royal streets all were lighted by burning homes, shops and back buildings that flared up and were destroyed as fast as Mama's cooking fire consumed a stick of kindling wood.

All five engine companies were furiously pumping water, but their efforts seemed no match for the shooting flames. Grabbing one of the buckets from Mama, Michael raced to the nearest water pump. He found it surrounded by jostling people all eager to help fight the fire.

"We'll never get near that pump! C'mon this way, Mike!" Losing sight of Mama and Massa Carter, he ran with David, catching sight now of lines of people stretching down to the Potomac, forming a human chain as they passed buckets of icy water, one hand to another, toward the nearest burning house.

People who'd never talk to one another ordinarily were working side by side. There was Philip's mother, her red hair all in tangles, grabbing buckets from Ned's mama and passing them on, the two women working together as smoothly as though they'd done it all their lives. Michael fell into place at the end of the nearest line, trying not to spill any precious water from the buckets as he handed them hurriedly on to David.

Just as it finally seemed the fire was dying down, new flames burst out a few hundred feet away, at the corner of Prince and Water street. Within mintues, both sides of Prince, previously untouched by the fire, could be seen burning furiously.

Groups of people left the bucket chain to head toward a more helpful position, but you could see how weary they were now, stumbling and hopeless in the face of this new outbreak.

Suddenly, Michael heard a sound that carried over the roaring of the fires and the screams of people struggling to put out the shooting flames or flee from the vicinity of suddenly burning buildings.

From the direction of the docks came a cheer that grew as it swept from throat to throat. Sailing up to the wharves were boats of every kind bringing fresh help from Georgetown and Washington across the river. Entire fire engines and their companies were being unloaded from ferries and racing toward the worst of the fires. Michael felt his throat grow hoarse as he cheered and cheered with the rest, tiredness forgotten now.

Only a few scattered fires were still burning as they headed in the direction of home. Hours had gone by since the first alarm sounded, and Michael suddenly realized how cold he was in his thin shirt. Their way was blocked by piles of soaked clothing and half burned furniture thrown every which way.

Mama was just as cold and tired, Michael saw, when they'd finally made their way home. She'd lost her shawl somewhere, and her dress was soaked from water spilled from the rapidly passed buckets.

"No matter," she said. "Thank the Lawd, the house was spared and all of them were safe."

Mama had taken a cold, but she didn't like to bother Massa Carter, she said, when he was so upset.

The day after the fire he'd had a terrible quarrel with Mista Harrison. They didn't need to eavesdrop to learn what it was about. Mista Harrison could be heard shouting all through the house.

Massa Carter had lost all his savings in the fire. A few months ago, he'd bought a frame townhouse that would bring him a nice rental income, he'd said.

Now it was burned to the ground.

Even worse, the house had had no insurance.

Michael didn't know what insurance was, but not having it made Mista Harrison awfully upset.

"It's bad enough you bought property in a town that's been going downhill since the War of 1812. But not even to insure it! A child would have had better sense!"

"I meant to buy insurance, I meant to. I just never got to it."

"Meaning to doesn't pay your losses. If you had no fore-thought for yourself, you could at least have had some on your son's behalf! That was David's inheritance that just went up in smoke."

When Mama heard the trouble, she grew awfully upset, too.

"Laws a mercy," she muttered to herself. "All he money loss. What if he take a notion to sell us now?"

"He won't do that, Mama. Who would cook and take care of his house? Anyway, he don wanna sell us. He like us."

Mama looked at him with a fond smile, but Michael could tell she was still troubled.

Michael couldn't believe it was just a few weeks since he'd been so happy at Christmas. The cold Mama had taken the day of the fire grew worse every day. The tea and honey she brewed herself didn't stop her coughing.

Massa Carter told her to go to bed and rest, but her cough-ing worsened. It scared Michael to hear her cough so, from deep in her chest.

What if Mama should die? He couldn't imagine being with-out her.

Massa Carter had done everything he could for Mama. He'd bled her three times and purged her with calomel, but her fever stubbornly refused to come down and her cough grew worse day by day. Her breathing had grown labored and rasped at her throat.

Michael refused to leave her side. Massa Carter understood. Mama was in God's hands now, he said solemnly.

Mama was ready to leave this life, she said.

"But they's somethin I gotta tell you firs, chile."

"Don try and talk, Mama. You'll hurt you throat more."

"Don fret bout that. I be with the Lawd soon, where all sickness done be healed. But I ain't neva tole you the truth bout you daddy, and I reckon it's right you should know it fore I passes on."

She stopped talking to cough. Michael was too stunned to say or do anything but smooth the pillow under her head.

"What you heard right. Massa Carter is your daddy."

"Why?" Michael wasn't even sure what he meant by his whispered question.

"I was married once, to a good man. Had us three chillens—two gals an a little boy weren't but three year old, las I seen em. They be growed now, if they still alive.

"Had a good massa, too. Tole us we uns could work for ourselves when we done our task, save up and buy our freedoms. Lawd, we done work hard, hopin on that . .!

"But then ol massa took with the pleurisy and die right sudden. We all sol diffrent ways. Ain't neva see one nother again."

Michael sat motionless as Mama turned restlessly on her mattress, still too shocked to interrupt.

"When I loss em, it hurt my heart so, I jus couldn't take up with another man. Then Massa Carter's wife done took sick after she bigged with David, just lay up in the bed the longes time, couldn have nothin to do with him in they bed, neither. He kep after me so—seemed jus no point not givin in. I knowed he'd get what he want from me sooner or later.

"I sure ain't wanted no baby by him, but the good Lawd seen fit to send you, and you been right a comfort to me, chile."

She coughed again, for a long spell.

"He fond of you in he way. But he neva gon think of you as no son. I pray he gib you you freedom one day, but he neva say nothin bout that, neither." Her voice had sunk to a whisper with her last words, and she fell into a troubled sleep.

Michael sat by Mama's side, still hearing her words in his mind. Massa Carter was his daddy after all. But he didn't care nothing about it, and just wanted Michael for his slave. He wished he could put it out of his mind. It was too much to think about with Mama dying.

For the first two days after Mama's death, Michael felt too numb even to cry. Aunt Sary came to wash Mama's body and see her laid out properly. Ned's daddy made Mama's coffin, and Massa Carter found a suit of David's for Michael to wear to the burial service.

People kept coming up to Michael, saying what a fine woman Mama had been, and not to grieve too hard cause she'd gone on to her reward now. Sammy couldn't get time off from work to go to Mama's funeral, but he ran all the way to Massa Carter's house to throw his arms around Michael, and tell him, "I'm real sorry bout you Mama, Michael. She wuz like a mama to me too. I reckon she with God, now."

Even David mumbled, awkwardly, "It's too bad about your mother, Mike."

When they returned from the burying, Michael stood a long time in Mama's room. Massa Carter had had her soiled bedding removed, and the room was as empty as if she'd never lived there at all.

Finally, it was time to lie down for the night, but he couldn't sleep. Long after he heard David snoring, he lay awake on his pallet remembering Mama.

When his tears came at last he felt sadness flow all through him, till his whole body shook with sobs he thought might never stop. The door creaked open, and Massa Carter crossed the room, crouching at his side.

"Don't cry so, Michael. Your mother's with the Lord, now."

He turned away from the man. He didn't want Massa Carter's comfort now. He could never feel the same toward him after Mama's last words.

Massa Carter was finally leaving the room, he thought, when he felt the doctor lift him up—his arms around Michael as he half carried him across the hall and laid him in his own high bedstead.

A moment passed before Massa Carter lay down next to Michael, still murmuring consolation and gently stroking his back. His resistance crumbled, and he allowed himself to take comfort from the man's strong, encircling arms.

Life had to go on, of course. He'd need to find another woman to do cooking and work around the house, Massa Carter said.

"You gonna buy someone?" Michael asked, wondering if it would be someone like Mama, who'd left her own family far away.

"No, I think not. It would be more than I could afford at the moment, and I'd rather not take on the responsibility of another slave in any case. I'd just as soon pay a year's hire."

A thought occurred to Michael. "Aunt Sary's a real good cook," he said. He wasn't sure if Massa Carter would hire a free colored woman, but she surely needed the money, he knew.

Massa Carter looked surprised. "She's an elderly woman. Is she still spry enough to work every day?"

"She can get around the house spry enuf. I reckon I could go to market so she wouldn't have so much walkin to do, though."

43

"It might work well, at that," Massa Carter thought aloud. "I doubt I'd have to pay as much as to hire a slave from her owner."

With Mama gone, there was a lot more work for Michael to do. Most every morning he went to market for Aunt Sary, as he'd told Massa Carter he would. Aunt Sary wasn't strong enough to do as much cleaning as Mama'd done either, so Michael did as much as he could. When you added in helping in Massa Carter's office, he had very little free time left.

Not that he minded working hard. It kept him from missing Mama so much. The main thing that bothered him was hardly ever having time to look at David's schoolbooks anymore, or even the Alexandria Gazette.

The other thing was that David was getting bossier and bossier, just when Michael was least in the mood to be told another thing to do. He didn't see much of him daytimes, but of course he couldn't help it at night, sleeping right in David's room like that.

Tonight was really too much, he decided. He was just falling off to sleep when David called to Michael to hand him the chamber pot. Sleepily, he fished it out and waited for David to finish so he could put it back in its place.

Then, in the middle of the night, Michael was woken up a second time to hear David say, "Hey, Mike, I need the pot again."

He was sitting up to get it when he thought angrily, "Why should I have to get it for him?" He wouldn't, either.

"Get it you ownself, David. It's under your bed." Let David say he was sassing him. He didn't care!

"You're supposed to get it for me."

"Why should I? You not a cripple, is you?"

"You're my slave, that's why. You're supposed to do what I say, not to sass me!"

"I belong to your daddy, not to you. And I work for him

44

all day. Don need to work for you all night."

"I don't care. You're a slave. You're supposed to do what I tell you to."

Suddenly Michael grabbed up his bedding and headed for the door.

"Hey! Where you think you're going?"

"To sleep in Mama's old room." He wondered why he hadn't thought of it sooner. The room wasn't being used for anything now.

"You're supposed to sleep here. You can't sleep anywhere you want."

"I don need to sleep at your feet like an ol hound dog." He closed the door behind him.

Michael thought surely Massa Carter would order him to keep sleeping in David's room, when David complained to him the next morning, but to his surprise, Massa Carter said he didn't see why Michael shouldn't sleep in Mama's room if that was what he wanted.

At first, Michael had to admit to himself it was strange being there without Mama. He wasn't sure he liked it after all. Not that he'd go back and let David boss him, though.

Then a few days later, something occurred to him that made him glad he'd changed sleeping places. Massa Carter had a whole cabinet full of books in the front room. He'd never dare take one out when the doctor might see him, but if he were careful his hands were clean, he could read in his own room by candlelight and no one would know. No one could see what he was doing once he closed the door to the room.

The first Sunday afternoon warm enough for fishing, all four of them went—Ned, Titus, Sammy and Michael. The fish were biting, and they grinned as they divided up their catch.

"You all wanna go fishin again tomorrow ebening after we

45

done working?" Titus asked.

"Not me," Ned said quickly. "I'm helpin my daddy. He's learnin me to do carpentry like him."

They all looked at him with new respect.

"He say with a good trade like that, I can help us all buy our freedom," he continued. "Daddy, he got it all figgered. He been workin fo his own self in the ebenings for years, got mos enuf money to buy his freedom. Then he can keep all he earns, won't be so long till he can buy Mama free, and she work for us too. Then I be next, and after me, Cassie. By the time we uns growed, we might all be free, Daddy says."

Just what Mama hoped, Michael thought with sudden bitterness, but said nothing. Why spoil Ned's happiness?

"Sure like to learn me a trade like dat," Sammy was saying, "but don spect Massa Hoffman ever 'low me to work for my ownself."

"How bout you?" Titus turned to Michael. "Docta Carter ever say anythin bout you learnin somethin like that?"

"Nah, he neva did. And since Mama died, there's so much work to do, don't s'pose I'd have time anyhow."

Not wanting to seem ignorant before them, he added, "I done learn lots jus watching him and helpin in his office. Bet I could bleed and cup people myself by now. But it's no use to me for nothin. I'd sure admire to be a doctor, but who ever heard of a nigger doctor?"

Michael left with Sammy when he headed back to the tavern. He wanted to talk to him without the others overhearing. He hadn't yet told Sammy what Mama had told him before she died. It was the first time he had a secret he hadn't shared with Sammy as soon as possible, but still he hesitated.

"What troublin you, Michael?" Sammy asked, sensing his friend's heaviness of mind.

"Fore Mama die, she tol me it true what folks wuz sayin. Massa Carter is my daddy. He made her go to bed with him when his wife too sick."

Sammy nodded, not surprised at all, Michael realized.

"He know she done tol you dat?"

"Nah. I sure ain't gonna say nothin, neither. What for? He don think of me as no son, thass for sure."

"He treat you good, though."

"I reckon." Michael paused, thinking as he spoke. "Least I always thought so, fore Mama tol me. But now I don know. He neva let me learn nothin, jus keep me slavin for him when I'm jus as much his son as—as David is. Jus don seem right to haveta call your own daddy Massa."

Once he'd said it to Sammy, Michael said it again to his ownself. Why should he go around calling his daddy "Massa Carter?"

Not that he'd ever call him "daddy," of course! But seemed that Doctor Carter might do just fine.

It took over a month before he got up the nerve. But one warm day, when the doctor asked him to get out the scalpel and bleeding basin, he just said "Yassuh, Doctor Carter," and that was that.

He thought the doctor looked at him oddly a minute, but he never did say anything about it.

It didn't make Michael any less of a slave of course, but somehow he felt just a little bit better about it.

Chapter 4

1828

Sammy sure would be happy when he told him what Cassie'd whispered that morning, Michael thought, as he hurried toward Mista Hoffman's tavern. He and Sammy had grown even closer in the year since Mama's death, and now he could hardly wait to repeat Cassie's words.

She and Marnetta had been giggling and whispering as they stood just ahead of Michael, waiting their turn at the water pump. As they turned to carry their filled pails home, Cassie gave Michael a poke. "Tell you bashful friend, Sammy, Marnetta thinks he sweet," she'd said, water sloshing from her buckets as she ran off.

Now Michael could hear shouts and drunken laughter from the tavern dining room as he neared the building, heading around back to see if Sammy was done working. Just as he reached the kitchen door, Lucy—a short, dark woman with a burn scar running down one cheek—ran to stop him.

"You can't see Sammy, now."

"He be done workin soon?"

"You can't see him at all, anymore," she answered after a moment. "Massa Hoffman done sold him."

"Sold him!" It couldn't be true!

"Thass right. Trader stayin here, buyin up niggers ta carry down ta Georgia, say Sammy look good'n strong, he gib six hundred dolla for him, so Massa Hoffman sold him."

Michael didn't know how long he stood there, frozen with shock, before managing to ask, "Where he at—in the slave pen?"

"Pens wuz full. Got him locked right in dat shed over dere. Trader tell Massa Hoffman he'd be much obliged if he could keep him dere till the auction Satiday mornin." She turned and headed back into the kitchen.

Looking carefully around to make sure he wasn't spotted, Michael ran to the rear of the storage shed. "Sammy, you in there?" he called cautiously, mouth up against the shed.

"Michael, dat you? Massa Hoffman done sold me!" Sammy's voice sounded muffled through the boards.

He had to help Sammy! "I'm gonna find a way ta get you outta there," he said.

"Ain't no use. Where'd I go?"

Michael couldn't take time to answer. He studied the shed, thinking as hard as he could. The door was securely fastened with a padlock he knew he'd never break.

The hinges, he thought. If he could just get the pins out, they could take the whole door off.

All he had to use was David's old penknife with the point broken off. It probably wouldn't work, but he had to try!

Kneeling by the bottom hinge he turned the knife this way and that, but it was no use. There was no way the broken blade could be foreced in to move the pin.

The wooden slats forming the wall were nailed top and bottom to the cross framing that supported the shed. Narrow cracks showed between them, but he knew he'd never pry the boards off with just the small pocket knife.

He ran his hands up and down the slats to see if any were loose, catching his finger on a protruding nailhead. That was it!

Holding the knife flat against the building, he eased the blade under the head of the nail, turning it back and forth til he'd worked the nail loose from the wall.

Most of the other nails were driven further into the boards, and not so easy to dislodge. As he worked at the fourth one the knife slipped, cutting painfully into his hand. He bit his lip to keep from crying out. They couldn't risk any noise.

It seemed hours before he'd finally removed enough slats for Sammy to force his way through the narrow gap. They didn't dare speak till they'd gotten half a mile from the tavern, moving cautiously and keeping their eyes peeled for the night watchman.

"Where we goin?" Sammy finally whispered.

"Down ta the river. We can find a fishin boat and row crost. If I puts it back fore mornin, no one'll know where you at. You can hide out there, till we figger how ta git you to a free state.

"Wisht I had a pen and paper," he added, "so's I could write you a pass. Prob'ly wouldn't be no good though. I can't make letters look like a white man wrote em."

They had to walk a mile past their old fishing spot before they finally found a boat they could use, tied to a tree by the river bank.

"Shit!" Sammy muttered. "Ain't no oars left in it."

They looked all around, but Sammy was right. He hadn't thought about the owner carrying the oars home with him, Michael realized. He sure didn't see anything else they could use either.

"We'll haveta paddle with our hands," he said finally. "You kneel down nexta me right in front of this here seat, and we can each lean ta one side. Ain't that far acrost."

It was a lot farther than it seemed it would be without the use of the oars, Michael thought, some time later. He wondered if Sammy's arm ached as much as his. They'd been kneeling side by side, pulling at the water with their cupped hands for what seemed like hours, but the wooded Maryland shore looked just about as far away as it had when they started.

It was nearly sunrise, Michael realized, with a sudden stab of panic. Grimly he put his head down, trying to pull at the water even harder.

Laughter cut through the air. Michael jerked upright. Rowing steadily toward them was a skiff carrying three jeering white fisherman. He knew it was all over, even before he made out their words.

"Hey Jake, looks like we caught ourselves some bigger fish than we was lookin for. Reckon they worth more'n a mess of catfish to someone."

His wrists burned from the rough rope as he and Sammy were dragged into the tavern, hands tightly tied behind them. Mista Hoffman, and a heavyset man Michael guessed must be the slave trader, sprang furiously toward them. Just behind them stood Doctor Carter, looking angrier than he'd ever seen him.

The trader twisted Sammy's ear in one beefy hand, bringing tears of pain to his eyes, as he reached into his pocket to reward the grinning fisherman.

"Thanks for the help, boys. Reckon I'd better lock this one up in a cell till the auction tomorrow." He yanked Sammy through the door, still gripping him firmly by his ear.

Mista Hoffman stepped toward Michael, his face red.

"Lucy told me you musta been the nigger broke into my shed." Reaching out suddenly, he grasped Michael firmly by the back of the neck, snatching up a three-foot length of rawhide from a nearby bench.

Raising the heavy whip, he spoke over his shoulder to Doctor Carter. "You don't mind, I'd liketa give him a good hiding, learn him a lesson bout helping slaves run off."

Michael looked up at Doctor Carter, trembling despite himself. The doctor ignored Michael as he replied. "He's my property. I'll take care of it myself."

"Better see that you do."

"I said I'd take care of it."

Michael came close to slipping on the cobblestones two or three times as he hurried after Doctor Carter, hands still bound behind his back. It wasn't till they reached the house that the doctor untied him.

"What do you think you were doing, boy? I thought you had some sense in your head!"

"Slave trader's gonna carry Sammy down South!" Michael said desperately. "It'll kill him! He never done no field work or nothin, jus worked in the tavern since he young."

"You can't be sure where he'll be sold. It could be he'll end up with a better master. Anyway, that doesn't justify helping him run off."

"He my friend! We like brothers. All his friends here. Ain't right to take him away and sell him!"

"Sammy's young," Doctor Carter said in a slightly gentler voice. "He'll adjust. In a few months, he'll have forgotten all about you."

Michael could hardly believe the doctor would say such a thing. "No he won't! What you think he is—a dumb animal? Ain't right to sell people like they animals!" He was nearly crying with anger.

"Maybe not, but there's nothing you can do about it. Mister

Hoffman was within his legal rights to sell him. All you've accomplished with your stunt is to get both of you in trouble."

One last hope of saving Sammy occurred to Michael, though he knew it was hopeless even as he said, "Maybe you could buy him?"

"You know better than that. I have no need for any more slaves, even if I could afford to buy him. You'll just have to learn to accept things the way they are."

He paused as if waiting for a reply, but Michael felt too miserable to argue any further.

"I meant what I said to Mister Hoffman, Michael," Doctor Carter said after a minute. "I'm going to whip you. You have to learn your lesson. Go bring me my razor strop."

Michael obeyed resentfully as the doctor took the leather strap, ordering Michael to follow him to the back yard. He raised his arm, then stopped a moment.

"Take your shirt off, boy."

"No!"

"I said take off your shirt!" the doctor repeated. "Do I have to tie you up again?"

Michael stared at Doctor Carter, overwhelmed by hurt and confusion. Though the doctor was often short-tempered, he seldom hit Michael, and had never before whipped him. Somehow Michael had thought Doctor Carter would understand how he had to help Sammy. But now the doctor was looking at him with nothing but anger in his face, waiting to beat Michael on his bare back with the razor strop.

Why should he have expected Doctor Carter to understand? Michael wondered bitterly. He was just the man's slave, no more to him than Sammy had been to Mista Hoffman.

"No suh," he answered, nearly ripping his shirt off and flinging it to the ground.

Michael leaned against the privy house as the stinging strap rose and fell, his face pillowed in his crossed arms, his cheeks wet with silent tears. That night he lay awake, almost welcoming the soreness in his shoulders if it would keep his mind off Sammy.

The next morning he went about his work without a word. He tried not to think about what was happening to Sammy, but he couldn't help it when he got to the water pump. He couldn't count the times they'd talked and played around this pump.

He had to see Sammy again! Dropping the buckets, Michael raced toward Duke Street and the slave pens. Outside the pens, huddled a short distance away, he found a small crowd of other people waiting for the slave auction to end, all hoping for a last look at a friend or family member.

The morning had nearly gone by when the gates to the pen were opened, and a line of handcuffed slaves, many sobbing openly, were herded through. Sammy was walking near the end of the line, chained to a bearded man of forty or fifty.

Racing up to him, he grabbed Sammy's hands in his own.

"They hurt you, Sammy?" he asked fearfully.

"Nah, jus gib me one or two licks."

The older man looked at the two boys a minute. "Trader wouldn't wanna mark him up fore he sold him. Jes lower his price if white folks think he a bad nigger."

"I be all right," Sammy said at last. "Sure am gonna miss you though." He stopped, choking back a sob.

"Me too," Michael whispered.

They were both crying too hard to speak now.

Before they could try to say anything further, Michael felt himself flung aside by the beefy slave trader. "Outta the way, boy!" the man growled, giving Michael a hard kick as he spoke.

He was still lying on the ground where the trader had thrown him, when he was suddenly pulled to his feet. He turned, startled, to see David.

"I told Dad I'd find you here. Are you out of your mind? You want him to whip you again?"

He stared up at David, starting to sob once more. "They're carryin Sammy down to Georgia. He done worked for Mista Hoffman since he six years old, and now he sold him down South. It ain't fair! It ain't fair!"

He twisted around. The chained slaves had begun to move, Sammy shuffling along with the rest. The line stopped a moment and Sammy looked back, rubbing tears away from his eyes with his manacled hand. As the trader yelled for them to continue walking, Sammy stretched his hands out as far as he could in farewell, then turned and trudged on with the rest.

David loosened his grip on Michael's arm and Michael glanced up at him. David looked troubled, as he watched Sammy move away. Maybe David was also remembering how they all used to play together, Michael thought. They stood silently, till the chained slaves had moved nearly out of sight.

Finally David spoke, in a gentler voice than Michael remembered in a long time. "I reckon you're right. It's not fair to treat him like that."

He cuffed Michael lightly on the shoulder. "C'mon home now, Mike."

"You've got to stop brooding about Sammy, Michael. I haven't seen you smile once in the past month."

Michael sighed. This morning Aunt Sary had told him just about the same thing as Doctor Carter was saying now. He wished he could stop thinking about Sammy so much, but no matter how he tried he just couldn't.

"Can't help how I feel, suh," he said.

Doctor Carter sighed too. "You've got to try and get over him. Have you finished grinding the calomel yet?"

"Almost, suh." He started methodically churning the pestle

56

against the sides of the mortar again, reducing the calomel to a heap of powder at the bottom of the bowl.

Two week ago, the doctor had suddenly said that he saw no reason why Michael couldn't learn to grind up medicines for him. He'd meant at least in part to raise his spirits, Michael guessed. Ordinarily, he'd have been excited to learn a new skill. He'd have wanted to run and tell Sammy, as soon as he was free for the day.

Now it seemed like just another job.

His friends chided him for being so down all the time, too. They all missed Sammy, of course. But seemed like they all had lots else to occupy their minds. They couldn't go no mourning day and night.

Michael was too down for anyone to want to be around, they told him.

He was having trouble sleeping, too, for the first time in his life.

Mostly he just tossed and turned, but six weeks or so after Sammy'd been taken away, he thought he might just as well look at one of Doctor Carter's books. He hadn't felt like reading lately, but now he found he could lose himself in a book for a while.

The Sunday following, they woke to a steady downpour. Doctor Carter called up to David to be sure and wear his waterproofed coat. They'd have a long walk from church to Sunday dinner at Uncle James and Aunt Alice's house, he reminded him.

Michael was glad to have the house to himself. He rarely bothered attending prayer meetings any more, and this rainy morning seemed a perfect time to finish the book he'd started two nights ago. The explorations of Lewis and Clark reminded him of the stories Mama had told him years ago about his own great grandfather, and he hurried to get the volume from the front room cabinet.

With Doctor Carter and David gone till late afternoon he could sit comfortably by the kitchen fire, he decided. He read quickly, moving a thin strip of wood he used for a marker down one line of print at a time. Soon he was engrossed in the exploration of the American frontier.

When he looked up again, Doctor Carter stood in the kitchen doorway looking right at him. How long had the doctor been watching him, he wondered. Surely it wasn't evening yet.

"I—I didn't hear you come in, suh,"

"Mrs. Harrison was indisposed. What are you doing with that book, Michael?"

"Jus lookin at it, suh."

Doctor Carter stepped into the room, looking down at him. "I don't see any pictures on that page. Are you looking at it or reading it?"

Never tell any white folks you can read, Mama had warned him. But just now, Michael felt sick and tired of playing dumb. He stood up, looking at the doctor proudly.

"I'm reading it, suh."

Doctor Carter picked up the book and looked at it a moment. "Who taught you to read?"

Michael shrugged. "No one."

"Michael, I asked you a question. I expect an answer, not sass from you."

"Wasn't trying to sass you, suh. No one just sat me down and learned me to read."

He hesitated before adding, "Some of David's friends like Tom and Robert learned me my letters. But that's back when they were chillen, so they didn't know they wuzn't s'posed to. And I heard you tellin David how to figger out his lessons, and tried to do what you said."

"I can't believe you could just have learned . . . " Doctor Carter left his sentence unfinished. "You've known how to

58

read for years, then. Why did you hide it?"

"Reckon I thought you wouldn't let me do it anymore if you knew," Michael said slowly. "And Mama tol me never let on to a white person I could read. Maybe she be wrong, though. Reckon if I go round pretendin I don know nothin, you're bound to think I'm dumber than I am."

"Nobody thinks you're dumb, Michael. I wish—" Doctor Carter left the kitchen without finishing that sentence either.

"Can you write, as well as read?"

Startled, Michael looked up from the medicine he was grinding. This was the first mention the doctor had made of reading since he'd surprised Michael the day before.

"Yassuh. But not so good as I can read."

Doctor Carter fished a scrap of foolscap and quill pen from a drawer of the desk where he wrote out prescriptions. "I'd like to see what sort of hand you write. I might as well make some use of your ability. If you can write a good, legible hand, you could copy out some of these prescription labels for me."

"Yassuh." Michael grasped the pen tightly in his fist, starting to spell out his name. He wished he could show Doctor Carter he could write a good hand. But he knew his letters always came out wobbly and uneven.

"You're holding the pen wrong, Michael," Doctor Carter said after a moment. "It's no wonder you find it difficult to form your letters. You'd write a lot better if you'd hold the pen correctly."

"Don know no other way to hold it, suh."

"Watch how I hold it, between my thumb and first two fingers."

"Feels strange this way, suh," Michael said, trying to imitate Doctor Carter.

"That's just because you were never shown the right way. With a little practice, it will seem natural to you. I'll see if I can find you something to practice on when you've finished

59

your work."

Michael had just finished carrying in wood from the shed that evening, when Doctor Carter stepped into the kitchen. "You can practice writing in this," he said, handing him a small package.

Michael could hardly believe that Doctor Carter had bought him a brand new copy book. He made certain the kitchen table was spotless before setting the book down on it. Holding a quill pen as the doctor had shown him, he painstakingly set about copying the first lesson.

After a while, he realized Doctor Carter had returned to the kitchen, and stood watching from a few feet away. Looking up at him, Michael smiled with sudden happiness. The doctor nodded approvingly, then slowly returned his smile.

Chapter 5

1828

Michael picked up the newly sharpened pen, then stopped a second, admiring the label he'd just written. In the month since Doctor Carter had given him the copybook, he'd spent nearly every evening painstakingly copying his letters in the book's ruled lines. The night before, Doctor Carter had finally told him his writing hand had improved enough that he could letter his medicine labels in the future.

The calomel he'd ground that morning was already bottled, and Michael had hurried back to the office after his noon meal, happily imagining Doctor Carter's surprise at seeing the labels finished on his return. He hitched the chair closer to the small desk, pushing aside the ruler he'd used to draw lines ensuring his letters would be even. He dipped the pen carefully in the inkwell, scarcely noting the office door open behind him as he concentrated.

The heavy ruler was suddenly snatched from the desk, smashing down in a painful blow across the back of his hand.

He jerked his hand out of the way with a cry of pain, nearly upsetting the inkwell as the ruler descended again, striking the desk with a sharp crack.

"What do you think you're doing, you damn nigger bastard!"

Michael jumped up, springing back out of the way. "Ain't doin nothin wrong!" He stared incredulously as Mista Harrison raised the ruler to strike him again, his face red with fury.

"What's going on here, James?!"

Michael breathed a sigh of relief as Doctor Carter's frame filled the doorway. "I wuzn't doin nothin but writing out the labels like you tol me to, Doctor Carter!" His words rushed out before Mista Harrison could speak.

Mista Harrison lowered his arm. "Like you told him to! You were fool enough to teach him his letters, weren't you!"

"I never taught him a thing." Michael listened in surprise as a note of pride crept into Doctor Carter's voice. "He picked up reading and writing by his own efforts. And in future, I'll thank you not to take it on yourself to correct the boy!"

"Someone should, George! You've let him get totally out of hand by your misguided softness." Mista Harrison stormed out the office door, his face still red with anger.

Michael stared up at Doctor Carter, rubbing his stinging knuckles. "I never done nothin to sass him, suh. He just bust in and started beating on me fore I even knew he wuz here. He always done hated me for no cause."

"There's no need to take on now, Michael." Doctor Carter hesitated, then clumsily patted Michael's head. "I know you're a good boy."

Now that his reading was no longer a secret, Michael could read openly in his free time, though he remained careful not to let Mista Harrison catch him again. He spent long evenings during the next few months with books borrowed from the doctor as well as David's schoolbooks. Some he found easy to understand, but others were difficult to puzzle out even with the help of Webster's school dictionary.

If only he could go to school and learn from a teacher! But that was impossible, of course. Schooling was only for whites.

Mista Stabler, the apothercary, was deep in conversation with his oldest son as Michael entered the shop. No other customers were there, but naturally he waited politely for the two men to finish talking.

"I had a most worthwhile journey to the Yearly Meeting of the Ohio and Indiana Society of Friends," Mista Stabler was saying. "Some of the Indiana Friends kindly showed me through one of the schools chartered for freed slaves. They're doing excellent work educating the freedmen there."

Michael could hardly believe it. There were schools colored people could go to up North! If only he could go to one.

Ned and Titus weren't impressed when he repeated Mista Stabler's remarks to them. "Don do us no good. We ain't never gonna get up North," Titus told him.

They had more pressing things on their minds, in any case. Titus allowed as how he worked too hard at the rope works, where he was hired out for the year, to worry over things that were never going to happen.

Ned was becoming almost as skilled a carpenter as his daddy, he said proudly. Sunday afternoons, he and Marnetta often went walking together. Everyone agreed they made a fine couple.

Michael himself was still sweet on Cassie, but it didn't stop him from wanting to learn any. "I sure wisht I could go to school though," he said again.

Titus laughed. "Ask you massa to send you up there, then.

He you daddy, ain't he?"

Michael shrugged off Titus' words. It wasn't a subject he liked to dwell on.

He couldn't stop thinking about what Mista Stabler had said, though he knew there was little chance he'd ever get to go up North to school. Even if Doctor Carter were ever to free him, Michael was sure he would never pay to send him to school. Since the fire two years ago, he often said his money was in short supply.

Just the other day, he'd snapped angrily at David for asking to take drawing lessons.

Mista Hollowell had hired a new teacher who would teach drawing to students at his school, David had said eagerly at breakfast.

"I've no money to pay for frivolity." Doctor Carter's voice carried clearly to the kitchen.

"It's what I like to do best, sir."

"You'd do well to spend more of your time mastering Latin and chemistry. Drawing's not going to help you any in medical school."

"I've never wanted to become a doctor." Michael had never heard David argue back to his father before. It didn't do him much good.

"I entered the occupation my father chose for me, and I expect you to do the same. I'll not listen to any more on this subject."

David had forgotten his algebra book and just as Michael expected, Doctor Carter wanted it carried to him.

The school lunch break must have started, Michael thought, as he stood at the back door of the big brick house on the corner of Queen and Washington. He'd begun to think no one heard his knock, when he heard a man's pleasant voice telling him to come in.

For a moment it was too dark to see in the hallway, then to his left he saw the long room filled with wide, yellow pine desks. Sitting at a larger desk at one end was a dark-haired man, busily sharpening a gray goose quill into a pen. There must be a hundred more on the desk in front of him, Michael thought in surprise.

"Can I help you?"

"Are you Mista Hallowell, suh? David done forgit his schoolbook, so Doctor Carter ast me to carry it to him."

"And you are?"

"My name's Michael, suh. I b'long to Doctor Carter."

"Well, thank you Michael. I'll see David gets it."

He knew he should leave, but stood watching Mista Hallowell. The schoolmaster was younger than he'd thought he'd be, with a boyish smile under a large, hooked nose. A sudden hope took hold of Michael. Quakers like Mista Hallowell didn't hold slaves, he knew, and spoke to colored people the same as they did to whites. Michael spoke up before he could lose his courage.

"You got an awful lotta pens there to make, Mista Hallowell, I could sharpen em for you. I know how ta make pens pretty good. I can do lotsa other work too."

The schoolmaster looked at him again, smiling. "I'm sure you could, Michael. But I'm still trying to get my school established. I'm afraid I've no extra money to spare for work I can do myself."

"I wouldn't want you to pay me no money, suh."

"What is it thee does want, then?"

"Could- could you teach me some, suh? Some of what you teaches in the school?"

He could hardly believe he'd come out and said it. But Mista Hallowell didn't look angry, only surprised and curious.

"Can you read, son?"

"Yassuh, and write too. Doctor Carter lets me write up his

medicine labels. But I'd sure admire to learn more. Theys lots in David's books I wish I could get splained to me."

He sure hoped Mista Hallowell would say he'd teach him. He had to give the matter some thought, the schoolmaster had said that afternoon. Michael hadn't been able to think of anything else since.

He hadn't even heard the knocker, he realized, suddenly becoming aware of voices in the front room. Doctor Carter must have opened the door himself.

"Michael!" He started quickly down the hall, realizing just as he reached the front room that Doctor Carter wasn't calling him, but talking about him to Mista Hallowell!

"I thought if you knew how eager the boy is for learning, you'd want to make some arrangement for him," Mista Hallowell was saying. "He seems to have a bright and inquiring mind. It's a shame to let it lie fallow."

Michael backed toward the kitchen a few feet. He couldn't make out Doctor Carter's exact words now, but he could tell he was angered.

"What possessed you to ask Mister Hallowell to teach you?" he demanded of Michael a few minutes later.

"I jus want to learn, suh. Didn't mean no harm by it."

Doctor Carter looked a little less stern. "I'd say you've already learned a good deal. Enough to be quite a help to me."

"Yassuh, thank you, suh. But theys jus so much more I want to know about."

"Mista Hallowell would be breaking the law to instruct you, Michael."

"Theys schools up North where they allows colored to go, suh. I overheard Mista Stabler talkin bout them once. I could go to school up there if you'd let me!" Suddenly his words were pouring out.

"I know you short of money, suh, but if you'd send me, I swear I'd work hard as I can and pay back every penny.

Theys so much I could learn if I could jus go to school. Mebbe I could even become a doctor like you, suh. It's what I wants more than anythin!''

Doctor Carter must have stared at him almost a minute before he spoke. "It's not possible, Michael. You're dreaming about something that doesn't exist. Even if you went to school, you'd never be able to use your education. Colored people up North are far worse off than those down here. And if you didn't belong to anyone, you'd have no protection in times of trouble. It's out of the question."

Michael was sure Mista Hallowell would never agree to teach him, after his meeting with Doctor Carter. To his surprise, the schoolmaster said a few days later that he thought he could give Michael instruction with a clear conscience. A law that shut people away from the light of learning couldn't be just.

1830

"Hurry and pack up my lancets and basin. Mrs. Cunningham's taken a turn for the worse. We'll need to call at her house to bleed her again."

Michael moved quickly to obey, but as he packed the instruments he couldn't help thinking,"It won't help her none."

"What!"

He hadn't realized he'd spoken aloud till Doctor Carter snapped at him, but lately he'd been thinking to himself that bleeding didn't seem much use at all.

Three patients had died of pleurisy in the past month, though Doctor Carter had bled and purged them all. It was a bad winter the doctor said grimly, but Michael thought maybe there was just more to know about curing people than Doctor Carter knew.

"What did you say?" the doctor asked again.

"Jus that I don think bleedin people's helpin them none,"

he muttered.

"You don't think! When did I ever tell you to think?"

"God gave me a mind jus like anyone else. Can't help thinkin bout what I see right in front of my eyes."

"Well, then, you can see for yourself that bleeding brings about relief from fever."

Michael shrugged. "But then they jus get sick again right quick. You bled Mista Mercer last month and he died, and Mista Jackson the same. And Missus Cunningham ain't gettin no better, it seem to me." He paused before adding, "Before Mama died, you bled her three times."

"I didn't kill your mother, boy!"

"Didn't help her none, either."

For a second he thought Doctor Carter was going to hit him, but the doctor just strode from the room, motioning to Michael to follow him with the kit. He didn't mean to sass the doctor and make him mad. But lately it seemed to happen more and more.

Since last year when Mista Hallowell started giving him lessons Friday nights, he'd come to realize there were lots of things Doctor Carter was wrong about. Up North was one of them. Mista Hallowell was from the North himself, and he knew of free colored folks who owned taverns and barber shops, and worked as preachers and schoolteachers.

It wouldn't be impossible to become a doctor if he worked as hard as he could.

He'd like to repeat Mista Hallowell's words to Doctor Carter, but of course that would mean telling him about the lessons.

"He has a magic lantern makes pictures right up on a screen and a pump what shows how air can push water right up through a tube." Michael couldn't tell his friends enough of the wonders Mista Hallowell had showed him—how you could puzzle out number problems using algebra, or see common

68

things enlarged right under your eyes with the round glass he called a magnifier.

He couldn't help but notice though that his friends seldom shared his excitement.

"You think you so special cause you learnin from books," Titus said now, as they sat on the doorstep of Ned and Cassie's house one warm Sunday afternoon. "Ain't nothin for you to be so uppity bout. You still nothin but a slave jus like the rest of us."

"He ain't uppity, either, Titus," Cassie spoke up. "I like ta hear what he done learn."

Michael smiled at her and gave her hand a quick squeeze. Since last year when he'd finally begun to get his growth, Cassie had managed to let him know she felt pretty sweet on him too.

He had to admit, it hurt to have the others call him uppity, yet he couldn't seem to keep his excitement over learning to himself.

Suddenly, the solution was right in front of him. He wondered why he hadn't thought of it sooner.

"Ain't nothin uppity bout readin, Titus. I'll learn you to read if you wants."

"Lotta good that'll do me," Titus said.

"Sure it will," Michael said, growing more excited as he spoke. "How bout you, Ned? You hopin to buy you freedom one day. Sure be a help to you to know readin and figgering."

"Makes a lotta sense," Ned agreed, after thinking it over a minute.

It made sense to Ned's folks, too, when Michael explained his plan. The young folks could meet for lessons in their home, his daddy agreed.

They couldn't all meet every Sunday evening, but before long Michael had a regular class of six or eight students. It wasn't hard to get hold of David's old schoolbooks and Mista

69

Hallowell let him have an old slate and chalk.

Titus was just as eager as the rest when he saw how Michael had won them over. Even free colored boys, like Henry and Charles, showed up from time to time. And Ned's daddy and mama often joined in with the young folks.

By the time 1831 was underway, Ned, Cassie and Titus had finished the first of Murray's readers and could make their letters well enough to be understood.

He was sure glad he had the lessons, and Sunday afternoons with Cassie, to look forward to, Michael thought, as he climbed the stairs to David's room. The rest of life seemed to be going from bad to worse.

He and Doctor Carter were having words more often, for one thing. Just yesterday, Doctor Carter had said that he didn't understand how Michael could have changed so much when he'd been such an eager, helpful youngster. Mista Harrison was probably right. He'd been much too soft in his management of Michael, the doctor said sourly.

The doctor had changed for the worse himself, it seemed to Michael. Since losing so many patients to pleurisy the previous winter, he'd started taking an extra glass or two of wine at dinner, which just deepened his gloomy outlook. And last month, Doctor Wilkins—a young doctor new in town—had moved to an office almost directly across the street from Doctor Carter. A number of his old patients were now seeing the new man. So added money worries were making him crosser than ever.

Then, to, he and David had been at odds lately. Just this morning they'd had a row over David's school report in Latin and Greek, and David hadn't left his bedroom since. Michael would just as soon stay away from David right now, but Doctor Carter had asked him three times to get the bed linens to be washed.

"What is it?" David said, as he knocked on his door.

70

"It's me- " Michael broke off in surprise as he stepped into David's room. Dozens of David's drawings lay scattered all over the floor, as if they'd been dropped or thrown in a rage. David was squatting on his heels, studying them.

"What do you want, Mike? These are private."

"I didn't meanta bust in on you. Your Daddy sent me up to get the bed linens fer the washin. You want I should get his and come back later?"

David hesitated a minute, then said, "Nah, that's okay. I just don't like people looking at my sketches, is all."

"How come you neva let anyone see em?" He hoped David wouldn't think it was nosey, but he couldn't help wondering.

"Just don't like people laughing at me, is all."

Michael looked at him in surprise. "I wouldn't laugh. They look real good."

He stared down at the pictures. Some were of houses or trees or ships, but most were drawings of people. He could tell some were older than others. There was Robert playing marbles, looking about ten years old. There were other boys as well, and several of Doctor Carter and Mista Harrison.

Suddenly Michael knelt down and picked up one of the drawings. "I neva knew your drawed Mama." He sat looking at the picture. There seemed only a few pen and ink strokes on the paper, but there was Mama just as he remembered— her kind, tired face smiling as she fixed him and Sammy lunch.

"Can I keep it, David?"

"Yeah, if you want to," David said, but Michael could see he looked pleased.

"You draw really good, David," he said again.

"Thanks," David said. "I'm afraid you're the only one who thinks so, though. Dad hates for me to draw. He says it's something that's all right for girls to do. Even Uncle James says I could spend my time to better advantage."

"Bet your friends think they good, though."

David didn't answer a moment, just stared at Michael with a funny look. He wondered what he'd said wrong, when David suddenly burst out, "I don't have any friends."

Michael couldn't believe it. Everyone had friends. "Sure you do. What about Tom and Robert—"

"Haven't seen them hardly at all since I changed schools. And no one at Hallowell's school likes me. They just make fun of my drawings, and call me a dunce. None of them'll give me the time of day. They don't even talk to me at lunch time."

Michael couldn't imagine not having any friends to talk to. And as far as he could see, Doctor Carter didn't understand David any more than he did him.

He'd never imagined feeling sorry for a white boy, but he felt sorry for David now.

Chapter 6

1831

Nobody could talk about anything else but Nat Turner and his terrible uprising.

Colored and white alike had been stunned when news reached Alexandria, on a hot August morning just a week ago, of the Southhampton, Virginia slave who'd killed nearly sixty whites in his terrifying revolt against slavery.

The man must have been crazy, Michael thought. Who didn't want to end slavery? But he couldn't imagine how anyone could just go out and kill all those people, even women and little children.

He couldn't understand, either, how white folks up here, who'd known the colored people in Alexandria all their lives, could suddenly look at them as if they were scared they might all be murderers like Turner.

Even whites like Mista Hallowell, who'd always been a

friend to the slaves, were afraid to rile up their neighbors. He'd sent Michael home as soon as he showed up last Friday evening. It just wasn't prudent to keep on with their lessons for the present, Mista Hallowell had told him.

Colored folks were plenty scared, too. No one dared be caught outside by the town watchmen after the ten o'clock curfew. They weren't even allowed to have a group of people get together.

Ned's folks said they didn't dare have the reading classes in their house anymore. Nearly everyone was afraid to come, anyway.

He wasn't scared to keep on, Michael told them. But only Ned and Titus finally agreed to continue. He hated to stop now when he was doing so well, Ned said. Titus said he'd keep on, too. He wasn't about to let Ned show him up.

They could meet right in his room, Michael told them. There wasn't any better place he could think of. He'd let them in the kitchen door, and no one would even know they were there.

That Sunday, everything worked out just as Michael had said it would. No one noticed Ned and Titus slip quietly into the yard from the back alley, and they finished a page of spelling and arithmetic well before the ten o'clock curfew.

The following week, Michael got hold of Woodbridge and Willards Universal Geography. "This here's a picture of our whole country," he told them. "They calls it a map. Here's where we at, right here along the border of Virginia."

"Where the free states at?" Titus suddenly asked.

"Pennsylvania, right here, the nearest." If only it was as near to get to as it appeared on the map, Michael thought. Probably they were all thinking the same thing, he guessed.

Before he could explain how to read the map, they were startled by loud voices from the front room.

"Just Michael," Doctor Carter was saying, "and he'd

hardly—"

"Gotta search all the nigra quarters in town," a rough voice broke in. "Can't take any chance of another Nat Turner here!"

Michael could barely breathe as the stomp of heavy footsteps sounded just outside the room. There was nowhere to hide the books and paper but under the thin mattress. Frantically they grabbed them up—but they'd moved too slowly. Half a dozen red faced men looked grimly in, as the door to the kitchen was kicked open in their faces.

"Got ya redhanded this time!" Sammy's old owner, Mista Hoffman, easily overpowered Michael, twisting his arm painfully as he tied his hands behind him.

The magistrate wouldn't sit till morning, of course. The cell they'd been thrown into was damp and strong with the odor of the chamber pot, but Michael wished just the same the morning would never come.

None of them could sleep. Ned sat huddled against the wall, absently rubbing his wrists where the coarse rope they'd been tied with had chafed them. "My folks sure gonna be sick bout this," he said at last.

Titus squatted over the pot for the third time that hour. "They gonna cut us bad, for sure," he moaned. Getting up, he turned suddenly on Michael. "You think you so smart, you sure got us in a heap of trouble."

Ned looked up a moment. "Shut you mouth, Titus. We all knew what we wuz doin. He sufferin same as us."

He wanted to thank Ned for speaking up for him, but he was shaking too hard to talk. He couldn't stop thinking of the constable's cowskin whip that could cut your back open with every blow.

Maybe Doctor Carter would speak up for them, and get them off without a whipping. He knew they hadn't meant any wrongdoing.

It was their only hope.

Titus and Ned's owners were in the courtroom, their faces stony with anger, as the three boys were hauled before the magistrate. Doctor Carter stood with his arms crossed, lips firmly pressed together. Mista Harrison stood next to the doctor. He wore the satisfied expression of someone who's been proven right at last.

They'd not only broken the law by meeting together and reading, but been caught redhanded with a map of the country, Mista Hoffman was telling the magistrate. "That one's been known for helpin runaways before. Wouldn't be surprised if he was plottin an uprisin just like Turner done!"

"We didn't mean to do nothin wrong, suh," Michael managed to say. "Sure ain't plottin nothin." Turning directly to the doctor, he added, "You know we wuzn't doin nothin wrong, Doctor Carter. Couldn't you speak to the magistrate for us?"

Doctor Carter looked at him a moment. He seemed about to say something, Michael thought, holding his breath.

Mista Harrison spoke up first. "You're a fool if you plead for him, George." His words were aimed at Doctor Carter, but they carried clearly in the small chamber. "You've never kept him in his place, and now you see the results. He's not only out of your control, but riling up other niggers as well! He needs to be taught a lesson!"

The doctor hesitated a moment longer, then slowly nodded. "You'll have to take your punishment, Michael. You knew the law. You brought this down on yourself."

After listening to the white men a few minutes longer, the magistrate spoke. There was no question they'd been caught reading and writing in outright defiance of the law, but he was prepared to be lenient in admitting that no proof of any conspiracy had been shown. No sense in damaging valuable property unnecessarily, he added, with a nod to their masters.

Speaking directly to the three boys for the first time, he

told them, "Your punishment will be that set for the teaching of reading or writing to nigras. Each of you is to receive thirty-nine lashes on your bare back, well laid on, at the public whipping post—immediately following this hearing."

The constable and his helpers halted them at the entrance to the jail yard to ready them for the flogging. Titus and Ned obeyed his orders in silence, stripping off their shirts and crossing their hands in front of them to be tied.

Michael began to follow their lead when he was suddenly overcome by fury. The law was wrong. Everything was wrong. It wasn't right to make them into slaves and pass laws to keep them like dumb animals! It wasn't right for these men to whip him!

"I won't!" he cried, twisting his arm from the constable's grasp. "I won't be tied up and whipped!"

The man laughed. "Mulatter ringleader thinks he's too high class to be whipped."

His helpers laughed along with him, as Michael struggled with unthinking abandon to fight off their blows.

For a second, he fought almost free of the encircling men. Then, with a wide grin, the constable doubled one massive fist, driving it full force into Michael's stomach. He doubled over fighting off sickness, as they tore his shirt in two, ripping it from his back.

His wrists stung as the constable knotted the rope tight as he could around each in turn, before lashing them together.

"Fraid the matter's out of your hands." The constable laughed again, gripping Michael tightly by the arm. "But we won't keep you waiting."

There was no point in struggling now. Head high, muscles tightly clenched to keep from trembling, he walked steadily across the open space to the whipping post.

A small crowd of onlookers had gathered from the adjacent market square—early market-goers, many of them slaves, small boys and rough-looking, jeering white men. A soft, nearly moaning sigh from his fellow slaves reached his ears, along with the loud catcalls of the watching whites.

At the far edge of the crowd he spotted Ned's father, his shoulders slumped with helpless misery. Michael turned his head. He couldn't bear to look him in the face.

Taking up the end of the rope trailing from Michael's wrists, the constable passed it through an iron ring bolted to the top of the post, above Michael's head. With a sudden strong yank he secured the rope to the post as firmly as he could. Michael gasped as his arms were pulled high above his head till they felt as if they would be torn from their sockets. He could barely touch the ground with his feet, and the backs of his legs ached.

He hung helplessly while the constable moved behind him, measuring a distance with his eyes that would allow him to wield the cowskin with the greatest possible force. Michael couldn't see him now, but he sensed the man running the untanned hide through his hands, drawing out the excruciating moment till the first blow would fall.

He heard the shrill as the whip cut through the air and gashed the small of his back. He cried out in pain. It was worse than any hurt he'd felt before, worse than any blow or knife cut he'd ever received. There was no way he could stand thirty-eight more such cuts.

Gasping for breath, he clamped his teeth onto his lower lip, biting so fiercely that blood trickled down his chin. His flesh burned like fire from the whistling cowskin, relentlessly cutting bloody stripes from his neck to his buttocks. With each blow he thought the pain could not possibly grow any worse, till the next stroke of the rawhide brought new agony.

He had no idea how many blows he'd been given before the torment grew too great to choke back his screams any longer. His shrieks ripped from his throat, mingling with the shrilling of the rawhide.

By the time the constable cut him loose, he was too weak to do anything but moan. He took one halting step. Everything spun around him a moment, and then abruptly went dark.

He came to in darkness, lying atop his familiar pallet. It was night, then.

He must have been carried back here, he thought weakly, but he had no memory of anything past the last, searing blow of the lash.

He hurt too much to try to think. His arms ached from being stretched above him and the raw rope sores on his wrists rubbed painfully on his bedclothes. Worst of all were the open cuts on his back, stabbing him with new agony as he tried to shift his body on the mattress.

He moaned once, then lay still, clutching the bedclothes tightly in his hand. Even breathing pained him, his breaths coming raggedly, like unwanted sobs, rasping the tissues of his throat.

He lay awake, barely hearing footsteps come and go. His head was raised from the mattress then, and a spoonful of bitter tasting potion placed between his lips. He shook his head weakly.

"Take it, boy. It's opium—to help you sleep." The doctor's voice seemed to come from a great distance away. Finally he swallowed, and after a time the pain dissolved into dreams again.

It was another full day before he felt well enough to ask Aunt Sary if she knew how Ned and Titus were doing. "They recoverin," she said, holding a cup of broth to his lips, "but you gotta stay way from em now. They massas both say they whup em again, they catch em talking to you."

He nodded bitterly. Now that the pain had begun to ease a bit, he could feel anger again, sharp and strong—at the men

79

who'd whipped him and the men who'd written the slave laws, at slavery and everything about it. And at Doctor Carter who saw nothing wrong with cutting him to pieces for trying to act like a man.

He couldn't talk to Doctor Carter. He went about his work in stony silence, choking on anger that felt like vomit at the back of his throat.

"You can't go on like this, Michael. You know perfectly well you brought your trouble down on yourself. I expect an improvement in your attitude," the doctor said finally.

He barely glanced at the man. "I'm doin my work, Doctor Carter. You can't expect nothin else from me."

It was a warm Saturday for October. That morning Doctor Carter had asked him if he thought he could get the shed whitewashed before colder weather set in. Michael hadn't bothered answering, but now he stood in the tiny yard, rapidly covering the shed with even, white brushstrokes.

He heard Doctor Carter call him twice before he laid down the brush and went inside to wait on him. Mista Harrison was calling on the doctor, as usual. Sullenly, he set the rum bottle and glasses on the table between the two men, turning to leave without a word. He'd reached the doorway when Mista Harrison sharply called him back.

"Just a minute, boy! I see what your master means about your attitude. It appears to me you're asking for another flogging. Didn't your experience last month teach you any respect for your betters?"

Two months ago he'd never have sassed Mista Harrison back, but now he felt too angry to watch his tongue. "I didn't see no betters, Mista Harrison. Don't make a man no better'n me jus cause he got a gun and a whip."

"You respect them because they're white men, boy!"

He knew he'd angered Mista Harrison, but he'd gone too far to stop now. "Ain't no reason I should, suh, no reason at all. You whites come and carry my people off from our own country, steal babies way from their mamas, kill people never done nothin to you—do any wrong thing you wants to jus cause you white. Ain't no reason I gotta respect that."

Both men seemed amazed into silence.

Mista Harrison recovered first, his face reddening with anger. "I'd take a rawhide to you for your insolence, boy, if I were your master! It's what he's asking for, George. Pay the constable to do it, if you're too softhearted yourself."

Doctor Carter shook his head. "That's hardly called for, James."

He turned back toward Michael. "You need to get over your grudge and think clearly, Michael. You can't lay blame now for what's happened in the past. Slavery's been with us a long time. Mista Harrison and I aren't responsible for it. You can't deny you've been well treated all your life, either. If I hadn't bought your mother and you at the slave auction someone else would have, who might have been a lot harder on you."

Only the last sentence registered. Michael felt frozen where he stood. When he spoke, it was with icy control. "You didn't buy my mother and me, Doctor Carter. You bought Mama, all right, but you got me for free. And got your pleasure out of my mama too."

He strode from the room without a single additional word.

In the yard he picked up the brush again, slapping white-wash furiously against the shed.

He'd been back at work just a few minutes when Doctor Carter appeared in the yard. "Put the brush down, Michael. I want to know who told you that story."

They were of equal height now, and he looked Doctor Carter straight in the eye as he spoke. "My mama did—fore she died. Are you tellin me she lied to me?"

A full minute went by before the doctor answered. "No, she didn't lie. But Michael, you can't expect—"

He knew better than to hope for anything else from the man now. "I don't expect nothin, Doctor Carter, nothin at all. You don't mind, I'd like to get on with my work now."

He cried out in pain.

He was tied up again, hands hoisted high above his head, and once more he couldn't hold back the screams as the rawhide cut into his flesh.

"Wake up, Mike!" David's voice released him from his nightmare. "You dreaming about being whipped again?"

He felt David sit next to him in the dark, gently laying a hand on his scarred shoulder. "They never should've done that to you. Just for reading a book!"

"Can't let us learn nothin. We might get to thinkin we human beins like them." He clasped his knees with his hand. "Jesus, I hate bein a slave!"

They sat in silence a few minutes. "Maybe Dad'll give you your freedom when you're older," David said finally.

"He'll never give me nothin. Wuznt nothin to him to see me whipped. I hate him! He's my own father, and he don't care no more bout it than if I wuz some mule he own!"

Even in the dark he sensed David's surprise.

"Dad is? Your father?!"

"Mama told me fore she died."

"I should've realized," David said finally. "You know, I overheard Uncle James fighting with Dad about you once. He kept yelling, 'It killed my sister when Hetty had him! I never understood what he meant before."

Michael started. "That's why he's always hated me!"

"Oh, I'm sure Uncle James doesn't really hate you, Mike. He can hardly blame you for things that went on before you were born. It's just his way to yell when he's mad."

David hesitated. "You're right about Dad, though. He ought to've treated you differently."

82

Chapter 7

1832

He was glad the holidays had finally dragged to an end. It was too hard to be so lonely at Christmas time. He'd known Titus wanted nothing more to do with him, but to be turned away from Ned's home where he'd always been so welcome!

Cassie had tried to ease his feelings, pulling him aside from the line at the water pump. "Ned say ta tell you he don't blame you none, Michael, but he can't go gainst Daddy now. You knows how hard Daddy always done work, savin up fer his freedom. He reckon come spring he gone have enuf saved ta buy hisself from Massa at last. He jus can't take no chance on not bein lowed to stay in the state after he free. You gotta understand that."

He understood, of course, but it didn't make it any easier to bear.

The first signs of spring were finally appearing. Two weeks of cold rain had stopped at last, and the mud in the alleys was drying up. Forsythia bushes were blooming sunshine yellow in the sheltered corners of front yards.

Thank the Lawd the town council had approved Daddy's petition to remain in the state, Cassie told him. Now that he'd secured his freedom at last, she was willing to talk with Michael again, sitting close beside him on the back stoop of the cabin.

With Cassie he could forget for a while the bleak future ahead, spending his days following another man's orders. They'd stopped talking now, and drew closer together as darkness fell. Michael trembled with sudden urgency as they kissed, his member swollen and hard with need for her. He could feel an answering firmness from Cassie's nipples as she pressed against him.

"They's time fore curfew to walk down by the river," he whispered urgently.

Cassie drew back a little ways. "I wants to, Michael, but I can't take a chance of gettin bigged less I knows what you plans for us. Reckon you know what I feel for you. You younger'n me, but you a man now. Is you willin to ast you massa to let us marry?"

He'd like nothing better than to be close to Cassie like this for always, but it wouldn't be enough. Not as long as they lived in slavery. "I can't Cassie. I can't jus marry and settle down long as I'm still a slave. I jus feel I gotta be free."

"We can work together, like Daddy done. Won't take so long fore we can buy our freedom."

"It'll be years, Cassie. We be old by then. I need to be free while I'm young enuf to do somethin more with my life." He hesitated, then said, "Ain't so far away to get to a free state from here. We could run off and marry up North where they ain't no slavery."

"You crazy, Michael? We be caught, mos likely, an sold down South! I ain't bout to try no such thing."

"We won't be caught if we careful. Think bout it at least, Cassie, please."

"You too hardheaded to talk to, Michael. Ain't no way you're gonna get me to try a fool thing like runnin away."

He walked aimlessly a long time after Cassie had slammed angrily into the cabin, barely looking out for the night watch in his misery. He'd never wanted any girl but Cassie, but he just couldn't resign himself to a life of slavery for her. If only she could understand how he felt!

It was well past curfew when he finally slipped through the alley and let himself in the back door.

"Where have you been till now?" Doctor Carter suddenly appeared in the kitchen doorway. "It's a good hour past curfew! Have you been teaching Ned and Titus again?"

You could smell the rum on the man's breath clear across the room, Michael thought disgustedly. "They afraid to even talk to me anymore. You satisfied, suh?"

The doctor lost his threatening expression. "Michael, do you think I take pleasure in seeing you unhappy? I'm partly to blame," he went on, as if talking to himself. "I should have put a stop to your reading the first day I found out about it."

There was no point even answering that. He turned to walk into his room.

"Michael, I asked you where you've been till now!"

He knew Doctor Carter would keep at him till he answered. "Jus walkin by myself. I wuz talking with Cassie fore curfew, but she gone in her home long fore it start."

Doctor Carter looked thoughtful. "You like Cassie, don't you, Michael?"

"Yeah, sure I likes her," he mumbled.

The doctor was looking at him as if it had been a lot longer than a few hours since the last time he'd seen him. "Why, you're near grown, aren't you, Michael? There's no reason the two of you couldn't marry. I expect my finances to be picking up in the near future. Aunt Sary's growing pretty old for the work she's doing. I'd be glad to purchase Cassie as soon as I can see my way clear. There's room for the two of you to live right here, at least till you start having children."

He bet Cassie would be pleased with the idea, he thought with a pang. She wouldn't even understand why it made him so suddenly furious.

"I ain't plannin on givin you no grandchildren to slave for you!"

The sudden, stinging slap on his face nearly knocked him to the floor.

"This is the thanks I get for trying to think of your welfare!"

He shrugged. "I s'pose you meant well, suh, but I ain't plannin to marry and father no babies to be slaves. I ain't about to lay that curse on a chile."

He couldn't sleep that night. Suddenly he rose from his pallet and slipped out the back door, running with no noise at all toward Cassie's house. She must have been expecting him back. She sat on the doorstep, not looking angry at all now.

They didn't need to say a word as they linked hands and headed toward the riverbank. The ground was cool, but he spread out her shawl for them to lie on, and they were warm, plenty warm in each other's arms.

Her dress was off now, and his own clothes tossed alongside. He felt her sweet, secret softness welcome him, and their joy grew and grew till they exploded together like a night full of shooting stars.

She held him in her arms as they dropped off to sleep afterwards. He woke with a start. The walls of his room stood close around him, the thin pallet hard and lonely.

He lay awake for a long time the, shaking with unshed sobs, his hopes seeming to dribble away like the seed slowly dripping down his thighs.

The following morning Cassie was even more set against Michael's plan to run up North. He was right about her favoring Doctor Carter's suggestion. He wished he'd never mentioned it.

"Wuzn't no need for you to sass him like that," she said angrily. "Least you could've done wuz ta ask me how I felt bout it. Pears to me you not serious bout me at all."

Plenty of other boys liked her fine, she added. Peared that she and Michael had just better stop wasting their time courting if nothing was to come of it.

He could get up North just as well by himself, he decided then and there. No point in waiting around for Cassie to change her mind. She never would. There was no future for them together.

There was no future for him here at all.

He wasn't an ignorant youngster anymore, he thought with satisfaction, laying the oars quietly in the bottom of the boat. There were still almost two hours left till sunrise as he beached the rowboat in a tall clump of tangled weeds on the Maryland shore, well hidden from view.

In the two weeks since breaking off with Cassie, he'd spent every spare moment preparing for his escape. Now everything was working out just as he'd planned. If only she'd trusted him!

Finding the oars had been the hardest part. Once he'd spotted a pair left out overnight by a careless boat owner, it had been easy enough to stow them away for his own use. It took a few minutes to master the use of the oars, but when he'd gotten the hang of them he rowed across the river easily enough.

Now he went over the rest of his plans once more. He'd studied the map of the country he'd torn from the geography so many times he knew it by heart, but he'd folded it small and shoved it to the bottom of his pants pocket just in case of need. He'd keep to back roads, he'd decided. There was too much chance of being spotted by someone he knew in the city of Washington. Better to skirt around it, then head due north towards Pennsylvania.

He'd given some thought to his pass before actually writing it out. The simpler the better, he finally decided. "My nigra man has my leave to go to market this morning," he'd written. The signature was scrawled quickly, so as to be nearly unreadable. He left the pass undated.

He hoped it would serve till he passed through Maryland, but decided to take along a blank sheet of foolscap on which he could write an additional protection if need should arise. The dried scrapings of ink were carefully folded into a scrap of old newspaper. He could easily mix them with water if he had to. The quill pen was too long to conceal easily, till he broke off the top half. The sharpened bottom now fit neatly in his pocket alongside his penknife.

He picked up the small parcel with his bread and slab of bacon. Sunday stretched before him, and with any luck he wouldn't be missed at all till Monday morning. It was close to seventy miles to Pennsylvania, as near as he could figure from the map. He could make it easily in three days time.

By Sunday afternoon he realized it would take longer than he'd first figured. The narrow dirt road, little more than wagon tracks, was not laid out anything like the straight path he'd envisioned, but threaded its way from farm to farm, detouring around patches of thickly overgrown woods and newly plowed fields. He'd lost two hours at the second fork in the road, he reckoned, following the branch that seemed to be aiming north some four or five miles, before realizing he was heading in a gradual curve back in the direction of the Potomac.

He had to keep to the road. It would be all too easy to lose his way in the woods, and he didn't dare be spotted cutting across an open field. He wasn't sure how far north he'd gotten as he lay hidden at the edge of one of the wooded patches that evening, but he knew it was nowhere close to the twenty or so miles he'd hoped to cover.

He was stiff and cold by morning. Now that Monday had come, he had to walk more cautiously, ready to conceal himself behind trees or underbrush at the sound of approaching wagons. Visiting between plantations was generally allowed slaves on Sundays, but now that the others had returned to their daily tasks he'd stand out like a sore thumb walking down the road alone. He had his pass, of course, but he'd sooner not have the need to show it.

He was stopped once that day, taken by surprise by a thin, silent hunter, who emerged suddenly from the woods, rifle slung over his shoulder and a freshly filled rabbit hanging limply from his left hand. He was sure his heart would give him away pounding so loudly in his chest, but to his great relief the white man merely gave his pass a quick glance and told him to go on his way then.

He woke Tuesday to gray skies and a raw, damp breeze. By midmorning, rain was falling steadily with no sign of letup. He crouched under a tree to eat the last of his bread, before the pelting drops could reduce it to mush. Only a small piece of the bacon was left now.

He prayed he was near the state border. He didn't dare approach anyone to ask for food or work in this strange country. There'd be berries in the woods later in the summer, but now there was nothing to be found.

The rain was still coming down as darkness fell that evening. He drew to a stop when he saw the ramshackle barn, just a few hundred feet from the road. It was safer to keep to the scanty shelter offered by the woods, but he was soaked to his skin and shivering with cold. The barn would at least give him some protection from the rain.

He hesitated, feeling so exhausted he could barely think straight. A sudden gust of wind bent the trees, as the rain began pelting down even harder. Mind made up, he crouched low, running across the open field to the barn.

It would be safe enough. He'd leave well before daybreak.

He hadn't taken account of how tired he'd grown. The sun had been up an hour when he woke with a start. The bearded man staring down at him was the farmer, he supposed, and the two younger men his sons.

His rain smeared pass did him little good. "We'll let the justice of the peace take a look at this," the man said simply.

The law was clear, the judge told him an hour later. A colored person found going at large was to be considered a fugitive unless he could prove otherwise.

His pass made little impression on the man. What was the name of his master? he asked sharply. Where did he live? Where was the market he supposedly was given leave to go to?

Michael didn't need to be told he couldn't come up with answers that would convice the magistrate. How could he? He didn't even know the name of the village they'd taken him to, some two dozen unpainted wooden buildings lining a few hundred feet of dirt road.

His only hope was to play dumb. "Don rightly know what it call, suh. Jus got turned round an loss mah way in the rainstorm. Sho wuz scairt ta go on in dat dark. Reckon ah can find mah way back now day here, suh."

He was beginning to think he might be believed at that, when the judge spoke casually. A search of Michael's person might help show if he spoke the truth or not.

The ink was nothing but a smudge of black powder in the wet newsprint, but he'd wrapped the map and foolscap with care. They lay smoothed out on a table alongside his broken quill pen.

There was no use pretending any more. His guilt was clear to everyone in the room.

He didn't want to give his name or where he'd run off from, but he had no choice. If his master couldn't be located, he'd simply be sold to pay the cost of jailing him.

The cell they locked him in was even more dismal than the one he'd shared with Ned and Titus. He could barely take half a dozen paces from one side to the other. There was nothing to do but count off the days till Doctor Carter came to fetch him and think about how he'd messed everything up—just when he'd been so sure he was on the verge of gaining his freedom at last.

At least Cassie had sense enough not to run off with him. That was the only good thing about it.

It was nearly a week before Doctor Carter arrived in response to the jailer's newpaper advertisement. Michael hated to admit it, but he was relieved to see him. He stood up quickly as the jailer unlocked his cell.

He didn't know what to say to the doctor. "Doctor Carter—" he began, uncertainly.

Before he could say anything else, Doctor Carter strode forward and slapped him across the face—an openhanded blow followed immediately by a stinging backhand to his other cheek. Once again the doctor struck him, rocking his head from side to side.

Michael stepped back, shaken, wiping a thin trickle of blood from the corner of his mouth.

"Keep your mouth shut, boy. I've had enough of your sass to last me a lifetime."

Doctor Carter wouldn't speak to him at all on the way back to Alexandria. When they finally stepped off the ferry, Michael turned automatically in the direction of the house. The doctor grabbed him by the arm, pulling him around.

"Where we goin, suh?"

Doctor Carter didn't answer but just marched him the few blocks from the dock to the jailhouse at the corner of the market square. Michael froze as they headed inside.

"You gonna have me whipped again?" His voice came out a little more than a whisper.

Doctor Carter stopped a moment. "No, I won't do that to you," he said, falling silent again as they entered the building. Michael followed him, equally silent. The doctor had let go of his arm, but what else could he do? He was trapped here just the same.

Inside the jail Doctor Carter spoke again, but not to Michael. "I'll thank you to lodge him here for the present," he said to the jailer.

The cell door slammed behind him, and he was left alone. There was no way to know how long Doctor Carter meant to keep him here. Possibly he even intended to sell him to one of the slave traders who made regular stops in Alexandria.

It didn't seem to matter. Nothing mattered at all anymore. He'd never escape from slavery. He knew it now.

Everything he'd tried had just made things worse. He'd gotten Sammy in trouble. Ned and Titus had been whipped because they listened to him. He was too stupid even to run away without getting caught.

He was a slave for life, and there was nothing at all he could do about it. There was nothing he could do to change anything at all.

He couldn't even care anymore.

The meals the jailer brought were mostly cornmeal mush and once in a while a strip of fatty bacon, but he didn't mind. He was never hungry enough to eat more than a spoonful or two anyhow.

He didn't bother to keep track of how many days had gone by. Once he pulled himself up to the window ledge and saw through the bars that the trees were in full summer leaf, but he didn't trouble to look again.

Several times, gangs of young men and boys were placed in his cell by slave traders for safe-keeping till the next auction day. He managed to answer if they spoke to him, but he could barely rouse himself to feel pity for their troubles.

Mostly, he slept. He woke late in the day, but by afternoon he'd feel too tired to stay awake any longer, and lie down again till the jailer brought his evening bowl of mush.

When he was up he sat barely moving, his legs stretched out on the floor in front of him. The jailhouse cat, a skinny gray tabby, took to curling up on his lap. He stroked her quietly, rubbing her rough fur by the hour as she slept.

Four men had been lodged in the cell with him the night before, the youngest a boy about Michael's own age, carrying his belongings wrapped in a faded bandanna. While the three older men dozed, leaning back against the wall, he paced rapidly back and forth, several times hoisting himself up to peer out the barred window. When their food was brought, he emptied his bowl rapidly. Michael glanced up at him a moment, then pushed him his own nearly untasted portion.

"Thanks," he said, flashing a sudden warm grin at Michael.

Michael could see the other boy wanted to talk to him further, but talking seemed just too much trouble right then. He stretched out right after the evening meal. Within an hour or so, the older men also lay ready for sleep, and finally the boy stopped pacing and joined them.

A sudden cry of pain, cut off by the sound of violent retching, broke into their sleep. It was still night, but enough moonlight seeped into the cell for Michael to see the boy doubled over, moaning as he vomited. By the time the jailer came on the run, he lay writhing helplessly, a watery stool now running from his bowels as well.

"Water! please water!" The words came out in a thin whisper. Michael held a dipperful from the bucket to his lips, but he took no more than a swallow before gagging and vomiting once again.

The jailer took one look and left to summon a doctor. The oldest of the men knelt by the moaning boy, holding his head and wiping his mouth from time to time. The others stared in horror. "Couldn't be de mush. We all et it," one mumbled.

It was midmorning before the jailer finally returned. The boy lay stretched out, barely moving, his eyes sunken into his face. The doctor took one look before announcing his diagnosis.

"Cholera."

They'd have to move him from the jail to a hospital across town, the doctor said, calling for a stretcher to be brought. He bent over the boy once more, then said quietly, "No hurry. He's dead."

The man who'd been nursing him broke into loud cries, rocking the boy's body in his arms like a colicky infant. He was most likely his father, Michael thought. He felt sorry for the old man, but he couldn't bring himself to feel sorry for the boy anymore.

At least he was free of slavery now.

Doctor Carter came that afternoon to take Michael out of the jail. Michael followed him as silently as he had the afternoon he'd been locked up.

The doctor looked at him a long moment before speaking. "I hope you've learned your lesson by now. It's cost me a pretty penny to pay the jailer for your keep, but nothing else seems to make any impression on you."

Michael shrugged, staring down at the brick sidewalk.

"Michael, I asked you if you've learned your lesson this

time."

"Yassuh, Doctor Carter," he mumbled. It didn't matter that the doctor had let him out of jail. He was still the man's prisoner just the same.

In the weeks he'd been locked up, a cholera epidemic had struck. A hospital had been hastily opened on the edge of town, although, like the boy in the cell, sufferers often died before they could even be carried there.

Doctor Carter was one of the physicians appointed to the cholera hospital by the town council, Michael learned. He followed the doctor about on his rounds, silently doing whatever he directed.

Few of the remedies tried by the doctors, whether purges, plasters or bloodletting made much difference. Patients died inside the hospital about as fast as if they'd never been brought there.

"How can you stand to go there every day?" David asked him one evening.

Michael shrugged. He wasn't afraid of the cholera. It wouldn't make any difference if it took him. He'd just as soon be dead.

If nothing else, the terrible epidemic kept him too busy to sit and brood. By the time the cholera had begun to run its course, Michael had gotten over the worst of his despondency. Not that he thought he'd ever be happy again. But if he kept his mind off anything but his work, he could manage to get through one day at a time.

He rarely said anything to Doctor Carter beyond "yassuh" or "nossuh" but the doctor didn't seem to notice. The doctor's own spirits had been at a low ebb since the onset of the epidemic. Most days he'd retire directly to the front room after his rounds at the hospital, slumping in his wing chair without even reading the newspaper, barely moving except to refill his rum glass from the decanter. Whole weeks went by he didn't bother opening his office to attend his patients' ordinary ailments.

It was only the necessity of finding David a tutor in Latin and Greek, to enable him to pass the University of Virginia entrance requirements, that had roused him from his lethargy at last.

Not that David would have cared much if he hadn't passed, Michael thought. Michael couldn't imagine anything more wonderful than going away to school, but you could see that David's heart wasn't in it. He admitted it himself.

"He says I've got to make something of myself," David said, as Michael helped him pack. "And if I'm not going to become a doctor, then I should study law. I suppose if I can't do what I really want, it's as good as anything else."

"What you really wanna do, David?"

"Just study art, that's all. If I could, I'd go to New York, Paris even, and become a real artist. But Dad would never hear of it."

"You could go anyway. You free. He can't stop you."

"Nah. It's just a dream, that's all. I wouldn't even have anything to live on."

"You could get work till you become a artist." A sudden hope grew in his mind. "Lissen, David, we could go to New York together, right now. No one'd think I wuz runnin away if I wuz with you. I could work and help you when we get there. I swear I would."

David sat on the edge of the bed without answering. Maybe he'll really say yes, Michael thought, as the moment stretched out. He must be thinking it over.

David sighed, finally. "I wish I could, Mike. But there's no way. I can't go against him like that."

He hadn't really expected anything else, he told himself. David might argue with his father, but in the end he never went against his father's wishes.

Now that the epidemic was over, the talk Michael overheard in town returned to other subjects. Much of it concerned the planned seven-mile-long extension to the Chesapeake and Ohio Canal, which started in Georgetown and was already navigable almost as far as Harper's Ferry. The Alexandria Canal Company had already started work on an aqueduct bridge across the Potomac that would carry a major part of the canal extension linking Alexandria and Georgetown.

Bringing canal traffic to Alexandria would ensure a return of prosperity to the community, townspeople felt. Doctor Carter agreed. He had decided to build a new duplex on the site of the burned townhouse, he told Mista Harrison. He'd have to borrow the money to put up the new building, but it would pay for itself shortly in rental income.

Michael didn't pay much attention to Doctor Carter's plans. He was beginning to make plans of his own once again. Maybe David couldn't help him, but one of the other white boys he'd played with as a child might well be willing to.

He'd bide his time till he was sure he'd come up with a foolproof escape plan. In the meantime, he'd act just as docile and respectful as white folks expected him to.

Winter was all but over before he came up with a plan that satisfied him, but when he did it was so simple he wondered why he hadn't thought of it sooner. He'd see if Robert would help him, he decided. It had been years since Robert had scratched out the letters spelling his name in the dirt by the water pump, but he thought he could be pretty sure Robert wouldn't give him away, even if he refused to help.

Robert worked in the saddlery shop, he knew, but he couldn't approach him there. Luckily, Robert liked to fish as well as anyone else in town. It took several Sunday afternoons hanging around the path to the river before he managed to fall in beside him as if by accident.

"You're crazy," Robert told him, after listening a few mintues. "Haven't you gotten yourself in enough trouble up to now?"

He shook his head. "I jus know this'll work," he insisted. "But I can't do it on my own. I gotta have someone white to help me."

Robert's line went taut. He pulled it in, carefully removing the hook from the mouth of the large perch flopping frantically in his hands. "It might work, at that," he said finally. "But I don't see why you expect me to help you."

"We played together when we wuz comin up, Robert."

"So? I ain't got nothing against you getting your freedom, Mike. But you're asking me to stick my neck out on your account."

Michael held his breath, waiting for Robert to continue, but Robert seemed in no hurry. He took his time baiting his hook and letting out his line again. Finally, he said, "Tell you what. You make it worth my while and I'll do it. I reckon ten dollars would be about right."

"Ten dollars! Where am I gonna get ten dollars from?"

"You'll have to figure that out yourself. Just let me know when you've got the money."

"You want to do what!?" Doctor Carter demanded.

"Hire my time, suh," Michael repeated. He'd thought it out for days. There was no way he could earn the ten dollars he needed to pay Robert in just his free time. He had to be able to work for himself days as well. Otherwise, he'd be an old man by the time he got away.

"You don't got near as much work for me as you used to," he said carefully. The doctor didn't have half the number of patients he'd had, either, but he'd better not say that.

"Nelly don't need my help marketing or nothin," he said instead. The woman Doctor Carter hired after Aunt Sary finally had to stop working last month rarely had a friendly word, but at least she was a strong and willing worker.

"How do you propose to earn money?" the doctor asked him finally. "I know you're a good worker, Michael, but you have no skills or trade."

"That ain't my fault," he retorted, before he could stop himself. Everyone else in town might be convinced that he'd learned his place at last, but he still found it hard not to blurt out his true feelings to Doctor Carter. The last thing he wanted was for the doctor to suspect that the real reason he'd asked for the privilege of hiring his time was to get the money to run away, rather than to save up to buy his freedom as he'd said.

Fortunately, the doctor didn't seem angered. "I've always meant to have you learn a trade of some sort. There just never seemed to be an opportune time."

"Yassuh," Michael said. "But they's lots of work I can do helpin out where they buildin the canal."

"I've always taken care of your needs, Michael. If you hire your time you'll have to pay for your board. I think you'll find it harder than you think to take care of yourself."

"I can board with Aunt Sary." He'd a lot sooner pay her for his keep.

"You'll have to pay me for your time anyway, Michael," Doctor Carter said sharply. "You still belong to me whether I allow you to hire your time or not. I don't want you forgetting that."

It was nearly a week before the doctor made up his mind. He'd still expect Michael to do the chores that were too heavy for Nelly, he said, but he could hire the rest of his time and board with Aunt Sary if he had a mind to. He'd expect Michael to pay two dollars a week for the privilege of hiring his time, he added.

Two dollars! It would be hard to earn much more than three,

and he'd have to pay Aunt Sary for his board, of course. The doctor was as good as robbing him, but he'd have to agree to his terms. What other choice had he?

Chapter 8

1833

He couldn't find steady work anywhere in town, so he went early every morning to the canal site or docks ready to do whatever job he could find. There was usually some ship-owner who needed extra hands to load or unload a cargo, or some errand he could run.

It wasn't easy to earn even three dollars a week though. Although there were plenty of odd jobs to be done, there was no lack of men and boys just as eager and willing as Michael to earn a few pennies: both free colored workers and slaves who—with the permission of their masters—tried to earn what they could for themselves when their regular task was done.

On a good day he might earn fifty cents, and once in a while seventy-five, but other evenings he went home with just a few pennies in his pocket. Sundays and evenings he often fished till it was too dark to see, saving out enough of his catch for Aunt Sary and himself, and carrying his surplus to sell the next morning in the market square.

His work left him little time for visiting with his friends, but it was just as well. They were all busy with their own lives. Cassie and Charles were planning on getting married. His family had talked it over, Ned told him, and decided to use whatever money they could save to help buy Cassie's freedom.

"It makes a lot of sense," Ned said soberly. "Charles' family's helpin em too. Otherwise, they chillen'll all be slaves when they born."

Michael wondered if Ned was disappointed to put off the time when he could buy his own freedom, but decided not to ask him. Ned would have told him if he'd wanted to. He'd just as soon talk about something else than Cassie getting married to Charles, anyway.

1833 was more than half over, and he still hadn't saved anywhere near ten dollars, though he'd been hiring his time all spring and summer. He could save up a lot faster if only he didn't have to pay Doctor Carter the two dollars every week. He knew Doctor Carter wouldn't agree to take any less, though. Even with the money he was turning over to him, the doctor still complained about his financial troubles.

Although the duplex was modest, it had cost more to build than he'd expected, Doctor Carter was telling Mista Harrison. He'd had to take out an additional loan to finish paying for it. On top of that he'd be getting the next semester's bill for David's university tuition before long.

"Not to mention that the talk is Council will be increasing the tax on real estate again to pay off the canal loan. The property owners of this town will be bankrupt before the canal is ever completed. I'd hoped to count on a steady rental income from the duplex, but with my expenses the way they are it looks as if I'll be forced to sell it instead. It's the only asset I have."

Michael stopped listening and went out to the yard to get another armload of firewood he'd just split for the doctor. He'd a lot sooner finish his chores and get on home to supper than stand around listening to Doctor Carter's woes.

Mista Harrison was talking as he walked back into the house. "You do have another asset, you know, George," he was saying.

"I couldn't consider it," Doctor Carter answered. He broke off as Michael approached politely to ask if there was anything else the doctor wanted done that evening.

"No, you can go on now, Michael."

"Yassuh, thank you, Doctor Carter. Evening, suh."

Mista Harrison's voice followed him as he left.

"Well, at least you seem to have taught him his place at last. I suppose that's something."

He had to earn more money before cold weather set in, or he'd have no chance of escaping this year. It had already grown too cool to fish most evenings. He'd have to find more work he could do than the odd jobs he'd managed to get so far.

It wasn't till he went to do his chores for the doctor the next evening that he came up with an idea. Lots of white folks in town hired the work they needed done. If he could borrow a saw and woodhorse from Ned's dad, he bet he could find lots of people needing firewood sawed before winter came.

Going from house to house looking for work was better than waiting around the docks. Even if they didn't need wood sawed, most people had some job they needed done—from carrying out ashes to whitewashing sheds and fences.

He asked for work at shops and taverns in town, too. Many of the shopkeepers had deliveries he could make. Sometimes he was paid with foodstuff rather than cash, especially by some of the colored craftsmen who had little money to spare, but that was all right. It saved having to buy dinner for Aunt Sary and him.

He'd have just over four dollars saved by the end of the week, he figured, as he carried in the doctor's firewood the last day of September. If he could put away at least a dollar a week, he'd have enough by mid-November. With any luck, freezing weather would hold off till Christmas time.

An urgent summons by Doctor Carter broke into his calculations. "You'll have to stop hiring your time," he told him abruptly.

He couldn't believe it! "Why? I been givin you two dollars every week, and doin everything you asked, ain't I? What more you want?"

"It has nothing to do with what I want," Doctor Carter said sharply. "I've received a summons to appear before the town council on the charge of letting you go at large and hire yourself out like a freeman."

"What's wrong with that? Plenty of slaves hire their time."

"That may be, but the law on the books forbids it, Michael. I hadn't realized it myself till I received the summons. But now that I've been charged, I can't ignore it."

He still couldn't believe it. "Who charged you? I ain't heard of no one else havin to give up hiring his time."

"It doesn't matter who it was. I know you're disappointed, Michael, but there's no help for it. You can move your things back here tomorrow."

"And do what? I don't want to stop earnin money for myself, Doctor Carter."

"This has nothing to do with what you want, Michael! Anyway, I would have thought you'd realize by now that it's not that easy to make your way on your own."

"It'd be a lot easier if you didn't rob me of pract'lly every cent I earn!" He should have held his tongue he knew, but he was getting too upset to watch what he said.

"I haven't robbed you, boy! I warned you when I first allowed you to hire your time I didn't want you to forget that I still own you, but it appears to me now that's just what you've done.

"I gave you a privilege, allowing you to hire yourself out and come and go as you please. Now it appears you haven't even appreciated it. I think this summons may have come just in time."

Once he'd started arguing back, he couldn't keep the bitterness he'd hidden so well all year from pouring out. "What you expect me to appreciate? You never gave me nothin. You think I should be grateful to work all day for you and be your prisoner just cause you took my mama to bed with you? That what you'd expect David to appreciate!?"

"You can't compare yourself with David, Michael." Doctor Carter spoke quietly, but Michael could see his lips were thin with anger. He stood looking at Michael a moment, then spoke deliberately.

"I'm not about to debate with you, Michael, so you can just keep your sass to yourself. I have enough trouble without your adding to it. I've had to mortgage this house to finish construction on the duplex, and I've debts coming due that I've no means of paying at present. I don't intend paying a fine to Council on top of that because of your disobedience!"

There was no way he intended to obey Doctor Carter. Once he gave up hiring his time, he'd never get the money together to pay for his escape. The only thing to do was to stall him, Michael decided.

In the meantime, he'd work twice as hard as before at earning money.

The day after their argument Michael went out to work as usual, leaving Aunt Sary's early in the morning and working till well after dark. He still had to do his chores for the doctor, though, if he didn't want to make him even angrier.

105

He hoped Doctor Carter might be out, but of course he was waiting irritably for Michael. "I see you haven't gotten around to obeying me yet."

"I can't right yet, suh," he muttered. "I told two or three folks I'd be by to saw up they firewood and clean they fireplaces, and they still expectin me. Don't reckon a few days gonna hurt nothin."

To his relief, Doctor Carter had nothing more to say. Four or five days passed before he asked Michael if he'd finished doing the work he'd promised, but Michael managed to put him off again. And that Saturday night he seemed just as willing as ever to take his two dollars, Michael noted.

The week after, Doctor Carter mentioned the matter only once, "Michael, my appearance before the town council is coming up at the next meeting."

"Yassuh," Michael mumbled, looking down at the floorboards.

The doctor looked at him sharply. "I don't intend telling you again, Michael."

"Nossuh," he mumbled again, still staring at the floor.

The next two weeks passed without any further reminders from Doctor Carter, and Michael hoped the whole affair had blown over. He wasn't about to bring it up by asking him what the council had said.

The last Saturday of the month, he'd finished up his odd jobs by late afternoon, when he was lucky enough to hear of a schooner which had just berthed at the docks and needed extra hands unloading. It was a good thing he'd gotten the work, he thought. Every extra cent was a help to him now.

It was a good two hours or so past his usual time when he finally let himself in the back door of Doctor Carter's house, but he supposed the doctor would be waiting for him just the same.

Doctor Carter had a visitor, he realized, hearing voices

from the front of the house.

"I wouldn't worry. He's always proved himself reliable," the doctor was saying in an odd tone of voice.

"Let's hope you're right," an unfamiliar voice answered. "It's well past eight now. I did accommodate you after all, paying you a day in advance, so you could get your financial concerns in order."

"Sorry to be late, suh," Michael told Doctor Carter after he'd entered politely. "They was a ship come in needed help unloadin."

Doctor Carter didn't seem concerned with his explanation, Michael realized. In fact, he was looking everywhere in the room except at Michael. The other man stood though, and walked up to him. He looked familiar, Michael thought, though he couldn't place him—a tall, middle-aged man with black whiskers that flowed onto his suit of black broadcloth.

"I've been waiting on you, boy. You don't belong to Doctor Carter any more. Reckon you might've heard of me—Mister Armfield of Franklin and Armfield. Run the biggest slave trading company in these United States."

He was frozen, too stunned to say a word. His only thought was to turn and run, but his feet were as impossible to move as if they'd been nailed to the floor.

The slave trader was still talking, he realized.

"Reckon this comes as a surprise to you, boy, but you ain't got nothing to be alarmed about long as you behave yourself. I promised Doctor Carter here I'd keep you in the county and find you a good master. He's right concerned with your well being."

He still couldn't speak, but it was just as well. It was better not to say anything till he could be sure his voice wouldn't betray him. He waited another moment till he felt calm enough to answer.

"Yassuh, Mista Armfield."

"Well, let's get going then, boy."

"Yassuh, Mista Armfield. Only thing, I don't have none of my clothes here, suh. And Missus Mercer, I cleaned her fireplaces this mornin, she say come by this ebenin and she could pay me then. I'd sho preciate if we could go by there, suh."

"I don't have time to traipse all over town with you, boy. I've delayed my supper long enough."

"Yassuh. Don't mean to put you out none, suh."

The trader looked at him a minute. "Well, I can see you're a good boy like Doctor Carter tells me. I reckon you know where our operation's located up on Duke Street."

"Yassuh, sho do."

"All right, you can go and collect your belongings then. Just show up by noon tomorrow. Don't you be late now, hear?"

"Yassuh, sho won't. Thank you, suh."

He stood where he was after the trader had left, staring at Doctor Carter in disbelief. It was true. He really had sold him. As it sank in, his fury at the man grew till he thought he could easily strike him, throw him to the floor and pound his head against the boards till he'd killed him. Trembling, he clenched his fists in his pockets, forcing himself to stillness.

Doctor Carter was speaking to him at last. "It needn't have come to this if you'd come to your senses sooner, Michael. You have your own obstinacy to blame, you know. I gave you every chance to obey me, but you completely ignored me. You've grown totally out of my control. I told Mista Harrison I'd never consider selling you to settle my debts, but you left me no choice.

"You knew my financial straits. Having to pay the fine and court costs was the last straw. I could have let the council sell you to one of the Southern traders to pay my costs, you know, instead of arranging your sale to a reputable company. I had to take a good deal less than I could have gotten from

Armfield, too, to include a restriction on reselling you outside this area in the bill of sale."

Doctor Carter thought he should be grateful! To be locked up in a slave pen—waiting his turn to be stood on an auction block and sold like a prize pig! He even expected him to believe Armfield's assurances about not selling him South.

He still didn't trust himself to say a word. If he opened his mouth to speak at all, he wouldn't be able to stop himself from telling the doctor just what a piece of lowdown white trash he'd shown himself to be. This wasn't the time to get in any more trouble mouthing off, he reminded himself.

He turned, heading toward the door.

"Michael, I'm not done talking to you."

He turned back toward the doctor a moment, taking a deep, calming breath. "You don't own me any more, Doctor Carter."

He closed the door behind him as quietly as he'd spoken.

"What do you mean, it has to be tomorrow? You got the ten dollars to give me?" Robert demanded, when he'd finally spotted him leaving McKnight's Tavern an hour and a half later.

He shook his head. "Six and a half's all the money I've got."

"Ten dollar's what we agreed on, Mike. You come back when you're ready to pay me the ten."

He caught Robert's arm as he started to walk off. "Won't be able to pay you nothin after this. He sold me to the big slave trader up to Duke Street."

"Sold you! I don't believe it! Ain't he your—?"

"He don't care nothin bout that. Sold me just the same. Mista Armfield, the trader, say he give me till noon tomorrow to get my belongings together."

"All right," Robert said at last. "Give me what you've got, then."

He'd had the two dollars clenched in his fist the whole time he'd listened to Doctor Carter, and now he took it out and handed it to Robert. "Ain't got the rest with me right now."

"Just don't forget to bring it tomorrow, hear! I'll meet you the same place we were fishing at, soon as it gets light."

He sorted over his few possessions rapidly. This time he wouldn't make the mistake of taking anything the least bit out of the way. He tied his extra clothing up in a small bundle, and added the package of food that Aunt Sary pressed on him. His fishing hook and line would be all right, and the small knife as well.

He'd studied the map so often he'd about memorized it, he thought. He'd have to rely on his memory, in any case.

He hesitated a minute over David's drawing of Mama, before reluctantly deciding he'd be safer without it. He left the picture where it was, tacked to the wall of the cabin. He could remember Mama without it. And Aunt Sary had loved her too.

It was barely light when he made his way silently down the path to the river, shivering in the cool morning air. No one else was in sight as he peered up and down the riverbank, and he thought for a tense moment that Robert could easily have changed his mind. He sighed with relief, then, as he spotted the skiff, nearly invisible among the tall weeds, still thick though they were dry and brown with fall now. Robert grinned as he straightened up from his hiding place at the bottom of the boat.

"You got the rest of the money?"

He counted it twice before handing Michael the oars. "Hope you know how to use these, Mike. Wouldn't look right if anyone was to see me rowin you." He stretched his legs out comfortably as Michael pushed the boat away from shore, casting out his fishing line once they were free of the entangling weeds.

Rowing supstream to Georgetown, Michael had to work too hard at keeping the boat on course to worry much over

110

all the things that could go wrong. Once they'd tied up the skiff up on the far shore though, he felt too frightened to move for a moment. If he was caught now, he'd be sold South for sure!

Calm down, he reminded himself, following Robert as he scrambled quickly up the riverbank. The plan would never work if he couldn't act natural!

It took just a few minutes till they reached the loading area that marked the beginning of the Chesapeake & Ohio Canal. Though it was still early, the quay surrounding the dammed up basin of Rock Creek was already loud with the braying of mules and the shouts of straining workmen.

The line of barges bumped and jostled in the crowded basin as men and boys hurried to carry their cargoes to adjacent warehouses. Children of the canal boatmen tugged at the reins of balky mules, while the womenfolk aboard the barges bent their efforts toward keeping curious toddlers out of harm's way.

They stood staring at the scene a moment before Robert motioned to Michael to follow him over the mule bridge to the canal towpath. Robert ambled along now, skirting piles of steaming droppings, and eyeing the line of barges with mule teams rehitched to the towline, waiting to enter the first of the locks.

He paused again, then smiled slightly, nodding at the fourth barge in line. "That's the one you want, Mike."

The boatman, a dark haired, wiry man, looked to be in his late twenties. Michael stood a few feet away, while Robert spoke to him as they'd planned. He kept his gaze on the ground, but out of the corner of his eye he caught a glimpse of the man's wife as she tended the younger of the two toddlers harnessed to the deck of the small cabin with short lengths of rope. She must be seven or eight months gone with child, he reckoned.

"Mornin, sir," Robert said. "My grandpa, lives up to Harper's Ferry, been doing right poorly lately. So Pa's promised him the loan of his boy, Moses, here, till he's back on his feet again. Pa 'ud be much obiged if you'd let him walk up the towpath with you. He's a good boy, won't be no trouble to you—got his own provisions and all. Just needs someone to keep a bit of an eye on him so he don't lose his way or nothin."

The man grunted, shifting a wad of tobacco from one side of his mouth to the other. "Well, reckon I could use an extra hand right about now," he said at last. "My wife ain't able to spell me at all, condition she's in. Reckon you can lead a mule team, boy?"

"Yassuh." Michael looked up as the man spoke to him. "I can sho do that, suh."

Robert turned to him. "You be sure and do what you're told to help em out, Moses, hear?"

"Yassuh, sho will, Mista Bill."

"My grandfolks don't live but a mile or two from the canal's end," Robert said, speaking to the boatman again. "Pa wrote out a pass for him to go on up there," he added, pulling it out of his pocket and handing it to Michael.

"Pa told him the way, but reckon I'd better make sure he remembers it right." Robert drew Michael aside, waiting to speak till the boatman had turned to check his towlines.

"Watch yourself with them, hear," he said in a low voice. "I don't wanna get in trouble with the law on account of your getting caught."

"I'll be careful." Michael manged a smile. "I sure don't wanna get caught, either."

"Okay, then." Robert started to walk off, then paused, turning back to Michael.

"That all the food you got, in that kerchief?"

He hesitated a moment after Michael's nod. "Christ, that

ain't gonna last you even to Harper's Ferry. Here. Reckon you'll be needing this more'n men." He strode off rapidly this time.

Michael stood still a few moments, clutching the fifty cents Robert had handed him, watching till Robert was nearly lost to view. Then he turned himself, hurrying to keep up with the canal barge.

So long as he was careful, he realized with relief, he wouldn't have much to fear from the boatman, Mista Wilkes, or his wife. Barge owners hitched up as soon as it was light enough to see and kept going till darkness fell a good ten hours later. Plodding along the towpath, guiding the mules on their towline some two hundred feet ahead of the barge, quickly grew tiresome. The Wilkes seemed glad enough to have an extra hand on this trip not to ask any questions.

It was lucky the mules weren't inclined to balk, he thought. Otherwise, Mista Wilkes would surely realize he'd never handled a mule team before.

Curbing his impatience to move away from Alexandria as fast as possible came hardest for him. On straight stretches of the canal, he reckoned they covered no more than two or three miles in an hour's time, but traveling the canal above Gerogetown meant delays of a quarter of an hour each time they entered a lock chamber, waiting till entering water raised the barge to the level of the next section of the canal.

By mid-afternoon they'd passed through seven lift locks, covering no more than eight miles, before encountering yet another series of seven locks ascending a steep slope just over a mile in length. They'd gone only five or so miles further by late evening, when Mista Wilkes finally tied the barge to the bank not far from a bustling tavern built adjacent to the canal.

Word could easily have reached the tavern well ahead of

the barge to be on the lookout for a runaway, he realized fearfully. Fortunately, the Wilkes showed little interest in the tavern. Missus Wilkes fixed her family's supper in the small cabin, and they retired shortly afterwards. Michael ate his own supper quickly, then curled up in the one thin blanket he'd brought along.

It was barely light when he awoke, hurrying into the scrubby woods bordering the towpath to make water. In the quiet morning, he could hear the roaring of the Potomac below him. He clambered over the rocks on the other side of the trees, till he could look down in amazement at the whirling water as it dashed and eddied through the narrow riverbed. It was hard to believe it was the same river he'd fished in so often at home.

He'd like to be moving as fast as that water himself, he thought. He smiled to himself, then, as he hurried back to help the Wilkes hitch up. He was a lot safer appearing to belong with the canal boat, however slowly it moved, than he would be on his own.

The locks were a little further apart, so they made better time once they'd left the tavern area. Still, it was another two and a half days till they reached the end of the navigable portion of the canal, just short of Harper's Ferry.

The Wilkes seemed sorry to see him leave, he thought, and Mista Wilkes asked him twice if he was sure he could find his way. "I'd see you up there myself, only I don't want to leave my wife on her own right now," the man told him.

Thank God for that! "Mista Bill tol me how to get there real good, suh," he said politely. "But I sho thanks you, suh."

He felt sorry to have to leave the Wilkes' protection himself. The hardest part of his route North lay ahead of him.

The terminus of the canal was twice as crowded and noisy as the starting point in Georgetown. Barges which had been hauled up the canal empty were hustled into the turning basin to take on cargoes of coal, corn, wheat and flour. A steady stream of wagons, covered with taut, weather-beaten canvas, clattered back and forth over the double wooden bridge that crossed the Potomac into the town of Harper's Ferry on the Virginia shore.

The surrounding land was densely wooded, with rocky mountains that rose steeply away from the shore—as different from the countryside he'd known as the turbulent falls were from the placid Potomac below Alexandria. He was just about thirty miles due south of the Pennsylvania border, he knew, but there was no way he could walk over those mountains.

He hadn't really planned past this point, he admitted to himself, but he couldn't just stand here gaping. The wagon traffic leaving the town was headed east, following a narrow turnpike along the river. He hated to retrace his steps, but there seemed no other road to follow. He hesitated a minute, then followed the line of traffic, keeping well to the edge of the highway.

He'd walked just about a mile when the road veered to the north, climbing uphill as it went. He breathed a sigh of relief as he climbed.

There was more wagon traffic than he could have believed, a steady stream of horse drawn vehicles from small flatbottomed farm wagons to brightly painted Conestoga freighters. Most carried full loads of flour, corn or wrought iron bars, the horse teams straining to pull them over the crest of the hill.

Downhill stretches gave the wagoners more trouble, he saw, as the heavy wagons had to be slowed down to keep them under control on the steep slopes. The drivers stopped frequently, cutting saplings from the roadside to tie to the rear of the wagon bed where they rubbed against the iron wheels sufficiently to slow their turning. He tried to keep well away from the halted wagons, though most of the wagoners seemed too busy to pay him much mind.

He'd been walking about an hour when the sapling wedged in the back of a mud spattered blue freighter slipped out of place, the heavily loaded wagon fetching up at the bottom of the slope some twenty feet ahead of him, leaning to one side against a stand of small trees.

He started cautiously around the stuck wagon, then froze as the brawny driver stepped into his path. "How bout giving us a hand here, boy," the man said.

He grinned in relief. "Yassuh, sho will."

In half an hour, they had the wagon back on the road again. The teamsters, John and Silas Schenken, were heading up to Frederick, Maryland, he learned, then on to York, Lancaster and Philadelphia, Pennsylvania along the old Wagon Road.

"Goin up that way, boy?" the driver asked.

He nodded. Surely the man would ask to see his papers now.

"My brother and me could use an extra hand along this stretch, if you care to stick with us," he said instead.

"Yassuh. Be glad to."

Evening was well begun when they pulled into the crowded yard of the wagon stand just outside Frederick, and five or six wagons were already parked outside the tavern building. Michael filled the feed trough and carried buckets of water while the two men unhitched the team, rubbing down the big horses and covering them with blankets before heading into the tavern. Michael followed them on in, feeling hungry enough to eat a bucket of hay himself. He silently thanked Robert for giving him back the fifty cents.

Supper cost twelve-and-a-half cents, but there looked to be more than enough to eat. He looked hesitantly around the big room before spotting half a dozen colored wagon drivers sitting at a table in the far corner. He quickly joined them, digging into the hot food hungrily, listening as the men talked of weather and road conditions.

He wished he dared ask if there'd be patrols checking colored travelers at the Pennsylvania border, but decided he'd better not. He'd heard of colored people betraying fugitives before, and his question would surely give him away.

The pass Robert had handed him could give him away now, too, he thought, as he was about to drift off to sleep. He sat up cautiously. The snoring teamsters lay stretched out in their bedrolls on the floor of the common room. He made his way quietly through the sleeping men till he reached the massive fireplace.

Crumpling the pass in his hand, he reached carefully for a stick of kindling wood. No sense looking suspicious, he told himself, if anyone else lay awake. A dirty newspaper, dated two days before, lay carelessly in the firebox. The National Intelligencer, published in Washington city, he noted, reading the masthead by the light of the dying fire. He glanced at the paper again, suddenly cold with shock.

"FIFTY DOLLARS REWARD!," the advertisement was headed, "for return of a mulatto man run away from Alexandria, D.C., known as Michael Carter, about 18 years of age, 5 feet 8 or 10 inches high, slender but tolerably broad shoulder, and walks with erect carriage. Tolerably bright mulatto complexion, with regular features, and likely appearance. Last seen wearing grey serge pantaloons and brown broad cloth coat. Of considerable intelligence and quick in his speech, the fugitive is acquainted with reading and writing, and may have provided himself with a pass. Reward will be paid to any person who will deliver him to the offices of Franklin and Armfield, Alexandria, D.C., or commit him to the keeping of any sheriff or magistrate where he may be claimed by the above owners. Nov 1."

Shivering, he pulled the paper out, crumpling it to a ball

as quietly as he could, slowly feeding it to the fire with his pass and kindling wood.

He lay awake, nevertheless, too fearful to sleep. Any of the men here could have seen the newspaper. The Schenkens could very well have seen it themselves, and be planning to turn him over to the authorities as soon as they entered Frederick.

Maybe he should slip away from the tavern now, he thought, and head due north towards Pennsylvania. On the other hand, if the two brothers didn't suspect him of being a fugitive, he'd be safer crossing the border in their company than on his own. He was still turning the matter over in his mind when sleep finally overtook him.

The only thing to do now was go on as he had been, he realized, as he opened his eyes the following dawn to see the wagoners already stirring and folding their bedrolls.

He felt he could scarcely breathe as they entered Frederick, relaxing only a little as they left the town behind. Remembering the wording of the advertisement, he walked with downcast look and posture, trying to speak as little as possible.

They spent the next two nights in similar wagon stands, joining the line of traffic heading northeast on the Great Wagon Road each dawn. The third morning, they'd walked less than an hour when a bone-chilling rain began, changing every so often to sleet. He didn't need to pretend to a downcast posture now, he thought, pulling his blanket over his head and hunching his shoulders against the driving rain.

Neither of the brothers seemed inclined to talk this morning, turning their energies to the task of traveling up the pike as speedily as they could. How long would it be till they reached the border, Michael wondered all afternoon. It couldn't be much farther, he knew.

He couldn't help but ask finally, "It be much further to

Pennsylvania now, suh?"

Silas Schenken turned his head toward him a moment. "Crossed over the state line a good hour and half ago."

He'd done it, and not even known! The cold forgotten, he breathed in the rain in great gulps, seeming to taste freedom on his tongue.

Straightening his shoulders, he walked down the road to Philadelphia with the two wagoners.

Chapter 9

1833

He couldn't find steady work anywhere in town, so he went early every morning to the canal site or docks ready to do whatever job he could find. There was usually some ship-owner who needed extra hands to load or unload a cargo, or some errand he could run.

It wasn't easy to earn even three dollars a week though. Although there were plenty of odd jobs to be done, there was no lack of men and boys just as eager and willing as Michael to earn a few pennies: both free colored workers and slaves who—with the permission of their masters—tried to earn what they could for themselves when their regular task was done.

On a good day he might earn fifty cents, and once in a while seventy-five, but other evenings he went home with just a few pennies in his pocket. Sundays and evenings he often fished till it was too dark to see, saving out enough of his catch for Aunt Sary and himself, and carrying his surplus to sell the next morning in the market square.

His work left him little time for visiting with his friends, but it was just as well. They were all busy with their own lives. Cassie and Charles were planning on getting married. His family had talked it over, Ned told him, and decided to use whatever money they could save to help buy Cassie's freedom.

"It makes a lot of sense," Ned said soberly. "Charles' family's helpin em too. Otherwise, they chillen'll all be slaves when they born."

Michael wondered if Ned was disappointed to put off the time when he could buy his own freedom, but decided not to ask him. Ned would have told him if he'd wanted to. He'd just as soon talk about something else than Cassie getting married to Charles, anyway.

1833 was more than half over, and he still hadn't saved anywhere near ten dollars, though he'd been hiring his time all spring and summer. He could save up a lot faster if only he didn't have to pay Doctor Carter the two dollars every week. He knew Doctor Carter wouldn't agree to take any less, though. Even with the money he was turning over to him, the doctor still complained about his financial troubles.

Although the duplex was modest, it had cost more to build than he'd expected, Doctor Carter was telling Mista Harrison. He'd had to take out an additional loan to finish paying for it. On top of that he'd be getting the next semester's bill for David's university tuition before long.

"Not to mention that the talk is Council will be increasing the tax on real estate again to pay off the canal loan. The property owners of this town will be bankrupt before the canal is ever completed. I'd hoped to count on a steady rental income from the duplex, but with my expenses the way they are it looks as if I'll be forced to sell it instead. It's the only asset I have."

Michael stopped listening and went out to the yard to get another armload of firewood he'd just split for the doctor. He'd a lot sooner finish his chores and get on home to supper than stand around listening to Doctor Carter's woes.

Mista Harrison was talking as he walked back into the house. "You do have another asset, you know, George," he was saying.

"I couldn't consider it," Doctor Carter answered. He broke off as Michael approached politely to ask if there was anything else the doctor wanted done that evening.

"No, you can go on now, Michael."

"Yassuh, thank you, Doctor Carter. Evening, suh."

Mista Harrison's voice followed him as he left.

"Well, at least you seem to have taught him his place at last. I suppose that's something."

He had to earn more money before cold weather set in, or he'd have no chance of escaping this year. It had already grown too cool to fish most evenings. He'd have to find more work he could do than the odd jobs he'd managed to get so far.

It wasn't till he went to do his chores for the doctor the next evening that he came up with an idea. Lots of white folks in town hired the work they needed done. If he could borrow a saw and woodhorse from Ned's dad, he bet he could find lots of people needing firewood sawed before winter came.

Going from house to house looking for work was better than waiting around the docks. Even if they didn't need wood sawed, most people had some job they needed done—from carrying out ashes to whitewashing sheds and fences.

He asked for work at shops and taverns in town, too. Many of the shopkeepers had deliveries he could make. Sometimes he was paid with foodstuff rather than cash, especially by some of the colored craftsmen who had little money to spare, ticeship with a qualified physician and knowlege of Latin—I couldn't admit a man of your race."

"I reckon I could learn Latin," Michael said slowly.

"Didn't you hear me, young man? Learn what you will, I'd lose all my other students if I were to accept a black into the school. I'd learn a useful trade if I were you, but if you intend to persist in your folly, you'll have to try somewhere else."

He'd known the Dean's words were to be expected, but his resentment welled up nonetheless. He worked at keeping his voice carefully polite as he asked, "Where else you have in mind, suh?" There had to be some school that would accept him, and this man might know of it.

The Dean shrugged, turning back to the paperwork on his desk. "I really couldn't say. You might try up in New England—it's a hotbed of abolitionism there. Dartmouth, maybe, or the Medical School of Maine, at Bowdoin. You're wasting your time in New York, though."

Bowdoin! The college that had admitted John Russwurm, the colored man who'd started Freedom's Journal. If there was a school of medicine there too, then that was where he'd go, he decided that instant.

He worked on the docks till the end of the week, then headed north out of the city. He stopped just once on his way—at a secondhand bookstore where he bought a battered Latin primer.

He worked his way as he had from Philadelphia, spending three weeks as a farmhand during the harvest season, before stopping for the winter in Springfield, Massachusetts, finding employment in one of the town's factories.

When he was done working for the day, he spent long hours studying the Latin primer. It was easy to see why David had disliked the subject. There didn't seem much sense in memorizing words in a language no one spoke. But learning Latin was necessary to enter medical school. By the time he left town in the spring, he'd mastered the last lesson in the book.

Brunswick, Maine lay on the Androscoggin River, its wide, unpaved streets crossing each other at right angles. It was easy enough to find the college, but he hesitated a long while outside the office of Professor Parker Cleaveland, Secretary of the Medical Faculty. He'd spend months getting to this point, but if he were turned away now, he knew he'd have to give up his dream of studying medicine for good.

There was nothing to do, finally, but knock on the door.

Professor Cleaveland seemed as surprised to see him as had the head of the New York school the previous fall, but at least he was willing to hear Michael out.

When he spoke at last though, he shook his head. "I'm sorry to disappoint you, but we need to maintain some standards of admission. It's true many of our students enter without a secondary school diploma, but not without any previous schooling whatsoever."

"Yassuh, but I read whatever I can, and I been studying Latin on my own all winter." He had to get the professor to change his mind!

Professor Cleaveland looked surprised, but after a moment shook his head again. "The Latin is fine, but it's not enough just to read whatever books come to hand. At the very least, you should have served as apprentice to a physician for two years, and read medicine under his direction."

Michael took a deep breath before replying. "I worked for a doctor almost eight years, suh, since I wuz ten years old—helpin him with bleeding and setting bones, grinding up his drugs, taking care of his instruments, doing any kind of work he needed done. And I read all the books he owned—Chesselden's Anatomy, and Domestic Medicine by William Buchan, and Doctor Rush's account of the yellow fever in Phila-

125

delphia."

"You might have said so to begin with. You have a written recommendation with you, I assume."

"Nossuh, I don't."

"Well, you'll need to write your preceptor and have his evaluation of your progress and moral character sent before we can go any further."

"I can't do that, suh." He hesitated, trying to choose his words with care, realizing then that whatever he said would give him away as a fugitive. "It- it wasn't a free state, suh."

Professor Cleaveland looked at him wordlessly a moment, removing his spectacles and polishing each lens in turn. When he'd replaced them, he continued studying Michael. Finally, he nodded. "I see. Then I expect we'll just have to give you a chance to show your worth as a student."

Although he'd dreamed of it for years, he could hardly believe he was signing the class register as a medical student at last. He dipped the pen carefully in the inkwell before forming the letters in his very best hand.

Michael C—he stopped, pen poised in midair. He had no desire to retain Doctor Carter's name, even if it weren't a precaution suggested by good common sense to provide himself with a new identity. He put a firm period after the C, thinking rapidly.

What name should he take? Brown or Freeman would serve, he supposed, but he'd met at least half a dozen men bearing each name in Philadelphia alone. If he was to choose a new name, he wanted it to be special to him. He couldn't stand hesitating much longer, though. Freeman was the better of the two, he thought.

He dipped the pen in the inkwell once more, then suddenly stopped again. He had a name special to him, his great granddaddy's, who Mama had told him so much about. He'd never

126

seen his name written out, of course, but he'd just spell it as it sounded.

Slowly he completed his signature, with careful black ink-strokes. Laying the pen down, he looked proudly a moment at the register book with his new name—Michael C. Mabaya—added to the student list for the term beginning in February, 1836.

1835

He'd been admitted to medical school at last, but he still needed to pay the tuition, he reminded himself. It took two three-month terms at the school to earn a diploma certifying that the student had qualified to practice as a physician. Students were expected to attend lectures in four subjects during the term, Professor Cleaveland told him.

He'd already paid the matriculation fee of three dollars. The fee for Obstetrics was just five dollars, but the fee for each of the other courses of lectures was fifteen dollars, payable to the professor the first day of class. Fifty dollars in all!

He'd left Philadelphia with eighteen dollars in savings—managing to stretch his wages by sharing the cellar room with Tim and making as many meals as he could from leftovers at the tavern—but on the road he was often paid with little more than his meals and a bed in a farmer's barn. Working in the factory last winter he'd earned a dollar a day, but his board was higher too, and he'd needed to buy a warmer jacket and pantaloons at the secondhand shop, as well as pay a cobbler to resole his wornout shoes.

He counted his money carefully. Fifty-five dollars—sufficient for one term of courses, not counting his costs for room and board. He'd need an equal sum for the second term, and Professor Cleaveland had explained that students were expected to obtain additional clinical training by working as unpaid medical apprentices during the nine-month term break.

There were five months left till classes started in February. He'd simply have to earn the difference by then. The Androscoggin River falls powered several mills, where he hoped he could find employment. First, though, he needed a place to stay.

Unlike the larger cities he'd been in, he could find no colored section or boardinghouse. At the two white boardinghouses near Mill Street that he finally approached, he was immediately turned away.

"No room here," a stout woman informed him at the first, though he could plainly see the "Rooms to let" sign in the window from the porch where he stood. When he politely pointed it out though, she flushed an angry red, mumbling that they'd all been rented as she closed the door in his face. Maybe she'd thought he couldn't read the sign, he thought bitterly, as he headed down the street.

The proprietor at the second boarding house didn't bother with a lie. The door slammed in Michael's face as quickly as it had opened.

There seemed no point even looking for another. Discouraged, he headed down the street, nearly missing the sign on the small, shingled building: "Good Food Eating House, Reasonable Prices, Meals Prepared for Our Premises or Yours." He hadn't eaten since breakfast, he suddenly realized, and it was well past noon now. If he couldn't find a room, at least he could get a bite to eat while he tried to figure out what to do.

He stood blinking in the dimly lit interior. There seemed no one else on the premises. He was turning to leave when the wooden doors from the kitchen swung open. The woman hurrying through them stopped a second in surprise as she caught sight of Michael, then her broad, dark face lit up with a smile.

128

"What can I do for you, chile?"

Within a few minutes he was sitting in the kitchen, finishing a bowl of fish chowder and talking to the eating house owners, Molly and Ben Brown. There were only two colored families in town besides them, he learned.

Of course he'd board with them, they assured him, before he could even ask. They'd plenty of room. Of their six children, only one had lived past infancy, and she and her husband lived in Albany, New York, now.

He was hired at the largest of the lumber mills the next morning. When classes started the third week of February, he'd put aside enough for the second term's fee, as well as the carefully counted out tuition he handed each of the professors.

There were eighty other students in the lecture room, and all of them seemed to turn and stare at him as he took his place in class the first day. It was difficult not to feel uncomfortable. Once they got to know him, though, he told himself, they'd realize he was no different from anyone else. Anyway, if he was going to learn anything about medicine, he'd have to keep his mind on the professors' words and not on the other students.

There was certainly enough material to be mastered. During the course of a school day, students heard lectures in Anatomy and Surgery; Obstetrics; Chemistry and Materia Medica— the effect of drugs and medicines on the patient; and the Theory and Practice of Physic which outlined the causes eminent medical thinkers had developed to explain human illnesses and their treatment.

By afternoon his hand would be sore from taking notes, but he was too afraid of forgetting some important fact not to write everything down. After helping Molly and Ben put the kitchen to rights, he'd settle himself by the fire and study his notes till he practically knew them by heart, often falling asleep with his head on the table.

With no previous schooling, he'd been afraid he'd fall behind the other students, but as long as he studied every day he had no trouble remembering the lecture material.

Actually, he had to admit to himself, not all of it was new to him. Like the rest of the class, he hung on every word of Professor Cleaveland's chemistry lectures, and he was fascinated by the talks on anatomy, which Professor Cobb illustrated with frequent references to the skeleton displayed at the front of the room.

Of Materia Medica, though, he learned little that he hadn't already absorbed in Doctor Carter's office. He made long lists of medicinal agents and their observed effects anyway, making sure he'd committed them to memory.

He had the greatest hopes for the theory of physic. It was wanting to understand why people took sick—and what made one person recover while another succumbed and died—that lay behind his desire to become a doctor, he thought.

Doctor Perry gave the lectures on the Theory and Practice of Physic. Much of the term was devoted to a study of the theories of the famous Philadelphia physician, Doctor Benjamin Rush, who had taught that all diseases—and fevers in particular—could be traced to a "morbid excitement induced by capillary tension."

"Thus, gentlemen, we see the importance of Rush's emphasis on the necessity for purging, as well as letting sufficient quantities of blood to bring about relaxation of the blood vessels, with consequent discharge of bodily poisons."

Michael puzzled over his notes that evening. Purging and bloodletting were what Doctor Carter had prescribed for most illnesses, without any better reason than that he'd been taught the methods by the doctor he'd trained under. Now Doctor Perry was explaining the reasoning behind the treatments.

But if Doctor Rush was right, he wondered, why didn't bleeding and cathartics cure more patients than they did? Try as he would to understand Rush's theory, it didn't make any more sense to him now than Doctor Carter's words had years ago.

He wondered if others in the class were as puzzled as he was. He doubted he'd find out, though. Despite his expectations of soon getting to know his classmates, after four weeks he felt as alone as he had the first day of the term. His attempts at greeting fellow students were met at best by a cool nod. After a few days he'd given up, coming and going in silence.

Doctor Perry continued his discussion of Rush's views the following day, noting that the eminent physician had recommended removal of sufficient quantities of blood to cause unconsciousness on the part of the patient.

Michael listened intently, still troubled by his questions. Suddenly, without being aware he'd planned to do so, he found himself on his feet.

The professor paused. "Is something the matter, Mister Mabaya?"

"Just, I'm having trouble understanding how sickness could be caused by the blood vessels being constricted, like Doctor Rush wrote," he said, suddenly acutely selfconscious.

"Then I suggest you pay closer attention to the lecture. I've gone over Rush's writings for several days."

"Yassuh, I been paying attention, Doctor Perry. Only, it seem to me if Doctor Rush was right in what he said, then people oughta recover when they're given treatments like he says. Only thing is," he hesitated a second, then plunged on, "I worked a long time for a doctor who always purged first thing, just like Doctor Rush recommended, and bled patients till they fainted too. I seen him treat all kinds of disease like that—pleurisy, and cholera during the epidemic. But it just

131

didn't seem to do much good. His patients died of their sicknesses just the same—even when he bled them two or three times."

Doctor Perry regarded him dryly a moment. "Mister Mabaya, may I remind you that this is a lecture hall and not a debating society."

He sank into his seat, hot with embarrassment, trying to pay no mind to the gust of laughter that swept through the room, forcing himself to pay close attention to the rest of the lecture. When the hour finally ended, he hurried out of the classroom.

"Mister Mabaya!"

Michael turned, startled. The student who'd come up behind him was a thin, intent young man, who usually sat in the front row of seats. He ran a hand through a head of unruly brown curls now, nearly dislodging the knitted skullcap he always wore.

"I- I just wanted to say I'm glad you asked that question. I've been wondering the same thing myself, only I never had the nerve to bring it up."

Slowly, Michael smiled. "Sure didn't find out the answer, though."

"Perhaps we will in time, Mister Mabaya. What's your first name, anyhow?"

"It's Michael," he said, smiling again.

"I'm Isaac—Isaac Marks. I'm glad to make your acquaintance," he added, holding out his hand to Michael.

The following week, Doctor Perry announced that he was organizing a tutorial for students wishing to study the theory of physic more thoroughly than they could in an hour's lecture period.

"You ought to take it, Michael," Isaac told him. "I've already signed up."

He nodded, thinking it over. The tutorial cost an extra three dollars, and he needed what money he'd saved to pay the second term's tuition. He'd earned a few dollars cleaning walks and driveways of snow in his spare time, though, and he guessed he could earn more when he had to.

"Reckon I will, too," he said. He'd come here to learn, after all.

The tutorial had been underway four weeks, when Doctor Perry told the fourteen students, "This afternoon we're going to read and discuss a paper given by Doctor Jacob Bigelow, of Boston, at the meeting of the Massachusetts Medical Society last year. I don't pretend to agree with many of Doctor Bigelow's views myself, but as aspiring physicians you gentlemen should be aware of them. They should be of particular interest to you, Mister Mabaya," he added, with a slight smile.

Michael looked up, startled, but decided he'd learn what the paper was about soon enough.

In his talk "On Self-Limited Diseases," Doctor Bigelow took issue with the views of Doctor Rush and his followers that the only way to cure most diseases was for doctors to treat them actively—mainly by blistering, bleeding and purging.

"By a self-limited disease," Bigelow had said, "I would be understood to express one which receives limits from its own nature and not from foreign influences; . . . to which there is due a certain succession of processes to be completed in a certain time; which time and processes may vary with the constitution and condition of the patient, and may tend to death or to recovery, but are not known to be shortened or greatly changed by medical treatment.

" . . . in many places, at the present day, a charm is popularly attached to what is called an active, bold, or heroic practice; and a corresponding reproach awaits the opposite course,

133

which is cautious, palliative, and expectant. In regard to the diseases which have been called self-limited, I would not be understood to deny that remedies capable of removing them may exist; I would only assert, that they have not yet been proven to exist."

The tutorial ran an hour past its usual time as the students argued over Bigelow's call for controlled experimentation on a large scale, in hospitals and charitable institutions, by treating similar diseases with a variety of remedies and comparing the results numerically.

"Even then," Isaac said, as they left the tutorial together, "we wouldn't understand why the remedies worked without knowing the original causes of the illness."

Michael nodded. He'd been thinking the same thing. Despite their differences in background, he and Isaac were often alike in their thinking, they'd discovered.

He'd been a lot less lonely at school since getting to know Isaac. By now, a number of the other students also exchanged a few words with him, but somehow he always felt they regarded him as an object of curiosity.

Isaac was the only one who talked with him just like he did with anyone else.

He often felt out of place with the other students himself, Isaac told Michael once. Most of them regarded Jews as being as different from themselves as they did colored.

There were other things on Michael's mind than what the others thought of him, at any rate. During the nine month term break, students were expected to resume their medical apprenticeship. Most of the students, naturally, were returning to their former preceptors. Isaac would be returning to his home town of Portland.

He obviously couldn't return to Doctor Carter! But he'd no idea how to go about securing an apprenticeship. Then, too, though he'd realized apprentices were unpaid, Isaac explained that most students paid their preceptors for the apprenticeship period—in some cases, more than the tuition for a term of schooling.

To his surprise, Doctor Perry offered him a solution to both problems.

His time was so taken up with his teaching duties, he told Michael, he'd little desire to take time from his medical practice to train an inexperienced apprentice. As he assmed Michael needed no further training in the preparation of purgatives and care of medical instruments, he said, smiling, he'd be glad to take him on as an apprentice without charge.

The lectures the following term covered much the same ground as the first. Doctor Cobb lectured the returning students in physiology, and they were fortunate enough to obtain a cadaver for dissection, the students straining to view the demonstration over one another's shoulders.

Completion of a thesis was the only other requirement for the second year students. At Doctor Perry's suggestion, Michael wrote his paper on "Observations in a Cholera Hospital, with a History of the Spread and Treatment of Asiatic Cholera."

Isaac did his library research on "A History and Comparison of the Causative Agents of Disease, as Proposed by Medical Theorists of the Seventeenth through Nineteenth Centuries."

The final examination was an oral one, students walking around the room to each of the four professors, to be quizzed in turn. Michael had spent days reviewing his lecture notes, but he needn't have worried, he realized with relief. He passed the examinations easily.

He thanked Doctor Perry once again, then ran the half mile to the eating house to bid the Browns farewell. Molly and Ben beamed when he showed them his diploma.

He'd like to see Doctor Carter's face if he could show it to him, he thought for a second, then shook his head, wondering at himself. The last person he ever wanted to see again was Doctor Carter.

Wrapping the diploma carefully, he joined the throng of departing students.

Chapter 10

1838

Some of the best doctors in the country were practicing in Boston, Isaac had remarked their last term in school. Michael had been delighted to discover that Isaac also planned to settle in Boston after finishing school.

Michael had his own reasons for choosing Boston, though. Home of the abolitionist newspaper, The Liberator, published by William Lloyd Garrison, Boston was reportedly one of the best Northern cities for colored to live in. And after the isolation he'd felt in Brunswick, he'd looked forward to being part of an active colored community again.

It hadn't taken long to find a place to live. And, as in Philadelphia, he was quickly introduced to organizations like the African Society and the newly organized Library Association by the other young men at his boardinghouse.

Earning a living as a doctor wasn't as easy, though his landlady was more than willing for him to hang his shingle offering his services. His degree of Doctor of Medicine was a source of pride to the whole colored community, she told him.

There was certainly a need for medical attention in the community too. But most of Boston's colored people were struggling day laborers, few of whom could afford needed medical care. Moreover, 1837 was a year of economic hardships and depression. And in Boston, as elsewhere, foreign immigrants often drove colored men out of work they'd done for years.

The colored benevolent associations were able to provide for some medical treatment. But Michael found he still had to hold down odd jobs to pay his living expenses and purchase the medical instruments and medicines he needed.

Then, too, despite his medical degree, he often felt the lack of sufficient skill and knowledge to do much more than make sufferers a little more comfortable.

"I know just what you mean, believe me," Isaac said, as they matched strides across the common—one of the few places they'd found they could meet together. Isaac had been fortunate enough to come to Boston with an introduction to a distant family connection, Joseph Bergman—an older doctor, nearing retirement, who was willing to take him on as an assistant in his practice.

"Most of what we do is just bleeding and purging whether it cures anyone or not. But why should he change? Most of his patients think you're no good as a doctor if you don't bleed them practically before you ask how they're feeling."

"Sarah and I heard Doctor Holmes lecture at the Lyceum last week," Isaac said, when they met again the following month. Michael smiled. Since meeting Sarah at Sabbath services four months before, Isaac never failed to mention her. It was obvious their feelings for each other were becoming steadily more serious. Michael suppressed a pang of envy at his friend's good fortune. He'd been introduced to plenty of attractive young women himself, but somehow nothing had come of it. He'd met no one he'd want to spend his life with.

"He's a remarkably clever speaker," Isaac was continuing. "And did you know he won two Boylston Prizes for his medical essays last year?

"But what I really wanted to tell you, Doctor Bergman told me that Holmes and some of the faculty from Harvard are starting their own medical school on Tremont Street. Doctor Bigelow's one of them. They're not planning to award a degree, just teach subjects a lot more thoroughly than they do in most medical schools. They expect a lot of Harvard students to enroll there between terms.

"Anyway," he added, before Michael could respond, "I went around there on my free time and talked to Doctor Holmes. Of course, neither of us could afford the time or money to take a whole term of courses, but they plan to let students take as many or few at a time as they like. And Holmes more or less said that practicing doctors would be admitted without tuition, as a courtesy—just by paying the matriculation fee. At the very least, we'd be able to observe some surgical operations at the Massachusetts General Hospital.

"So what do you think? Can you take time from your practice to go there with me?" he asked, winding down at last.

Michael laughed. After nearly two years in Boston he still spent the better part of his time on whatever jobs he could find, to eke out the meager income from his medical practice. "I reckon I could," he said.

Doctor Oliver Wendell Holmes was a short, energetic man, and a lot younger than Michael had realized. He couldn't be more than a few years older than Isaac and him, he thought, but of course Holmes had the advantage of Paris training, the best medical education available.

He could see Doctor Holmes' surprise, too. It probably had never even occured to Isaac to mention his color, but he could see it mattered to Holmes. It mattered a good deal.

Seconds ticked away on the clock in the large, book-lined room, while Holmes still studied him in silence. Michael returned his gaze, bracing himself for the inevitable rejection.

"I take it you intend practicing in your own country when your training is complete?" Holmes abruptly asked him instead.

Michael blinked in surprise. "Yes sir, of course," he said.

Doctor Holmes nodded. "There should be no problem with your attending sessions at Tremont, then."

The surgical amphitheater at Massachusetts General Hospital was roofed with a high dome, designed to supply the maximum amount of light to the chamber. The students and observing physicians waited attentively, eyes fixed on the operating chair.

The patient lying in the chair had been dosed with opium beforehand, they knew, but remained conscious, eyes darting in terror from the surgeon to his assistants. The black stubble of his whiskers stood out against the pallor of his skin.

He looked to have been in vigorous health before being injured, Michael thought. The observing students had listened carefully to the House Surgeon, as he had described to them how the bone had been shattered above the elbow by a blow from a suddenly rearing horse. Amputation was the only possible course for an injury of such severity.

As the surgeon began his work of binding the arm above the wound, the man suddenly struggled and thrashed about in the chair. The surgeon stopped. "Will you have it off, or do you intend to die of your wound?" he asked.

The man moaned an assent, and the assistants stepped forward to hold him immobile as the surgeon cut swiftly into the shattered arm, several inches above the injury. Only a few minutes passed before the bloody limb lay discarded in a pan, and the doctor skillfully commenced tying off the blood vessels.

Michael closed his eyes a second, praying he'd never be forced to perform such an operation. Glancing at Isaac, he could see he felt the same.

December of 1839 was raw and chilly, but the debate that evening at the Adelphic Union Library Association was heated. Setting aside their usual literary topics, the speakers for the evening addressed the topic "Resolved: That the Colored Citizens of this State Should Support the Candidates Selected by the Liberty Party, as the Most Direct and Appropriate Expression of our Continuing Struggle Against Slavery."

Michael listened intently as the opening speaker urged his audience to both campaign and vote for the new anti-slavery party, formed only one month previously in Warsaw, New York.

His opponent, equally convinced, took the position that a party organized around one cause—however worthy—was bound to lose at the polls, and that the more effective method was to vote for men of conscience, whatever their party.

"Neither of your positions can be supported in good conscience." The dark, stocky man in the second row was the first on his feet after the session had been opened to audience participation. "I hold with Mister Garrison. Campaigning and voting for any political party under the present Constitution of this country means cooperation with the forces of slavery. Slavery is countenanced in the Constitution itself— the very basis of government in the United States—and until the Constitution is amended, no man of conscience ought participate in political processes under it."

There was a buzz of whispered commentary, but Michael found himself on his feet before anyone else could respond.

"Doctor Mabaya," the moderator recognized him.

"We're part of this country as much as any other people. Our whole struggle is to win our equal rights as citizens, right along with freedom for those of our people still held in slavery. I don't see how we can do that if we hold off from voting and participating in politics till the government is made perfect. We here in Massachusetts live in one of the few states that even allows us the ballot box, and it seems to me it's our duty—as well as our right as free men—to make use of it." He sat down again, wondering if he'd expressed his thoughts as best as he could.

Across the aisle from Michael, a slender young woman rose to her feet. "I want to voice my agreement with the doctor," she stated firmly. "The foundations of our country will never be changed if colored citizens scorn to use what political power they have. If I might add another point, Mister Moderator, I know it's not on the agenda for this meeting, but we colored women have worked and contributed as much as our brothers, without even the limited say that you have. I propose it be resolved that the Association recognize the justice of extending the vote to women equally with men."

Michael stared at her, his attention hald equally by her words and her looks. Her long, blue dress buttoned under her chin, setting off a high cheeked oval face, her smooth skin the color of burnished mahogany. Her wide set eyes sparked with pride and determination as she spoke.

Like Mama must have looked, he thought for a moment, before she was worn down by work and sorrow.

He nudged Ted Johnson, the young carpenter who had the adjacent room at the boardinghouse. "Who is she?" he whispered.

"Her name's Rachel Gardner," Ted whispered back. "Her father has a used clothing shop over on Southac."

He headed toward her when the debate ended, not even

142

waiting for Ted to introduce them.

"I don't remember seeing you here before," he said, smiling.

"I teach adult classes, most evenings. But I didn't want to miss this meeting."

They stood talking together till they realized they were nearly the last people left in the room. Michael looked for Ted to tell him not to wait, then realized Ted had already left without him.

He nearly ran down Southac Street to his boarding house once he'd walked Rachel to her door. The shabby houses seemed to glow with beauty. He was young and free, living in a city that offered the most opportunity of any in the country—and the most wonderful girl he'd ever met had promised to see him again the following evening.

The American and Foreign Anti-Slavery Society was formed a few months later, in May of 1840, splitting off from Garrison's New England Anti-Slavery Society in its commitment to political action and support for the new Liberty party.

They both wanted to do whatever they could to support the anti-slavery party, Michael and Rachel agreed. They joined with other enthusiastic young people—writing and printing handbills, and organizing political meetings and talking to as many people as they possibly could about the importance of voting the Liberty ticket in the November election.

Evenings when they weren't busy with the new anti-slavery organization, or attending lectures at the Library Association, were spent visiting in Jacob and Mary Gardner's front room, above the family clothing shop. Rachel's two older brothers generally stopped by with their families, drinking coffee and arguing politics while their toddlers fell happily asleep on the handiest lap.

The discussion this evening seemed a continuation of the

one he'd heard in Jake's barber shop earlier that week, Michael thought. Like his parents' clothing store, the hair cutting establishment run by the older Gardner son was a community gathering spot as much as a place of business.

"You're wasting your time trying to get the colored vote out for the Liberty slate. There's not a chance of winning at the polls," Jake said now. "At the most, the Democrats will get a few less votes."

"Every vote they lose on account of their support for slavery is a sign to them," Reuben Gardner answered. "Take away enough votes, and the Whigs and Democrats will have to recognize the moral force of abolition and move to reform their own stands."

He was right, Michael thought. He started to say so, then stopped just in time to catch hold of Reuben's eighteen month old daughter as she reached for his coffee cup, lifting her onto his lap.

"That's enough talk for one evening," Martha, Reuben's wife, announced, taking her daughter from Michael. "It's time to get this child home to bed."

Rachel walked down to the street with Michael. "I'm afraid my family's going to frighten you off," she teased, smiling up at him.

Michael laughed. "I like them too much for that. I've always wanted to be part of a family," he said, suddenly serious.

"But I can't wait to be alone with you, either," he added softly, pulling her closer to him as they kissed.

They'd be married at Christmastime, they decided, in the African Methodist Episcopal Church, where the Gardners family worshipped. Sundays, after church services, they took long walks together—holding hands and talking by the hour, making plans for their life together.

They'd have to board with Rachel's parents to begin with,

144

but if they could put by a little each week, they'd be able to rent a place of their own before too long, they told each other.

Rachel's salary from teaching was small, but it was steady, she assured Michael. He wished he could say the same. He had a growing number of patients in the colored community, but too many had to put off paying for medical treatment till they were back on their feet again. His earnings as a doctor were still undependable at best.

He hadn't realized they even knew that many people, Michael thought. The Gardners' front room was crowded with friends and relatives, come to celebrate their wedding that afternoon.

He smiled at Rachel, thinking she'd never looked more beautiful than tonight, her movements graceful in the long white dress her mother had worn at her wedding. She smiled back at him a moment, then turned to hug her brother and sister-in-law.

He could scarcely believe they were married at last. He wanted nothing more now than to be alone with her, but they'd have to wait for that till the last guest had gone. They'd nowhere else to go than Rachel's old room that now belonged to both of them. He turned himself to grin at Ted Johnson, one of the first friends he'd made in Boston.

It was close to midnight before the last of Rachel's aunts had left and his new inlaws bid them goodnight, Rachel's mother giving her a final embrace before following her husband into their bedroom. Michael felt suddenly shy as they closed the door to their own bedroom at last.

He could see Rachel felt the same way as she looked at him, suddenly solemn. Hesitantly, he closed the distance between them, taking her hands in his. She smiled up at him then, before they kissed softly, then pressed together more closely, their awkwardness disappearing.

She was beautiful all over, he whispered to her as they lay

joined together, caressing each other with lips and finger-tips, learning each other's bodies at last.

As happy as they were, his lack of a steady income preyed on Michael's mind more once they were married. They both hoped for children, of course, but if Rachel were forced to give up teaching, supporting a wife and child would be precarious on his earnings alone.

He redoubled his efforts to earn money, feeling guilty at taking time even to attend an occasional lecture at the Tremont School, though he knew it would make him a better doctor.

He wouldn't have wanted to miss Holmes' demonstration of the use of auscultation and percussion in patient examination, though. Although use of the stethoscope had become accepted in France, it was viewed with skepticism by most American doctors. Doctor Holmes' essay on "Direct Exploration" of the body, written shortly after his return from his studies in Paris, was one of the earliest in introductions of the new instrument to American medicine.

Listening to the sound of human heartbeat magnified through the earpiece, Michael felt awed by the instrument's potential for revealing the state of the patient's vital organs to the physician.

"Let me remind, you, gentlemen," Holmes added, "observation of one case, however meticulous, is but an isolated phenomenon. But recording the details of each examination, however routine the results, will turn your casebook into an instrument of diagnosis as useful in its own way as any invention of science."

Holmes himself had worked as a visiting physician in the Boston Dispensary—a charity clinic for treatment of the city's poor—shortly after finishing his medical studies, and had observed more medical histories in a year there than he might have in ten years of private practice, he was fond of adding.

Michael walked home that evening, thinking hard about the charity clinic. In addition to the opportunity for observing a wide variety of cases, the doctors who were hired there were assured of a steady salary.

To be appointed took the recommendation of established practitioners in the medical community, though. It would be unlikely for a colored doctor to win a position at the clinic, he thought.

"You could speak to Doctor Bowditch," Rachel suggested that night.

"You're right." As always, her suggestion was a good one, he thought. Doctor Henry Bowditch was nearly as respected in the medical community as Doctor Holmes, but was unique among his fellow physicians in his devotion to the abolitionist cause. He and Rachel had spoken with him briefly at several anti-slavery meetings.

He'd be glad to recommend him, Bowditch told Michael immediately, but he'd need at least one additional referral.

"Why not ask Holmes? He has as much influence as anyone in Boston."

Michael smiled. "I doubt he'd be willing to use it for a man of my color, though."

"He might surprise you," Bowditch said, after a moment. "I've known Wendell for years. He's always been fairminded. I doubt he'd reject a qualified applicant out of hand."

Sitting across from Doctor Holmes a week later, Michael wasn't so sure.

Doctor Holmes tapped his fingers on the desktop, studying Michael. "I don't deny you're qualified for a position at the Dispensary, but I'm puzzled by your application," he said finally. "You told me two years ago, when you asked to attend lectures at Tremont, that you intended practicing in Africa. Surely, your preparation is complete by now."

"Africa?" He was completely bewildered. "Why would I

go to Africa?"

"I distinctly remember asking if you intended practicing there," Holmes said stiffly. "I naturally assumed you were affiliated with the American Colonization Society."

So that's what the man meant! He must have been stupid to have missed his meaning, Michael thought. He sat up straighter.

"I'm afraid we've had a misunderstanding, sir. You asked if I intended to practice in my own country. This is my own country, Doctor Holmes."

There was doubtless no point in pursuing his request further, Michael thought, but he'd be damned if he backed down of his own accord. He stayed seated, returning the older doctor's gaze. To his surprise, after a few moments Holmes' lips curved into a rueful smile.

"As I'm popularly supposed to be a man of letters, Doctor Mabaya, it would seem I must take the blame for imprecise use of language. I'll recommend you to the Dispensary committee for the next available opening."

He'd been working three months at the Dispensary before Rachel knew for certain, early in the fall of 1841, that she was carrying their child. He took her in his arms, kissing her joyfully, thankful that their happiness was no longer mixed with worry over how he'd be able to take care of his family.

Chapter 11

1842

The facilities of the Boston Dispensary were old and poorly maintained, but still better than anything a young doctor could provide for patients on his own. Many of the slum dwellers who were provided treatment at the clinic were so ill-fed and housed, it was a wonder any of them could recover from illness, Michael told Isaac when he met him at the monthly meeting of the Boston Medical Society in February, 1842.

"We can do some good vaccinating for smallpox or relieving the ague with quinine, but what a lot of these folks really need—especially some of the families who've just come over from Ireland—is halfway decent food and a way to keep warm in the winter. I never realized any white people lived that poorly," he added.

Isaac nodded thoughtfully. "I know. I've heard that Doctor Holmes made the same criticisms when he worked at the Dispensary, but nothing changed. Most doctors seem more interested in medicating diseases than trying to prevent them to begin with.

"It's too bad you can't attend Holmes' sessions on microscopy," he added, changing the subject.

"I wish I could, but I just don't have the time now. I've been seeing patients referred by the African Society in the evenings, and Rachel and I've been trying to get things ready for the baby."

Isaac smiled. "I remember." He and Sarah had been married two years now, and were already the proud parents of a year old daughter. "There's nothing to equal the joy of your first child."

Michael nodded. "But to tell the truth, I'm scared too. Not so much about childbirth. Rachel's always been healthy, thank God. But I can't help worrying about becoming a father. You know how I came up. I sure never learned anything about being a good daddy from Carter. I don't know a damn thing about being a father."

Isaac smiled, resting his hand on Michael's arm a moment. "So who does? You'll know when the time comes, Michael, believe me."

She'd have the baby at home, of course. Though no one knew why, many women just as healthy and strong as Rachel entered the obstetrics ward of Massachusetts General or other leading hospitals, only to die of the dreaded childbed fever.

Home birth was safer, but he couldn't help being anxious even so, though he tried not to let on to Rachel. His mother-in-law's disapproval of their intention for Michael to remain with Rachel through the birth didn't ease his mind either, though he'd surely had as good training as any midwife.

When she finally felt the first labor pain, just after midnight the second Saturday in May, he felt a moment of panic.

His hand shook a second as he lit the oil lamp. Rachel smiled up at him then, squeezing his hand a moment. He squeezed back, relaxing a little, then kissed her softly before going to rouse his mother-in-law as he'd promised.

Her pains stayed a quarter of an hour apart much of the day. He felt tender and helpless, with little he could do but rub her back where she told him it ached and give her sips of luke-warm tea.

It was early evening till her water broke and her pains grew stronger and closer together. Rachel's mother held her knees then, urging her to bear down hard as she panted with exertion. Michael felt more useless than ever, even as he carefully washed his hands, rinsing them with clean water from the pitcher.

It seemed a long time till the infant's head crowned at last, thrusting through the opening of the birth canal. The child appeared to be strong and healthy, he saw with relief. He slipped his finger carefully into the outlet of the birth canal then, gently easing the tiny shoulder through the opening till he held their newborn son in his hands.

Rachel lay back, looking exhausted but radiant, as he cut the cord with his scalpel and cleaned the birth fluids carefully from the infant's nose and eyes before placing him in her arms.

He felt overcome with happiness as he sat watching while Rachel offered the baby her breast for the first time. She smiled back at him with answering joy.

"Are you sure you don't want him named after you?" she asked softly.

He smiled. "Nobody would call him anything but Junior then. I reckon we'll name him Peter, like we decided."

He took his son from her then, cradling him in one arm, careful to keep his head supported. He ran his fingertips gently over the soft spot at the top of the baby's head, stroking the wisps of black hair, the tiny flat nose and small, perfect ears. Stretching out a finger, he sat marveling as the infant grasped it in his fist, gripping tightly till his tiny body relaxed in sleep.

Isaac was right after all, he thought then, as he tenderly placed their sleeping child back in Rachel's arms.

"Peter Benjamin Mabaya. It's a good, strong name," Rachel said, carefully slipping the baptismal certificate into the family Bible.

It was, he thought. They'd chosen Peter in honor of Rachel's great grandfather, who'd won his freedom after serving in the Continental Army during the American Revolution.

After some thought, he'd suggested adding Benjamin, after the Quaker schoolmaster, Benjamin Hallowell. "I might never have passed medical school, or even been able to escape from slavery, without some of the things he taught me," he told Rachel soberly.

His own children would grow up free, thank God, and be able to attend school as well. Even here in Boston, though, colored people weren't treated equally with whites. The buildings of the schools colored children had to go to were old and crowded, and the instruction was inferior to that given white youngsters, Rachel said.

A number of parents had become concerned about the poor quality of the colored schools, she added, and were talking about petitioning the School Committee to stop requiring their children to attend separate schools from whites.

He agreed with them, Michael told her. Peter was still a baby, but when the time came he wanted him to get the best education he could—as good as that of any other child in the city.

It could just as easily have been him who was hunted down, Michael thought, as he and Rachel walked home from the meeting organizing the new Freedom Association. Only a few weeks previously—on the 20th of October, 1842—the colored community had been shocked out of its security by the arrest of George Latimer, like himself a fugitive from slavery.

Efforts to free the man by obtaining a writ of habeas corpus had failed, and he'd been held prisoner while preparations were made to return him to his former master. White abolitionists and colored joined in the effort to regain Latimer's freedom. Leaders of the anti-slavery movement—including the brilliant young speaker, Frederick Douglass, who had escaped slavery himself only a few years earlier—denounced the Boston police as kidnappers at public meetings.

Despite the obvious justice of their appeal, only the efforts made by the entire colored community to raise the funds demanded by Latimer's owner for his ransom had secured his freedom at last.

Along with their efforts at raising money, the committee that sprang up to free Latimer had collected nearly 65,000 signatures on a petition to be presented to the Massachusetts legislature, protesting the involvement of law enforcement officials in doing the work of slave catchers.

Petitioning wasn't enough protection, though. The Association they'd just helped organize would stand ready to help fugitives directly in their flight to freedom. Preparations were being made to have emergency assistance ready within the colored community—in the form of food, clothes, a place to stay or whatever else was needed.

He'd volunteered his own services as a doctor, of course. It was the least he could do. He was a fugitive himself, after all. He could tell from the pressure of Rachel's hand on his that she was thinking the same thing.

The Massachusetts legislature recognized in the favor of

the cause of justice. The petitions presented the previous winter had resulted in the passage of the Personal Liberty Act. From now on, it was unlawful for officals of Massachusetts to cooperate in any way in the capture or return of fugitive slaves.

They'd given thanks in church, of course, but Michael added his own thanks in the privacy of his heart. Though he doubted Franklin and Armfield were still seeking him after all these years, he felt reprieved from danger nevertheless.

Once again, he felt justified in placing his faith in the promise of freedom held out by his adopted state.

Now that their free time was no longer filled with passing out petitions and attending meetings, Michael and Rachel were able to think about moving into a place of their own. It was time, they both agreed. Peter was nearly a year old, and would be walking any day now. He was already growing too big for the cradle at their bedside. And much as they both loved the Gardners, they were ready for a little privacy as well.

They found a brick row house at a rental they could manage, only a few streets away from Rachel's parents. They walked through the house together, delighted with the kitchen, with its cook stove, and the sunny front room. An archway led to a small middle room that would hold an examining table and cabinet of medical instruments. The house was much like Doctor Carter's, Michael thought, wondering at his sudden satisfaction.

With two bedrooms opening off the second floor landing, there'd be plenty of room as their family grew, he and Rachel agreed. The Gardners presented them with the bed in which they'd started their married life, and they carefully counted out some of their savings for a table and chairs and chest of drawers.

Now that they had their own home, she'd decided to start

teaching again one or two nights a week, Rachel said, as they put away dishes and pots in the newly scrubbed kitchen. Many adults in the community were hungry for any additional learning they could get, and she was eager to start instructing them once more.

"There's room for half a dozen students right at the kitchen table, and I'll still never be out of earshot of Peter. Don't you think so, Michael?"

He turned, smiling at her. "I think it's a wonderful idea. We're out of earshot of your folks now, though," he added softly. "Let's go on up to bed."

The discussion among the doctors leaving the medical society meeting was more than usually heated. Like Isaac and himself, most of the men Michael overheard were still discussing Doctor Holmes' paper on "The Contagiousness of Puerperal Fever," published only a few weeks previously in the April, 1843 issue of The New England Quarterly Journal of Medicine and Surgery.

"I'm sure Holmes is right," Michael said, "Half the doctors at the Dispensary treat patients all day long without ever thinking of washing their hands."

Isaac nodded. "I know. His paper definitely shows that it's doctors and midwives themselves who're responsible for the increase in cases of childbed fever we've been seeing. Yet half the doctors in Boston are attacking him for it rather than change their ways."

"It's hard to see how they can. He's studied such a large number of cases. And he shows a clear difference in the amount of the disease among women attended by doctors who practice good sanitation and those who ignore it."

"I don't think he leaves any question that childbed fever is contagious, even if he can't explain the exact means of transmittal. But you'd think more doctors would at least act

155

on his findings. Some over at Massachusetts General still go right from performing an autopsy to the lying-in ward."

Michael nodded. "I'm just glad that Rachel had our baby at home."

"I feel the same way about Sarah. Have you and Rachel gotten settled into your new home yet?"

"Just about. It's good to have a place of our own. Rachel was saying the other night," he added, "how you and I've been friends for years, yet our wives have never even met. The two of us just see each other at medical society meetings or lectures. Now that we have our own home, we were hoping you could come to dinner sometime." He spoke the last words hesitantly, suddenly afraid that he'd pushed their friendship too far and not much wanting to know it if he had.

Isaac was hesitating, too, Michael realized. He seemed to be searching for words as he ran his fingers through his hair. Then he smiled. "Why not? I'm sure Sarah would like to meet Rachel, too."

1844

Night had already fallen by the time Michael found the narrow alley he'd been dispatched to. He walked slowly over the frozen dirt, his eyes searching for the address he'd been given.

"What in the hell you after doing here, nigger!?"

Michael whirled around, straining to see down the dark alley. "I'm a doctor from the Boston Dispensary. I'm looking for a family named Garrity, who have a sick child," he said, clearly and carefully.

"Sure, and I'm Tim Garrity myself," the man's rough voice shot back. "but I'm not after having no black nigger meddling with my boy!"

His eyes had adjusted to the darkness now, and he could see the man step down from a low stoop and stride toward him. In one hand he held a jagged two foot long board that

156

appeared to have been torn from the house behind him. If he had any sense, Michael told himself, he'd turn and leave the alley this minute, but the message he'd been given said the child was near death.

"I was sent here by the Dispensary, Mister Garrity," he repeated. "The other doctors will have gone home by now. Can you tell me what's wrong with your youngster?"

Garrity stood speechless a moment, then turned abruptly, lifting the pointed board in a gesture that seemed midway between threat and signal to follow. Michael hesitated a second, then followed after him as he hurried into the dark doorway.

The room they entered was nearly as frigid as the January night outside, cold air seeping through spaces between the bare wooden wallboards. By the light of a small cook stove, which looked to be the only source of heat, Michael could see the child, a boy four or five years old, lying on top of a pile of blankets and old clothes pushed up close to the stove. A woman clutching a baby sat huddled by the sick youngster, holding him to her with her free hand.

Garrity stopped, his shoulders sagging, barely motioning toward the child, his gaze turning bleakly from Michael to his son.

Michael hurried toward the boy, setting down his kit as he knelt alongside the makeshift bed. The youngster broke into a spell of high pitched coughing, his body tossing back and forth as his hands clutched at his mother. He fell back again, choking and gasping, his whole body straining with the effort to draw in another breath.

"Can you tell me how long he's been sick, ma'am?" The woman shook her head wordlessly, staring at Michael a moment, then drawing the child tighter to her.

It didn't matter, Michael thought, feeling the child's drenching perspiration even in the icy room, as he laid his hand

157

on his forehead. The boy's ill-smelling breath rushed out, the indrawn breath that followed harsh and loud as he struggled to fill his lungs with air.

Diptheria. And it was evident the membrane had already spread into the larynx. The obstruction of the breathing passages was nearly total. Even in the dim light, he could see the youngster's lips were already turning blue with suffocation.

There was no way to stop the boy from choking to death, he thought, despairingly.

No, that was wrong! If a cut were made into the boy's windpipe, he could be kept from suffocating. The operation had been performed successfully in France, the professor of surgery had told their class in medical school. He'd never even seen it done, though, and the facilities could hardly be worse than this shanty.

The boy drew another gasping breath as he hesitated.

"Can you do something for him, then?" Garrity's voice was dull and hopeless.

If he did nothing, the child would surely die before much longer, Michael thought. He'd have to try the operation.

"He's suffering from diptheria," he answered, looking at the man and his wife in turn. "His throat's closing up from the disease so that he can't get air into his lungs. All I can do is to cut into his windpipe to stop him from suffocating. He'll have a chance of recovering then."

"No damn nigger's gonna butcher my son!" Garrity started toward him, his unshaven face growing dark with renewed anger.

His wife spoke for the first time. "I'm not after losing another one if there's hope of saving him. You go ahead, then," she said to Michael.

He nodded. "I'll need your help to steady his head, ma'am."

She stood up wordlessly, setting the infant in a basket at

one side of the room, while Michael hurriedly removed his coat and selected the instruments he needed from his kit.

Quickly he rolled the worn blankets tightly, piling them under the child's shoulders till his head hung far enough back to keep the blood and mucus from running down into his lungs. "Easy, boy," he whispered to the unhearing child. The youngster's struggles grew feebler, and Michael prayed he was too far gone to feel the scalpel.

"I'll need a better light, if you have one," he added, relieved as the woman produced a battered oil lamp.

He checked his preparations once more, aware of Garrity still standing angrily behind him as he showed the boy's mother how to position his head. He turned to him, then. "Mister Garrity, you'll have to hold his hands and feet still," he said.

The man stared angrily another moment, then abruptly moved to the child, clasping the boy's hands in one of his own and holding his ankles together with the other.

There was nothing to do then but cut as carefully as possible down the skin of the youngster's neck, till he'd opened an incision a little under two inches in length—sufficient to expose the windpipe. Setting down the scalpel, he pulled the severed edges of skin back from the cut, holding them in place with his spread fingers.

He had no thought for anything but what he must do next, as he slid the small, hooked tenaculum behind the windpipe, drawing it forward till it was clearly exposed to view. Holding the windpipe steady with one hand, he cut quickly across it with the scalpel, just above the Adam's apple. The child cried out weakly, but quickly subsided.

Wiping the blood and pus from the wound, he positioned a narrow metal catheter tube in the open windpipe, watching carefully to make sure the neck remained arched, keeping the lungs free of the bloody fluid.

He held his own breath then, his eyes fixed on the protruding pipe. The youngster arched his body to draw another struggling breath. Slowly, his thin chest rose and fell, as air entered the tube and reached his lungs.

He sat motionless by the boy as his breath whistled in and out of the thin pipe. The blue discoloration slowly faded from the child's face, till his skin returned to a nearly transparent pallor.

"Will he live, then?" The woman's question was a whisper barely louder than the boy's breathing.

If only he could promise her that! The disease still had to run its course, though, and the child's chances were slim. "It's too soon to say for sure, ma'am," he responded finally, as gently as he could. "The diptheria's still in his body. He'll need to be moved to a hospital where he can be kept warm and given medication for the disease."

Both parents fell silent, their eyes fixed on their youngster as he finally sank into a restless sleep. Michael kept his own eyes on the boy as he wrapped his instruments, replacing them in his kit. After a moment he reached for his coat, placing it over the sleeping child before settling down to keep watch again.

Mercifully, the child slept through the night, the tube rising and falling with each new breath. Kneeling at his side, his mother murmured an unceasing supplication, her gaze still on her son as her fingers moved of their own accord on a string of worn, wooden rosary beads. A gray dawn showed dimly through the walls before she rose to nurse her infant and brew a pot of strong, bitter tea.

Michael took the cup she handed him, grateful for the warmth of the liquid as he drank, aware of Garrity's gaze still grimly fixed on him. "Can you get the use of a cart, Mister Garrity?" he asked after a moment. "We'll need to carry him to the hospital now that it's light."

The woman sat in silence as her husband drove the borrowed cart, the sick youngster—wrapped in the blankets now—
lying weakly across her lap. Michael winced as the iron wheels clattered on the uneven cobblestones, and the woman shifted her body to cushion the child from the jolting.

He took his eyes from the boy's windpipe a moment. "Give me the baby to hold, ma'am, so you'll have your hands free to support his neck."

She spoke abruptly as she handed him the infant. "We lost two to the croup last winter and another on the ship coming over. These are the only babies left to us." Her voice trailed off, and she fell silent again.

He nodded, not knowing what to say. How could she endure losing so many, he wondered. It would be more than he could bear if he and Rachel were to lose Peter.

Doctor Bowditch was the admitting physician on duty at Massachusetts General. He stared at the child's windpipe a moment, then quickly barked out orders. "Start him on a teaspoon of iron and mercury once an hour, and swab his throat well with peroxide of hydrogen."

The boy's mother kept her eyes fixed on Bowditch's face as he spoke. "Can you cure him?" she whispered.

"God willing," he answered shortly. He looked at the woman's desperate face a minute, then added, "He's already sent his help in the form of Doctor Mabaya here. Your son wouldn't be alive this moment if he hadn't reached you in time and dared attempt a tracheotomy."

She nodded, then hastened to accompany her son as hospital attendants lifted him to a stretcher. Michael stood exhausted a moment as the child was carried towards the ward, then turned to head for home.

"Doctor!" He turned back, startled at Garrity's voice. The man stood speechless a moment before his words tumbled out hoarsely. "I'll be after thanking you then, doctor," he said finally, turning on his heel and hurrying after his family.

"I'd never have had the nerve to do it myself," Isaac said, as they left the meeting room. To Michael's surprise, half a dozen other men at the February medical society meeting—most of whom had never even spoken with him before—had approached him with similar words of congratulations for undertaking the tracheotomy.

He shrugged now. "There wasn't anything else I could have done. I'm just thankful he's recovering. Doctor Bowditch thinks he'll be able to go home in another week or two."

Isaac nodded. "There's nothing worse than watching a child die."

Michael nodded soberly in turn. Practicing medicine made him only too aware of just how many illnesses threatened children's lives. He couldn't keep from worrying over his own son, though Peter continued to thrive and at nineteen months had passed the most dangerous period of infancy.

He tried to keep his concern from Rachel, especially now that she was again with child, though he knew how easily she sensed his feelings.

"She's a beautiful baby," Sarah said, smiling at Rachel. "And Abigail's a pretty name for her."

Isaac nodded. "Is that a family name too?"

Michael shook his head. "We just liked it. Her middle name's after my mother, though, so it's Abigail Hetty."

"Can I hold your baby?" It was the Marks' first visit since Rachel had given birth six weeks earlier, and three-years-old Ruth stared wide-eyed at the infant.

"If you sit down, I'll put her in your lap for a bit." Rachel smiled at the little girl. "She'll be a big help to you when yours comes," she added to Sarah, over Ruth's head.

Sarah smiled. "I think you're right. I just wish the next

162

few months were over."

"We can't stop protesting now," Rachel said, pushing a copy of the petition to the School Committee across the kitchen table to her brother. "I know we've made progress in a lot of other areas. We can ride inside the horse-cars and hear lectures at the Lyceum. But what's more important than our children's schooling?"

"I'm not arguing with you there," Reuben answered. "I'm just not sure going to school with white children's the answer. It seems to me we'd be better off working to improve schools for our own race, and getting colored teachers hired who'll respect our children's ability."

"The Smith School's nothing but a cellar." Rachel leaned forward earnestly as she spoke. "You can barely see to read there, even during the day. And it's so damp, it's no wonder the children are sick half the time. The parents have been complaining about it for years. But the School Committee will never bother improving it as long as our children are the only ones forced to go there."

"I'll sign it," Jake said, picking up the pen. "Even though I don't think anything will come of it."

"Then we'll have to keep working till we do get the schools open to all children on an equal basis, just like they did in Salem last month. Rachel is right."

Michael stopped talking a moment as Peter left his cousins to stand solemnly watching the grownups, one thumb stuck in his mouth. He removed the thumb gently, putting his arm around his son. "Anyway, even if the School Committee does fix up the colored schools, it's still telling our children they're not as good as whites or they wouldn't be set off by themselves. I don't want anyone telling Peter he can't learn as well as any other child when he's old enough for school."

"Or Abigail either," Rachel said sharply. She smiled at him

163

then. "There's no reason why she shouldn't get just as good an education."

"Or Abigail either," Michael agreed, smiling back at her across the table.

Chapter 12

1846

The amphitheater at Massachusetts General Hospital was packed, the doctors seated shoulder to shoulder on the raised tiers. Every spot was filled, to the very top row occupied by first year medical students.

"Every doctor in the city must be here," Isaac murmured.

Michael nodded, without taking his eyes from the reclining operating chair and the chief surgeon, Doctor John Warren. The patient, a pale young man of twenty years, lay awaiting the removal of a large, congenital tumor on his neck. In his years as a surgeon, Doctor Warren had carried out dozens of similar procedures.

What drew the crowd of medical men this day, the 16th of October, 1846, was the announcement that a new chemical substance was to be tested—one purportedly able to render the patient insensible to pain.

The substance had been brought to the notice of Doctor Warren by a Boston dentist, William Thomas Green Morton, now standing ready with the apparatus he had designed to assure proper inhalation of the fumes.

As the medical men watched intently, Morton held the inhaler to the patient's mouth, inserting the neck of the glass globe between his lips. For several minutes, the young man breathed in the fumes given off by a soaked sponge within the globe. His arms and legs thrashed for a moment, then he abruptly fell unconscious.

The audience was completely silent as Doctor Warren cut into the man's neck, removing the tumor and ligating the veins, while his patient remained oblivious to the scalpel.

Regaining consciousness afterwards, the dazed patient testified that he had indeed been free from pain.

"It's a miracle," Isaac said as they left the amphitheater. "The most amazing discovery. What a blessing for surgical patients."

Michael nodded. "It certainly is," he said, shuddering a second as he thought of the first operation they'd watched here and the terrible cries of the injured man as the surgeon sawed through his arm.

He continued his thoughts in silence as they walked down the stairs. "If only we could make similar progress against illness. But we have no real idea what even causes most fevers," he added finally.

"We know diseases can be transmitted from one person to another," Isaac said thoughtfully. "Holmes definitely showed that illness is contagious, at least in the case of childbed fever."

"But there's still no real explanation of what brings the disease about. We know hand washing helps prevent contagion, but not why."

"You remember Cotton Mather's hypothesis that fevers are

caused by tiny animals that can only be seen through a microscope?"

"I remember you included his views in your thesis, but I thought they were discredited nowadays," Michael answered, puzzled.

Isaac smiled. "You're right. Most medical men today who don't hold with Rush's views believe that diseases—epidemics especially—stem from miasmas or bad air. There's been some interest in the idea in Europe though. Holmes mentioned it in the sessions he gave on microscopy.

"Jacob Henle—a German—published an essay five or six years ago arguing that infectious diseases can be spread by a live parasite, even if they originate from a miasma. And there's been some work done with the microscope itself. Alexandre Donne, in 1837, reported that he'd actually seen microscopic organisms in matter taken from syphilitic lesions. In his view, they're the cause of the syphilis. It was published in French, of course, but Holmes translated it for us. I'll show you my notes . . . "

"These are amazing," Michael said, finally looking up from Isaac's notes. "I had no idea you could see anything like this through the microscope."

Isaac nodded. "Leeuwenhoek sketched these animalcula, he called them, that he saw through his instruments over a hundred-fifty years ago. They're what gave Cotton Mather the basis for his reasoning that illness could be carried by them from one person to another. He even cited another Dutch microscopist, a man named Blancard—here, it's in my notes— 'that the microscope discovers the blood in fevers to be full of animals.' "

"I'd never heard of it before," Michael mused, still amazed. "And you say that Frenchman made the same finding in syphilitic lesions just ten years ago? I'd sure like to find out more about their work."

167

Isaac smiled. "I was hoping you'd say that. I've been wishing I had more time to really do some reading on the subject. The last two or three years a lot of my free time's been taken up with work on the committee to get the synagogue established. And of course I've been a lot busier in my practice since Doctor Bergman retired.

"I know you're busy yourself. Between the two of us, though, maybe we could dig into the subject."

Michael nodded. He was busy. In the past few years he'd been called on by the Freedom Association, and the newly founded Committee of Vigilance, to treat a growing number of fugitives. And the number of private patients he saw after his hours at the Dispensary had also grown, even including some of the Irish immigrants who'd been coming to the city in increasing numbers.

It was a good thing he did have more patients, he thought, with their third child expected in a few more months. They had the added expense, too, of the monthly payments they'd started making last year toward the purchase of their home.

The sketches and writings on animalcula that Isaac had just shown him were too fascinating to ignore, though. He had to learn more about them and the part they might possibly play in human illness.

"With two of us, we ought to be able to learn something more about it, at any rate," he answered at last.

The small table in the Mabayas' front room was cluttered with old medical books and handwritten notes. Michael laid the translation Isaac had brought on top of them, looking at him with growing excitement.

"This finding by Schonlein fits rights in with Donne's conclusions on syphilis."

Isaac nodded eagerly. "I know. Schonlein's work shows a pretty clear connection between the skin disease favus and the presence of animalcules."

168

"The studies we've found so far all agree with Mather's theory," Michael said, echoing his enthusiasm.

"Mather wasn't even the first to propose the idea," Isaac mused. "Fracastor postulated a contagium virum responsible for the spread of epidemics three hundred years ago."

Michael nodded, trying to clarify his ideas in his own mind, even as he spoke with growing eagerness. "They had no way of finding out if their ideas were right or not, though, even though it makes sense that if diseases are contagious there must be some way they're carried from one person to another. But this research that's been done using the miscroscope, especially these studies the last ten years or so, definitely show the presence of animalcules in diseased specimens."

"Yet there's been hardly any attention paid to them. Most doctors here have probably never even heard of them." Isaac paused, running his fingers absently through his hair.

"I think we should write an essay describing the research we've found," he added at last. "We could submit it to read at the medical society meeting this fall, or even to one of the journals."

"You think we'd have a chance of getting it accepted?" Michael asked, suddenly realizing he hadn't given very much thought to what might result from their reading.

"Why not? Nobody's really tried to tie any of this work together. It ought to be given wider attention, and that's what we'd be doing."

Michael nodded. "Sure wouldn't hurt to try," he said, smiling.

"Daddy!"

He turned as his two oldest children crowded into the doorway with Ruth and Miriam Marks.

"Daddy, Mama said to tell you we're gonna eat dinner soon as she gets Elizabeth asleep," Peter said, coming up to his father.

"I'm helping her," Ruth announced. "I helped my mama all the time when Miriam was little."

"Me too. I wanna help too," Miriam chimed in.

Abigail grabbed her hand. "C'mon. I show you who we change my baby."

Ruth paused a moment before following the younger girls upstairs. "They think they're big as Peter and me, now that Abigail has a baby sister."

"She's sure in a hurry to grow up herself," Michael said, smiling at Isaac.

"I know, believe me. I can hardly believe she'll be starting school this fall. And Peter will be school age in another year, won't he?"

Michael nodded. "He'll be six next May. But I don't know what we'll do about school. Most parents are keeping their children out of the colored schools, but the School Committee still refuses to abolish separate schools.

"Rachel and I've started teaching Peter his letters, and he already knows most of the alphabet," he added, glancing at his son proudly. "But that's just a stop-gap solution."

"The School Committee turned down your last petition too, then?"

Michael nodded. "According to the Committee there's such a mental and moral distinction between the two races that our children can never go to school together," he said bitterly, listening to the chatter of the three little girls as they climbed the stairs.

"Animalcules! Would you care to be more specific, Doctor Marks? Were the tiny beasties postulated by Reverend Cotton Mather black cats or other familiar witches' spirits, perhaps?"

Michael winced as a wave of laughter greeted the jibe. He and Isaac had spent much of their free time during the past summer working on their paper, "Historical and Recent Evidence for the Animalculaer Explanation of Epidemics," spurred on by the news that it had been accepted for presentation at the October medical society meeting.

Though increasingly convinced themselves of the validity of the animalculaer hypothesis, they'd expected their presentation to draw considerable questioning. They hadn't expected outright mockery though.

Isaac was flushed with embarrassment, Michael saw. He disliked public speaking at best, but they'd reluctantly decided the paper would be better received if Isaac were to read it. It was obvious, though, that he was too flustered now to make any effective response to the heckling.

He rose himself, turning to face the portly doctor who'd just spoken. "Being wrong on witchcraft doesn't mean Mather had to be mistaken about everything, Doctor Potts. He was one of the first supporters of smallpox innoculation, you'll remember. In any case, I think we've found enough modern research that supports his theory to make it worth paying serious attention to."

Several of the other doctors were nodding, he saw with relief. Questions started coming then about the findings of Bassi, Schonlein and the other researchers they'd cited, and he was glad to see that Isaac had recovered his self-possession enough to answer them.

He could feel Isaac's discouragement as they left the meeting room, though. He put his hand on Isaac's shoulder a moment. "C'mon, don't let Potts upset you. He's as scared of new ideas as most folks are of an outbreak of cholera."

Isaac managed a smile. "But even the men who took us seriously don't think the studies we found are of much importance. They feel the research showing microorganisms in favus and silkworm disease is a fluke, or at best a scientific curiosity with no real applicability to most epidemics."

"Well, they're right that research on animalcules is just at the beginning," Michael said gently. "There's a lot more work needs to be done to really establish a connection between microorganisms and disease."

"Nobody seems very interested in doing it, though."

Michael nodded. "There's no reason why we shouldn't," he said slowly. "We've put so much into this already, it's a shame to let it drop now."

"There's nothing I'd like better," Isaac said after a moment. "But we haven't any facilities for that kind of work."

"Sure we do." Michael stopped walking in his eagerness to share the new idea suddenly crowding into his mind. "Look, right here at Massachusetts General there's patients suffering from a dozen different diseases. And the doctors are still bleeding two out of three of them. We wouldn't have any trouble in getting specimens to study. We'd just need to get the use of a microscope, and Doctor Holmes might be able to arrange that."

"I think he'd be willing. He seemed pretty interested tonight. Anyway, what can we lose by asking?" Isaac smiled, his enthusiasm returning at last.

Doctor Holmes was not only willing to arrange for the use of a microscope but had managed to find them a small store room at Massachusetts General Hospital that could be cleaned out enough to work in. They sat the microscope on a sturdy table next to the window, positioning it carefully for the best possible illumination.

Despite their impatience to get started, spring of 1849 was only a few weeks off before their workspace was set up and they could arrange enough time together to begin. It was an additional two weeks till they were able to obtain a specimen from a patient suffering from syphilis, in the hope of discovering for themselves the animalcules described by Donne.

Their microscopic examination of the man's blood revealed

a bewildering variety of forms, both moving and stationary. A sample of pus from an open sore showed the microorganisms more clearly, as well as taking longer to dry up on their glass slide, but still left them looking at each other in puzzlement.

"I can see animalcules that resemble a corkscrew the way Donne described," Isaac said finally, "but there must be half a dozen different kinds of organisms in this specimen. How could he determine which caused the disease?"

Michael nodded, still lost in thought. "What we'll have to do is examine specimens from as many different kinds of disease as we can get hold of," he said finally. "And we'll need to look at as many samples of the same disease as we can, too. Then if we find distinct types of animalcules appearing in specimens of each illness, we'll have a good idea that those are the organisms causing the different fevers."

"It's a good scheme," Isaac agreed. "We've got an awful lot of work ahead of us, though."

At eight in the morning there were still two hours till the official opening of the annual Anti-Slavery Bazaar, but the market on the ground floor of Faneuil Hall was already crowded as members of the Female Anti-Slavery Society bustled about getting their booths in order. Cartwheels clattered on the pavingstones outside as additional exhibitors tethered horses and unloaded wares. Peter and Abigail watched wide-eyed as a daguerreotypist and his assistant set up their bulky equipment alongside a window, a large sign on a tripod advertising "Framed Daguerrean Miniatures, Twentyfive Cents a Portrait."

Michael lifted Elizabeth from her perch on Rachel's hip, glad to be spending the day with his children. Over the past summer, he and Isaac had met in their workroom at least two or three evenings a week, as well as most Sunday afternoons, taking advantage of the illumination provided by the long summer days. The long hours he was spending at the research had become an increasingly sore subject between Rachel and himself.

Just yesterday evening she'd told him sharply, "The children and I deserve a little of your time, too! I know the studying you're doing with Isaac is important to you, but it's not more important than your own family."

She was still upset today, he knew, as she hurried off with her mother and sister-in-law to arrange their displays. "Mama go bye-bye," Elizabeth called, wriggling in Michael's arms.

"I can carry Lizabeth, Daddy," Abigail said eagerly.

He smiled down at his older daughter. She had grown just since the beginning of the summer, he thought with a pang. Rachel was right. He hadn't paid much attention to his children the past few months. "She's pretty big for you, honey. Let's just hold her hands, and let her walk."

"Here comes Granddaddy," Peter called. "I bet he's gonna take her."

"I bet you're right," Michael smiled, greeting his father-in-law, who hugged Abigail and Peter before hoisting his youngest grandchild onto his shoulders.

The bazaar grew more crowded as they strolled from stall to stall, chatting with friends and examining the fancy needlework, knitted baby garments, hand-smocked dresses, picture puzzles and wooden toys offered for sale to raise funds for the anti-slavery cause. Hungry fair-goers were already lining up to buy plates of baked beans with Boston brown bread and slices of freshly baked pie. Michael stopped to look at a display of campaign literature for Martin Van Buren, presidential candidate of the Free Soil Party, the newly formed coalition that included old Liberty Party supporters as well as Conscience-Whigs and Free Democrats.

"Come on, Daddy," Peter urged him. "I want to find a book

I can read myself." He smiled at his son as they started down the row of books and broadsides. Two tables were stacked with poetry selections, from religious verses by Phyllis Wheatley to anti-slavery stanzas by John Greenleaf Whittier and James Russell Lowell. Frederick Douglass' Narrative of his life in slavery was still selling briskly, three years after its publication.

Michael paid for a copy of the 1848 New England Anti-Slavery Almanac, while Peter looked through the "Slave's Friend," a magazine for children. "It's still too hard for me," he said, disappointed.

"How about this?" Michael asked him, selecting a broadside headed "Slavery's Alphabet."

"I think I can read that," Peter said, after a moment. "A is an Af-?" He looked up.

"African," Michael prompted gently.

Peter nodded, starting to sound out the words again with Michael's help. "A is an African sold far from home. B is the babe from his mother's breast torn. C is the cotton field slaves have to hoe. D is the driver whose whip makes blood flow." He stopped proudly. "I read most of the words myself, didn't I?"

"That's right, son," Michael answered, equally proud.

"Daddy!" Abigail tugged urgently at Michael's sleeve as he counted out three cents for the broadside. She was staring wide-eyed at the drawing at the top of the alphabet, he realized, a spread-eagled slave tied hand and foot to stakes driven into the ground, his huddled family looking on helplessly as an overseer plied the lash.

"That man is so mean, Daddy!"

He looked down at her wide, stricken eyes. "I know, honey," he said, kneeling down and putting his arm around her. She looked back at him, her face still urgent with questioning.

"Daddy, why do the slaves stay there when they're treated so mean? Why don't they come here, like you did?" she whispered finally.

"That's a dumb question!" Peter said. "If they could just come up North when they wanted, they wouldn't be slaves."

"Don't call your sister dumb!" Michael said sharply. "It's a good question."

He turned back to Abigail. "Most of them are afraid to run away, because the slave-owners watch the roads, and they have guns and dogs. And slaves aren't allowed to learn to read, so they have a real hard time finding their way up North even if they do escape. That's why we need the Underground Railroad to help people get free. I was lucky," he added. "My mama told me how important reading was, and I was able to get some little white boys to teach me my letters."

She nodded, clutching his hand as they started down the aisle again. "Were you sad to leave your mama when you ran away?"

"She died when I was a boy," he answered gently. "But I would have been awfully sad to leave her if she was still alive."

"What about your daddy? Were you sad to leave him?"

He stopped, hesitating before answering her question. He'd never believed in keeping the truth from his children, though. "My daddy was the white man who owned me," he said finally, "and I wasn't at all sad to leave him."

Peter was looking at him now, as stunned as Abigail had been. "Daddy, you mean the man who owned you is our other grandfather?"

"He's your grandfather as far as blood goes, son. But he'd never call you a grandson of his, any more than he called me his son. You don't need to worry about him. Your mama's daddy is as fine a grandpa as you could want."

Peter nodded, but Michael could tell he was still troubled.

176

He looked at his children's sober faces, seeking a change of subject. "I tell you what. It's almost time for the Garrison Junior Choir to sing. We'd better head over so we can hear your cousins. Then, if your mama can leave her booth a little while, maybe we can get a portrait made of our family. There's not such a long line now," he added, waving toward the daguerrotypist.

The three children were asleep as soon as they fell into bed, exhausted by their long day at the bazaar, but Michael lay awake though it was well past midnight. He could feel Rachel tossing restlessly beside him. Though they hadn't resumed their argument, he'd felt the strain between them even as they held each other in love-making.

"Daddy! Daddy!"

He was out of bed instantly at Abigail's screams, gathering her into his arms as Rachel hurried after him. "It's all right, honey. You had a bad dream, is all," he soothed her.

"Daddy, I thought you were a slave and that mean man was hitting you with his whip, and I yelled and yelled, but he wouldn't stop," she said, sobbing again.

"Hush, it was nothing but a bad dream," he said, rocking her gently and stroking her back. "Massachusetts is a free state. Nobody can carry me back into slavery from here. I tell you what, honey. You can come sleep with Mama and me the rest of the night." He carried her across the hall as Rachel soothed Peter and Elizabeth.

"I should have known better than to show her that alphabet," he whispered miserably to Rachel, after Abigail had fallen asleep between them.

She reached for his hand over Abigail's sleeping form. "Don't go blaming yourself. You can't keep things like that from them. You're a good father, Michael," she added softly, squeezing his fingers in hers.

The conversation at the October medical society meeting was grim. Cholera had swept through Europe earlier that year, and now seemed likely to scourge the American continent, a number of medical observers were predicting.

The Boston City Council had already been alerted, and in common with other city governments had directed the Board of Health to oversee the cleanup of courts, lanes and alleys in the poorer sections of town.

These sanitary measures would be adequate to prevent any serious outbreak in the city of Boston, several of the doctors confidently argued. "Cholera is a disease of dirt, dissipation and debauchery, gentlemen," Doctor Potts was telling a circle of solemnly nodding physicians. "Our respectable citizens have nothing to fear."

Michael stopped to listen, recollections of the epidemic seventeen years before suddenly vivid in his mind. There'd been plenty of respectable citizens who'd succumbed to cholera then.

"Cholera might breed in filth, Doctor Potts," he said, "but it can still be passed from one person to another once an epidemic gets started."

"By your imaginary animalcules, Mabaya? I'll confine my belief to what I can see with my own eyes. The foul surroundings our lower classes seem content to live in are the only places you'll find cholera striking."

Michael shrugged as he walked on with Isaac, who seemed lost in thought.

"I wonder if we could find a distinctive organism if we examined a specimen from a cholera patient," Isaac said at last.

Michael stopped short, remembering the boy who'd shared his cell and how he'd gone from vigor to agonizing death in a few short hours.

"Just pray we never get a chance to. You ever seen anyone

178

die of cholera, Isaac? That's one disease I don't want to mess with."

The threat of cholera remained, but with the onset of winter Michael had little time to worry about it over much. Recent famines in Ireland had swelled the numbers of immigrants arriving in Boston, with a corresponding increase in patients in need of the medical services of the Dispensary. Along with the clinic's other doctors, Michael was kept busy treating the usual onslaught of seasonal ailments, aggravated by the crowded living conditions of the new arrivals. The number of patients he was called on to treat in the evening hours also had grown, and their illnesses seemed unusually stubborn and lingering, with influenza and bowel ailments rampant.

Word reached Boston the first week in December of the packet ship *New York,* anchored in quarantine off Staten Island. Seven steerage passengers had died of cholera during the Atlantic crossing, and a number of new cases were reported among the remaining three hundred.

In common with other medical men and anxious citizens, Michael awaited further word of the disease, but the cold winter weather seemed to have halted the cholera's spread.

The snowy weather was welcomed by the children, who flocked to the lower slopes of Beacon Hill, sliding down the snow covered cobblestones on home-made sleds. Michael's old friend, Ted Johnson, helped his two sons and Peter fasten a shallow packing box to a pair of smoothly sanded runners.

Fresh snow fell throughout February. Ted and Lydia Johnson sat around the kitchen table with Michael and Rachel on a cold Sunday afternoon as the children hurried out to slide, followed by reminders to the boys to watch out for Abigail.

Two evenings before, Michael had been called on by the Vigilance Committee to treat Ellen Craft, a fugitive who'd arrived in Boston with her husband, William, just a few days earlier. The Liberator had already chronicled the Crafts' daring escape, with the light-skinned Ellen—dressed in man's attire—masquerading as a Southern aristocrat, her husband playing the part of her faithful body servant. His friends hung on Michael's words nevertheless as he desribed his meeting with the young couple.

"They sure had their wits about them," Michael said admiringly. "Luckily, she's just suffering from exhaustion."

Ted grinned at him when he finished speaking. "You had your wits about you yourself when you got free of slavery, Michael, and so did my Lydia here."

Lydia smiled. "I was lucky. Butter wouldn't melt in my mouth when I talked to my old mistress. Just got her thinking I was so content slaving my life away for her, she carried me along to wait on her while she was summering up North. Second week there she sent me to the cobbler with a pair of her shoes she'd worn through the soles of. I left those shoes with that man, and just kept right on walking till I'd left old mistress behind too."

They all laughed at her familiar story.

"Well, it was a lucky day for me when I met you," Ted said, reaching for her hand. "I've been fortunate since then, too. I've had steady work, and I'm just about set to open my own shop."

Michael nodded, gazing around the warm kitchen at Rachel and his good friends, listening to Elizabeth starting to sing to herself upstairs as she woke from her nap. "I couldn't have been more fortunate myself," he said, with a quiet happiness.

Chapter 13

1849

"Evening, Doctor Mabaya."

"How you doing, Michael?"

Michael returned his neighbors' cheerful greetings, enjoying the walk home in the mild evening air. Winter had given way to spring at last, and clusters of women visited on front stoops or picked over the cartmen's selection of fresh vegetables. Men walked with new optimism now that the thawing of the harbor had reopened jobs for laborers on the city docks.

Peter and Abigail ran to meet him as he climbed the few steps to his front door, with Elizabeth right behind them, calling "Daddy's home." He hugged his older children, smiling at Elizabeth's cheerful chatter as he scooped her up for a kiss.

At two, Elizabeth wanted to do whatever Peter and Abigail did, Michael mused, smiling. Neither had been as eager as their baby sister, though, who ran to meet family and friends alike with arms held out for a hug.

Welcome as the warmer weather was, the end of winter meant a likely end to the respite from cholera. Many medical observers considered the persistently lingering winter ailments a sure forerunner of cholera, Michael knew. New cholera outbreaks had been reported since the beginning of April, and it seemed only a matter of time till the epidemic reached Boston.

By the end of May, cholera was reported as far north as Wisconsin, and spreading through the western territories along the trail of the California gold-rush.

"The papers say nearly one person in ten has died in St. Louis," Michael said to Isaac in horror. "And there's hundreds of cases in New York and no end to the epidemic there."

Isaac nodded soberly. Although it had been well over a month since the last time they'd been able to meet in their workroom, both men found themselves preoccupied by news of the cholera epidemic.

"New England was only lightly hit in the '32 epidemic," Isaac said at last. "And New York is far filthier than Boston."

Michael nodded in return, recalling the wandering herds of pigs that had so astonished him during his few weeks in New York. "I reckon you're right. Let's hope so, anyway," he added, finally turning to adjust the microscope.

Cholera might have touched Boston more lightly than New York, but that was no help to the man who lay newly dead before him, Michael thought bleakly. The young seaman was one of three cholera sufferers he'd found in the North End boarding house he'd been summoned to earlier that evening. A second, gray-haired sailor lay comatose, his eyes sunken pits in his ebony face, legs drawn up with cramp. Feeling his icy hands, Michael knew he wouldn't last out the hour.

The third man was still stirring, weakly calling for water. Michael held a mug to his lips, letting him sip as much as he wished. There was little else he could do for him, much as he prayed that at least this one of his patients would live.

No two doctors seemed to agree on the best treatment for cholera, but most believed that purging with calomel was the very minimum that should be done to drive out the vitiated humors. Michael couldn't bring himself to purge the man, already weakened by his constant puking and discharging bowels. He laid a hot water bottle at the seaman's feet, then sat helplessly at his side, reminding himself of Doctor Bigelow's belief that a draught of water or turned pillow might be the best treatment a physician could give, while allowing the disease to run its natural course.

Slowly the seaman's condition improved, his cramps diminishing and his stopped urinary tract beginning to function again. His hands and feet regained their customary warmth as he fell into a restorative sleep. Michael remained by his side till he was sure the man would live, before heading wearily across the city toward home.

Cases of cholera continued to strike as the summer wore on, mainly among the poor and recent immigrants. By mid-July, Michael felt exhausted with overwork and strain.

He put his weariness aside though, to accompany Rachel to the Negro School Abolition Society meeting. Though recently organized, the Society members were men and women who had devoted several years of effort to securing equal schooling for their children, including Garrison's assistant on The Liberator, William C. Nell.

Michael listened to the discussion intently. Repeated petitions to the School Committee to do away with separate schools had been denied, though, like Rachel and himself, a majority of colored parents refused to subject their children to the humiliation and inferior education of the segregated schools.

Peter now attended a primary class taught by Rachel and

183

several other mothers, concerned that their children not fall behind in their schooling. The class was meant as a temporary measure, though it often seemed to Michael that they might go on petitioning fruitlessly till their children were grown and parents themselves.

His frustration was shared by other parents on the committee. The year before, Benjamin Roberts, a printer and active abolitionist, had entered his daughter, Sarah, in the primary school nearest her home, despite being refused a ticket of admission by the Primary School Committee. When the little girl was excluded from the school, Roberts brought suit against the city of Boston, for violation of its own law that children should attend school closest to their residence unless special provision had been made otherwise.

Although the suit had been denied, it had been appealed to the Massachusetts Supreme Court, and was scheduled to be heard that fall. The noted abolitionist lawyer, Charles Sumner, was representing Roberts. Sumner's assistant in the case was Robert Morris, an active member of the committee for equal school rights. Still in his mid-twenties, Morris had filled the colored community with pride when he passed the Massachusetts bar examination two years before.

The Society members listened hopefully now as Morris summarized the status of the case.

"We've got the law on our side," Michael told his inlaws an hour later, as he and Rachel stopped by to pick up their children. "I don't see how the Court can deny Sumner's arguments."

Jake, also visiting his parents, looked up from his coffee cup. "You're fooling yourself if you believe that, Michael. The Court'll read the law any way it pleases to keep our children from going to school with whites."

Michael shrugged, too tired to argue with Jake. "Let's hope you're wrong," he said, trying to lift up Elizabeth without

184

waking her, as Rachel called Peter and Abigail from their play.

He was even more tired the following evening. The narrow streets still held the stifling heat of the day as he finally reached his front door, loosening his collar as he entered the house. He stood in the hallway a moment, wondering at the unusual quiet.

Rachel's footsteps sounded on the staircase as she hurried toward him. "Thank God you're here. Peter and Abigail have been puking all afternoon."

He rushed upstairs after her, pausing only to hurriedly wash his hands, before kneeling by the children's beds. Abigail broke into weak tears, hands clutching her stomach. "It hurts, Daddy. Make it stop hurting."

Peter lay doubled over in his own narrow bed, rocking from side to side, trying not to cry out Michael saw with a pang, even as he suddenly spewed vomit into the already filled chamberpot. He steadied his son's head, wiping his mouth gently as he subsided again.

"Have their bowels been running?" he asked Rachel, doing his best to steady his voice.

She nodded. "Michael, is it—?"

He couldn't bring himself to say it either. "It may not be," he said, stroking Abigail's forehead, wincing at the coldness of her skin. She clutched at his hand. "You'll be all right, honey," he murmured, praying it was true.

It hurt to be able to do so little for his own children. He placed warm cloths gently over their stomachs, adding a few drops of laudanum to ease their cramps to the weak broth Rachel brought them.

He looked up once the children had quieted a bit, realizing he hadn't heard the sing-song babble of their youngest since he'd been home. "Is Elizabeth still at your mother's?"

She shook her head. "Sleeping on our bed. Mama felt bad herself this morning so I took her along with me. Two of the other children got sick in class, too. We sent them all home before noon."

He nodded. "Don't let her in here. We don't want her catching whatever Peter and Abigail have," he said, his voice faltering momentarily.

She nodded in return, taking his hand in hers. He squeezed her hand, then turned back to their sick children.

He changed the warm cloths hourly during the night, encouraging the children to sip the lukewarm broth. By morning Rachel had emptied the chamber pot three times, and the two youngsters had fallen into a fitful sleep.

He stayed by their side as Rachel left to care for Elizabeth, gently touching their outflung hands and thanking God as he felt them warm in his own. By evening their spasms were gone. Rachel knelt next to him as the children slept peacefully now, her eyes glistening with relief and thankfulness.

They spelled each other at the children's bedside through the second night. Michael lay on top of the coverlet at Rachel's insistence that he get some rest, still too wrought up to sleep. Finally he drifted off, lulled by Elizabeth's even breathing as she curled up in her trundle bed, set up for the night at her parents' bedside.

He woke to her sudden, shrill crying, clasping her in his arms as Rachel rushed into the room. He looked at her in misery as Elizabeth abruptly vomited, her small body doubling over in his arms.

Once again he struggled against the disease, trying desperately to drive the chill from his daughter's body with warm cloths and ease the pain in her stomach with the tincture of opium.

This time his efforts were in vain.

She couldn't keep down even a swallow of broth, and her cries turned to weak sobs as her watery stools flooded the bed. Rachel held her close, rocking her ceaselessly as the night wore on. By morning she was too weak to cry, her closed eyes sunken in her face.

"Do you think, if you bled her?" Rachel whispered to him, finally.

He shook his head. "She'd just die the sooner," he said numbly, admitting to himself as well as Rachel that they were going to lose Elizabeth. He rubbed her icy hands and feet, praying that he was wrong and knowing that he wasn't.

Rachel held her another hour before a final breath escaped her pinched lips and she lay lifeless in her mother's arms. Michael stroked her hand a last time, shaking with sobs as Rachel finally laid her on the bed, gently covering her tiny body with a blanket. He reached out to Rachel then, his head falling onto her breast, feeling her tears falling onto his face and mingling with his own.

The older children had gotten up, he realized after a moment, and stood shakily in the doorway. Abigail came weakly into the room, her voice still a whisper. "Daddy, I don't want Elizabeth to die."

He couldn't stop crying enough to speak. He held out his arm to Abigail, drawing her close, as Peter came into the shelter of his mother's arm. The four of them held each other tightly then, their small circle swaying as they sobbed.

The remainder of summer passed in a round of misery. Michael returned to work, doggedly pushing himself from one bedside to another, offering whatever help he could to patients suffering from cholera as well as the usual variety of summer ailments. No matter how tired he was by evening though, he was pierced anew by the emptiness of their house without Elizabeth's running footsteps and cheerfully babbling voice.

Family life went on, of course. Outwardly the evenings passed the same as before, but he knew he was often silent and morose, even in the midst of reading to Abigail or helping Peter with his lessons.

By the end of summer the epidemic had abated. There was time once again to think about resuming the research and going ahead with interrupted family plans.

He couldn't bring himself to do either.

He shook his head in response to Isaac's gentle urging. "How can I spend time worrying about animalcules when I can't even keep my own baby alive?"

He had no heart for worrying about household affairs either.

He couldn't find comfort even in church, despite the urging of their pastor, Reverend Snowden, and Rachel's parents that he be reconciled to the will of God.

Rachel took him to task at last. "You have two other children who need you to be a father to them. And I need you too, Michael. Don't you think I'm grieving for her too? But we've got to trust in God's mercy and go on living."

He nodded, knowing she was right. It still wasn't easy to do.

"We've both got to be strong now," she added, her eyes suddenly filling with tears as she looked up at him.

He held her close then, not talking, doing his best to bring some comfort to both of them.

The School Abolition Society continued to meet through the fall, completing plans for the establishment of their own alternative school to the segregated city ones, though still hopeful that a favorable Court decision would make their work unnecessary.

In October the school opened its doors, with Rachel teaching the youngest primary students. With just the two children, she could easily teach the full school day she said, with only a slight trembling in her voice. Though not yet six, Abigail could easily keep up with the lessons in the first reader.

Sarah Roberts' case finally came before the Massachusetts Supreme Court on December 4th. The teachers dismissed the temporary school for the day, so that parents could take their children to the hearing if they wished. Michael and Rachel arrived an hour-and-a-half early with Abigail and Peter, dressed in their Sunday clothes and admonished to be on their best behavior.

The doors finally opened, and they crowded into the courtroom with the other colored spectators. Michael listened to the proceedings intently, leaning forward in his seat as Sumner summed up his arguments to the Court.

"This little child asks at your hands her personal rights. So doing, she calls upon you to decide a question which concerns the Constitution and laws of the Commonwealth.

"According to the Constitution of Massachusetts, all men, without distinction of race or color, are equal before the law. In point of fact the separate school is not an equivalent. Compulsory segregation from the mass of citizens is of itself an inequality which we condemn.

"The school is the little world where the child is trained for the larger world of life. And since, according to our institutions, all classes, without distinction of color, meet in the performance of civil duties, so should they all, without distinction of color, meet in the school, beginning there those relations of equality which the Constitution and laws promise to all."

It was a strong argument, Michael thought. He glanced at Rachel and the other members of the Society, seeing his feelings echoed in their faces. The Court would have to rule in their favor.

Enthusiastic meetings supporting the cause of school equality were held throughout the winter. He and Rachel took the children to hear Garrison, Wendell Phillips and other speakers, both white and colored, at the African Meeting House.

The likelihood of a favorable ruling was frequently discussed in the community, particularly among the parents of school age children. He talked it over with Ted once again as they sanded the walls of the new attic bedroom for Peter. Even the children were discussing the Court case, Michael noted, overhearing his friend's oldest son, Teddy, explain to the others how they might soon be able to attend any public school "just like any other boys."

Justice Shaw finally announced the Court's decision in April of 1850. Despite their hopes, the ruling allowed each school system to decide the question of segregation for itself, leaving the Boston Primary School Committee free to go on requiring separate colored schools. The colored schools provided met the legal requirements for equal rights, the Court ruled, stating that in its opinion race was as legitimate a distinction as sex.

"We're not giving up yet," Robert Morris told Michael that Sunday after church. "There's a good possibility of persuading the legislature to enact equal school laws."

Michael nodded, still disappointed by the Court ruling. Peter was disappointed as well, he thought, glancing at his son's face as they walked home from church. He put his arm around his shoulders. "He's right. We'll have to keep on protesting till we get equal rights, even if it takes longer than we hoped."

Peter shrugged, looking up at his father. "Who needs to go to their schools anyway? You never even went to school, and you became a doctor just the same."

Michael stared at his son as he formed an answer, suddenly seeing himself at Peter's age—learning his letters in the dirt by the water pump, sneaking looks at David's schoolbooks, scared he'd find out and tell Doctor Carter on him. He remembered James Harrison, a few years later, smashing him across the knuckles with a ruler when he'd discovered him using pen and ink.

He saw himself at sixteen, then—proud to be able to teach

Titus and Ned, till they were dragged out and tortured with the rawhide for daring to get a little learning. For a second he was too filled with remembered fury to speak.

"I didn't run up North to raise you like I came up!" he said harshly. He saw Peter looking at him in surprise.

"I couldn't go to school because the law didn't allow it. And I was strung up and whipped when I tried to teach my friends. I don't want you ever to go through what I did," he added, a little more calmly.

Peter nodded, still staring at him in shock. "But they have colored schools here we can go to if we want. It's not like when you were in slavery," he said timidly.

Michael walked on without speaking, turning Peter's words over in his mind. "No, we aren't in slavery here," he said at last. "But we'll never be really free either as long as we're only allowed to go to certain schools, or told we can't go somewhere we want to, just because of our color. As long as we can be kept in our place like that, we're still only half free. I want you to remember that," he added, putting his arm around Peter again as they walked on home.

1850

With the school fight at a stalemate, national issues came to the forefront of attention in the colored community. Emotions had been rising in the country since the end of the war with Mexico over the admission of new states to the Union as free or slave. Texas had already entered as a slave state, but Southern congressmen threatened secession over the House-passed Wilmot Proviso prohibiting slavery in any other territory acquired as a result of the Mexican War. A proposed compromise, drafted by Kentucky Senator Henry Clay, would admit California as a free state while the territories of New Mexico and Utah would neither permit nor prohibit slavery.

"The slave trade would be ended in the District of Columbia. That's supposed to make us willing to accept Clay's scheme to force the return of runaways!" Jake said, throwing down his newspaper in disgust.

Michael nodded, in common with the other men crowded into the barbershop. Like the rest, he was filled with horror at Clay's inhuman proposal to empower the Federal government to capture and return fugitives to slavery as part of his compromise.

"He'd hold the Union together with our blood," Ted said. Michael laid his hand on Ted's shoulder, knowing his friend was imagining Lydia being dragged back into bondage, then nodded his own agreement with Ted's bitter words. "That's exactly what he'd do. It's still hard to believe that Webster would back him up."

The others murmured agreement. The Senate speech of Massachusetts Senator Daniel Webster supporting Clay's proposals—including the enactment of strict fugitive slave laws—came as a shock to his constituents, even those who had never thought of themselves as abolitionists.

"The man's a traitor to our cause." Michael turned at the new voice. Charles Sumner—a frequent visitor to the barbershop—stood in the doorway, his voice carrying clearly through the crowded shop.

There was another murmur of agreement.

"But will Congress be convinced to pass it?" There was a moment of anxious silence after Ted's question.

"Even if the Congress should pass such an infamous, unconstitutional bill, it will never be enforced in our Commonwealth," the lawyer responded, his voice strong with conviction.

He had to be right, Michael thought, hearing Ted's sigh of relief beside him as the discussion continued.

Along with the rest of the colored community, Michael anxiously followed the Congressional debates. In May, Clay's resolutions were referred to a committee of the Senate. Michael scanned the newspapers daily for word of the committee's report.

"Even if Congress should pass it, President Taylor will never sign it," Reuben said, when the committee finally reported two compromise bills. Michael nodded. The President had declared his opposition to the bills. Reuben had to be right.

There was little to do, except wait and hope that the cause of justice would prevail. It was a relief to turn his mind back to the research on animalcules. In the months after Elizabeth died he hadn't had the heart to return to the workroom, but now he found his interest rekindled at last.

As he predicted, it wasn't hard to obtain specimens to study. Writers in several medical journals, including an editorial in the fall 1849 *Philadelphia Medical Examiner,* had suggested microscopic organisms as the cause of the recent cholera outbreak. Doctors at Massachusetts General were interested enough in their research to assure them as many specimens as they had time to examine.

It wasn't nearly as easy to see the microorganisms as they had thought it would be, though. Much of their time in the workroom two years before had been spent working out ways to observe the animalcules. Through trial and error, they'd found that their specimens would last longer under the microscope when the glass slide had a hollowed depression ground out to hold a drop of the sample material. They were still at the mercy of the weather, though, depending on daylight bright enough to reflect from the mirror through the objective lens of their microscope.

With the beginning of summer, cholera returned, though fortunately not so serious an outbreak as the year before. Cases occurred in Boston as everywhere else, but they could give thanks that the numbers were fewer.

Isaac once more brought up the subject of obtaining specimens from cholera sufferers for examination.

Michael didn't want to consider it.

"If we're serious about looking for microorganisms, we ought to be examining from cholera patients," Isaac urged. "You know the *Medical Examiner* mentioned a German report of microscopic fungi found in the stools of cholera sufferers. We'd have a good chance of confirming those findings."

Michael shook his head. His memories of the disease were too painful even to study it under the microscope.

"I know how you feel, Michael, believe me," Isaac said finally, "but I still think we ought to study it while we have the chance."

"You don't know. You've never lost a child," he said sharply. He held out his hands apologetically then, seeing Isaac's hurt look. "I didn't mean to snap at you. It's just that even talking about cholera brings everything back to mind again."

"I know. I'm sorry, Michael. But if we could discover the cause, then there'd be a chance of finding a remedy for it."

He sighed, giving in. "We're a long way from that, Isaac. I reckon you're right about studying it, though."

The news spread within hours over the telegraph lines. President Taylor lay dead in the White House, a victim of the cholera. Millard Fillmore was sworn into office the next day, the tenth of July, 1850.

Men and women in the colored community gathered on stoops and streets, fanning themselves in the warm July evening, discussing the new President's views on Clay's compromise in worried tones. They didn't have long to wait. As his first official act, Fillmore replaced Taylor's Cabinet with men who had led the fight for the dreaded bills, naming Massachusetts Senator Daniel Webster as Secretary of State.

Worried discussions continued in the streets, shops and

churches, but despite Michael's concern over the proposed bills there was little he could do but attend the frequent meetings of protest. Otherwise, life went on as usual. He continued to care for his patients, stroll with his family on fine evenings and continue the search for microscopic organisms.

Though the numbers of cholera cases were fewer, there was no trouble collecting specimens of excreta from victims of the disease.

Still inwardly reluctant, Michael placed a drop of rice-water stool on his cover slip, carefully turning it over and positioning it on the concave slide. For once, the lighting conditions were perfect. He peered into the eyepiece at the sample. Among the tiny animalcules was a form he hadn't seen before—barely visible, slightly curving rods, slowly twisting as he watched.

Isaac bent over the eyepiece in turn at Michael's call. "That could be the cause of the disease," he whispered finally.

Michael nodded, suddenly filled with unexpected excitement.

The front room was dark, the silence broken only by the sound of Ted's even breathing as he crouched to one side of the window. Michael slipped his stethoscope into the cabinet of medical instruments without lighting a lamp, then joined Ted at his post.

"Ellen's all right," he murmured. "Rachel's gotten her to drink some broth, and she's resting now."

"Thank the Lord," Ted whispered, without turning his head.

Little more than a month had passed since the Fugitive Slave Bill had been signed into law on September 18, but the cruel legislation had already brought crisis to the Boston community. On the 26th of October, two slave hunters arrived in the city, obtaining warrants for the arrest of William and

Ellen Craft, whose daring escape in disguise had thrilled the colored community two years before.

The young couple's public appearances at abolitionist meetings had made their whereabouts easy to pinpoint. With the first news of the slave hunters' arrival, the Vigilance Committee had moved into action to thwart their capture.

Hiding the two in separate—and frequently changed—locations would make their capture that much more difficult. Ellen Craft had been brought to the Mabayas shortly after darkness fell, half ill from the strain, and quickly given a bed in Peter's attic room. Since then, at least half a dozen committee members and friends had joined in keeping watch.

Michael returned to the kitchen, repeating his report on the young woman's health. There was a general sigh of relief around the kitchen table, where William Nell, Jake and Reuben sat in a semblance of a normal visit.

"We've got the placards Benjamin Roberts printed posted all around the city," William Nell said, continuing his report of the steps taken to protect the Crafts. "They describe both those wretched fiends down to their last chin whisker. Not a soul will see them without knowing them for exactly what they are. And members of the Vigilance Committee will have them under watch every minute they're in our city."

Michael nodded his agreement with the Committee's scheme for members to follow the slave hunters wherever they went, publicly denouncing them as kidnappers.

"That's all right as far as it goes, but it's not enough," Jake said. "We need more than Garrison's moral suasion to protect us." Reaching into his pocket, he pulled out a revolver, the gun-metal gleaming with newness.

"I'm not going anywhere unarmed as long as the Fugitive Slave Law stands," he said into the sudden silence. "None of you ought to either. You especially, Michael. You've a double reason, as a fugitive yourself."

Michael stared at the pistol with reluctant fascination. "I've given it some thought," he admitted, "but I just can't see myself shooting anyone."

"Jake's right, though," William Nell said quietly. "I've supported Garrison for years, but his doctrine of nonresistance is useless against the kind of scum who earn their bread hunting their fellow men. It's likely William Craft would have been taken by now, if it weren't known he's well armed and prepared to defend himself. We've as much right to protect ourselves against them as if we were attacked by wild beasts in the forest."

"I'm not arguing with that." Michael stopped, trying to put his thoughts into words. "I think we've got every right to defend ourselves. It's just I've spent my whole life trying to heal people—" He broke off, not sure he could explain his feelings even to himself.

Jake rose, putting away the revolver. "If that's how you feel, then you ought to run for Canada before it's too late. I'll go take over for Ted," he added, leaving the room before Michael could make any reply.

"Jake's right about one thing," Ted said soberly a few days later. "None of us are safe in this country anymore."

Michael nodded bitterly, sipping the hot tea Lydia had brewed while he examined Teddy and Jim, both abed with measles. "The Vigilance Committee tactics worked, though. We've driven the slave hunters out of Boston," he said after a moment's thought.

"Only because Lewis Hayden threatened to put a lighted torch to a keg of gunpowder and blow them up right along with himself and his whole family if they made a move to force William from his house. How many of us have that kind of nerve? I'm thinking about Canada more and more these days."

"Not me," Lydia put in. "This is our home right here. And you know how hard you worked so's to open your own shop."

"Lydia's right," Michael said. "Why should we let ourselves be forced out of our own homes? We've just won a battle against the slave forces, after all."

Ted shook his head grimly. "The Crafts still had to flee to England. All we won them is a little time."

Lydia reached for her husband's hand. "I still say we should stay. Anyway, ain't no one going to know where to look for me. I haven't been up giving speeches like William and Ellen."

With the immediate crisis past, Michael gave in to Isaac's urging to devote some time to tying up the loose ends of their research. Since spotting the new animalcule they'd focused their efforts on cholera, repeating their observations a number of times.

The microorganism they'd found showed up in each specimen of stools they'd examined from a victim of cholera—swarming, barely visible bugs seeming to dart swiftly among the other animalcules.

At Isaac's suggestion they'd looked at specimens of their own healthy stools for comparison. There was no sign of the microorganism. Its association with cholera was clearly indicated.

Although cases of cholera had once again dwindled with the coming of fall, their work wasn't over. They'd been urged repeatedly by Doctor Holmes and other physicians at Massachusetts General to present their findings in a paper.

"I promised we'd give it at the March meeting," Isaac said. "That gives us less than three months."

Michael smiled. "I'm as eager to get it written as you are. Let's just hope the slave hunters stay clear of Massachusetts from now on," he added grimly.

198

Chapter 14

1851

The Vigilance Committee's tactics were working after all, Michael told Ted, as the new year arrived with no further attempts to recapture Boston fugitives. Ted had to agree. They could all breathe a little easier now that the threat from slave hunters seemed to be stemmed.

The winter continued without incident as Michael spent long evenings with Isaac working on drafts of their paper.

"I won't be spending this much time much longer. It's just that it's only five weeks till we present the paper," Michael told Rachel apologetically, after an especially lengthy session the first week of February.

She came up to him, already in her nightclothes. "I'm not angry. I'm proud of you, Michael," she said softly, linking her fingers behind his head as she smiled up at him.

He put his arms around her in turn, holding her tenderly,

careful of the new life growing within her at last.

He'd seen his last patient for the evening a week later, when Jake rushed through the front door, breathing so heavily he could barely gasp out his message. "A fugitive's just been taken and locked up in the Courthouse!"

At the hastily assembled meeting of the Vigilance Committee, Michael listened grimly to the rest of the details. The fugitive, Fred Wilkins—who'd taken the name Shadrach shortly after his escape from slavery—had been arrested only hours earlier that day, the 15th of February. A United States marshal had seized him at his place of work, Taft's Cornhill Coffee House, acting so swiftly to secure him behind bars that he'd been locked in his cell at the courthouse still wearing his waiter's apron.

Robert Morris and several white lawyers who were active members of the Vigilance Committee immediately volunteered to defend him. In a repeat of their earlier tactics, the Committee assigned volunteers to keep Shadrach's owner under constant watch.

It didn't seem enough. Michael felt filled with frustration as the meeting adjourned.

The hearing at which the Federal commissioner would determine whether to send Shadrach back to slavery was set to begin without delay. The following evening Lewis Hayden called the colored members of the Vigilance Committee to a second meeting.

Robert Morris reported to the waiting group. Michael had never seen the young lawyer so grim.

"Richard Henry Dana's agreed to act as defense attorney. I'll be assisting him. Dana will do everything he possibly can to secure Shadrach's freedom, but the fact is the law's got us tied hand and foot.

"You all know how the Fugitive Slave Law reads. No jury trial's allowed, no testimony by the fugitive in his own defense. All the commissioner needs to make his ruling is a sworn affidavit by a slave owner that the man's his property, and in case there's any hesitation on his part the law pays him double to enslave a fugitive as to free him."

Morris paused a moment before adding quietly, "It's time to take the law into our own hands."

Michael held his breath as Morris outlined the plan. During the court recess, he'd arrange for the doors to the courtroom to be opened to a waiting rescue party who'd carry Shadrach from the courtroom.

Lewis Hayden took the floor then. "I'll be in charge of the party that rushes the courtroom. We need to have a carriage ready and waiting, and I want every man who's not afraid to act tomorrow up here now."

Michael was on his feet before he'd finished speaking.

It was almost too simple to work, Michael feared, as the hours passed the following day, though so far everything had gone as planned.

By afternoon, Hayden had gathered a crowd of some fifty unarmed colored men, many of them brawny laborers and seamen. When the lawyers' request for a recess was granted, they thronged through the suddenly opened doors, jostling and shoving their way through the spectators, surrounding Shadrach so completely he was hidden from the view of law officers as they hurried him to the waiting carriage.

The crowd melted away as the horses sprang forward, hoofs striking sparks on the pavingstones as the carriage sped swiftly out of sight.

They'd moved so suddenly no pursuit was possible, but it was still too risky to try to take Shadrach out of the city before darkness fell. Hayden's own home on the lower slope of Beacon Hill was too closely watched now to make a safe place of refuge, he agreed.

Nothing was more natural than a sick man entering a doctor's residence, though. The carriage pulled up near an alley entry a few streets away. Moments later, a blanket wrapped man, shivering as with fever, was helped through the door bearing the neatly lettered sign, Michael C. Mabaya, Doctor of Medicine.

Only Peter seemed too excited for fear as he watched importantly from an upstairs window. The men who'd come to stand guard talked among themselves in low, worried tones as they kept a simultaneous watch for officers of the law and the promised arrival of Lewis Hayden. Abigail hurried after Rachel, helping her carry hot stew to the frightened fugitive, but her eyes were bright with fear as she stopped to slip her hand into her father's.

Michael's concern scarcely diminished when Hayden finally appeared to transport Shadrach from the city on his way to Canada. Not till word was received that they'd arrived safely in Concord, where sympathizers waited to see the fugitive on the next leg of his journey, did he turn to Ted, grinning with relief.

Ted's face remained sober. "Thank the Lord, he's made it to safety, but you can bet the next fugitive taken won't be left unguarded a minute. This isn't our country anymore, Michael."

Nothing Michael said could change Ted's mind.

"After all your work, Ted. It could take you years to get another shop."

Ted shook his head. "No shop is as important as my Lydia's freedom."

He wouldn't listen to Lydia's arguments either. "Shadrach wasn't up giving speeches, just waiting table and minding his own business."

Even Lydia had to admit it. Once they'd made up their minds, Ted got what he could for his shop and their furniture. They were packed to leave for Canada just a week after

Shadrach's rescue.

Rachel and Michael had their friends to dinner the night before they left. After all their years of friendship, it was hard to believe this was the last time they'd be sitting and talking together around the kitchen table.

"You ought to leave yourself, Michael," Ted urged him once again.

He shook his head. "I still think the people of Boston will never stand for kidnapping."

"There's a lot who won't go along with an unjust law," Ted agreed. "But half the businessmen in Boston signed that letter to Webster supporting his speech last year. Over eight hundred signatures, Michael, in support of the Fugitive Slave Law!"

Michael nodded soberly. It was true. Even Doctor Holmes had signed the letter of public support for Webster's position last March, he remembered bitterly. For a moment he felt rigid with anger, his determination not to be forced into flight stronger than ever.

"This is still our home," he said quietly. "My whole life is here. I'm not letting anyone scare me into leaving."

There was nothing more to say. Lydia and Rachel embraced, crying. The children looked at each other awkwardly, shuffling their feet. Peter had tears in his eyes as he bid Teddy and Jim goodbye, Michael saw, though he turned his head quickly away from his father's glance.

He shook hands with Ted again, wishing him luck, then suddenly embraced his friend, tears in his own eyes now.

Scores of additional fugitives fled to Canada within the next few days, many of whom had called Boston home just as long as Michael. He looked soberly around him at church the following Sunday. Whole pews sat empty. He took Rachel's hand as the congregation filed quietly forward, closing up the gaps left by their fellow worshipers.

They'd have to go over the paper at his house, he told Isaac the next day. It made him uneasy to spend evenings away from home when he might be called on to give assistance to fugitives passing through the city at any time.

Isaac nodded, not speaking again till they turned the corner half a block from the house. "Are you safe here yourself now, Michael?" he asked then, his words coming in a rush.

He laughed bitterly. "Safe? None of us is safe anymore. All it takes is the word of two whites to send a man into slavery even if he was born as free as they were."

He softened his voice then, seeing the concern on his friend's face. "I'm safe enough, Isaac. No one's still looking for me after all these years."

They managed to finish the paper to their satisfaction a week-and-a-half prior to the medical society meeting, sitting around the cluttered front room table to go over it together.

"Our observations definitely show a correlation between the presence of the organisms and that of cholera," Isaac said with satisfaction.

Michael nodded. "We still can't say for certain though that the animalcules are the cause of the cholera. It could be they result from the cholera, or there could even be a third cause for both."

They'd been arguing the point since they first sighted the microscopic animalcules. Isaac smiled. "Well, that's why we've titled the paper a preliminary finding. It's enough to convince me though. And I doubt we could ever find enough evidence to convince men like our friend Potts.

"I suppose you saw his letter," he added with sudden bitterness.

Michael looked at him in puzzlement. "I haven't seen any letter of his."

"Well, it's unsigned, of course, but I'm sure he wrote it.

You've got the journal right here," he added, lifting the *Boston Medical and Surgical Journal* from the table.

"I've had it a week, but I haven't had a chance to look through it."

Isaac was already thumbing through the pages. "Here." He handed Michael the opened journal.

"The lowering of standards in our profession is nowhere so aptly and unfortunately revealed as in the upcoming March program of the Boston Medical Society. Four years ago, unforewarned, members of our society were subjected to the unfounded drivel of doctors Isaac Marks and Michael C. Mabaya in their attribution of the sufferings of the sick to unseen and invisible animalcules.

"This pair now returns to our forum to lecture us on 'Preliminary Findings of Animalcules in Association with Cases of Asiatic Cholera.' Doubtless such folly is all that can be expected from these two—Marks, a Jew, one of the infidel children of Abraham, and the negro Mabaya, scant years from his jungle ancestors.

"Yet in recent years, our profession has been hard pressed by attacks from the frauds of allopathy, homeopathy and hydropathy. It profits us even less to open ourselves to public ridicule by allowing the humbug and fraudulent to speak from the platform of our own society. We do ourselves little service by thus draping quacks in the trappings of medical respectability. Signed, A Concerned Boston Physician."

Michael stopped reading, unaccountably disturbed. There was no point in saying so and upsetting Isaac further though. "Well, we always knew what Potts thought of us," he said slowly.

The start of the March medical society meeting was still two hours off as Michael carefully read through his copy of the paper a final time. They'd eaten supper early, and the children stood watching as he thumbed through the pages, checking their completeness.

"Are you going to show the other doctors your little animals, Daddy?"

He smiled down at Abigail. "I'm going to tell them what they look like, and we'll show them drawings we made with the camera lucida. You can only see the animals themselves under the microscope and we can't bring that to the meeting."

"I'd like to look in your microscope, Daddy," Peter said suddenly.

"You can come with me next time I go to the hospital," he said, pleased at his son's interest.

Rachel adjusted his collar and retied the bow of his cravat for the second time. He smiled at her fussing. "It looked all right the way it was. Anyhow, they've all seen me plenty of times before."

"They haven't seen you up reading a paper before," she said, kissing him quickly.

It was only a short walk from his house to the Harvard Medical School, standing adjacent to Massachusetts General on the bank of the Charles River. He'd left plenty of time, but Isaac was already waiting at the door of the meeting room, clutching the borrowed magic lantern. They set it up together, checking the angle of the lens, setting the small stack of sketches they'd painstakingly drawn alongside.

The first arrivals were already filing in by the time Isaac had adjusted the lantern. Isaac would operate the equipment to project their illustrations, much to his relief, while Michael read the paper.

"You nervous, Michael?" he whispered, as they took their seats in the front row.

He'd told Isaac earlier that it wouldn't bother him any to present the paper, but he had to admit to a little disquietude now. "Some," he nodded back. He held the pages stiffly in his lap, mentally reviewing them once again, paying only perfunctory attention to the reading of the minutes and call for new business.

His uneasiness lingered as he rose. He kept his eyes on the paper as he read, only relaxing into his customary eagerness to share his ideas after the first few minutes had passed.

The room was almost completely quiet as he described the unique animalcules they'd discovered in the rice-water stools, the silence punctuated only by the scraping of chairs as an occasional latecomer found a seat. The magic lantern worked better than they had hoped in the dimly lit room as Isaac showed their painstaking drawings of the animalcules.

"Microscopic examination of stools from persons unafflicted by the disease showed no evidence of the animalcules, while these microscopic organisms were present in every stool specimen obtained from a victim of the cholera."

He could feel the interest of the audience as he outlined their findings, arriving finally at their conclusion that there was a definite association of the animalcules with cases of cholera, which further research might well show to be causative.

At least half of the thirty or forty men in the room clustered around them to ask further questions as the official meeting adjourned. He took turns with Isaac detailing the methods they'd used to study their specimens under the microscope.

The doctors on the outskirts of the group had begun to drift away as Doctor Holmes finally asked, "How do you anticipate translating your findings into medical practice, assuming your theory of causation proves correct?"

Michael looked at Isaac, smiling ruefully. It was another point they'd argued between them. Isaac had always been a lot more optimistic than him about the possibility of their research leading to a means of preventing the disease. He stepped back, listening as Isaac began to frame his answer.

"Michael! Michael, I can't believe it's really you!"

He turned, startled at the call, then stood completely still, staring at the man behind him. The stocky shoulders were not held quite as straight now and his hair had turned to gray, but he'd know him anywhere.

He was stunned to silence, then slowly his voice came back, cold and controlled.

"Yes, it's me. How are you doing, Doctor Carter?"

Another long moment of silence stretched between them.

Doctor Carter finally spoke. "You really are a doctor then, Michael. There was a letter in the Boston Medical Journal . . . I had to find out if it could be you."

Slowly Michael nodded, still struggling with shock. "Yes, I'm really a doctor. You've come a long way to satisfy your curiosity, sir."

Doctor Carter held his hand out tentatively, then slowly drew it back as Michael ignored it. "I came to see you, Michael. I thought I'd never see you again, after—after you left the way you did."

After you sold me you mean, Michael thought, memory of their parting flooding back. For a moment he was standing once again in the doctor's front room, anger swelling inside him.

"You needn't have bothered, Doctor Carter. You're not going to drag me back into slavery!"

The older man shook his head, his face dismayed. "Michael! You can't really believe that was my intention in coming here."

He shrugged, still filled with unreasoning anger. "It's no more than I'd expect from a man who'd sell his own flesh and blood to a slave trader."

Doctor Carter winced as if he'd struck him. When he spoke again, his voice trembled. "Michael, please don't humiliate me in front of these men."

208

Startled, Michael glanced over his shoulder. In his surprise he'd forgotten they weren't alone, but now he saw that the semicircle of doctors had drawn closer, none of them making the slightest pretense of doing anything but listening to their words.

Slowly he brought himself back to the present. He looked back at Doctor Carter. The doctor's shoulders had slumped, and his hands, hanging limply now, betrayed a slight tremor.

Doctor Carter had aged, Michael thought slowly. For that matter, he was far from a boy himself. There was no reason to let this old man upset him. Whatever links had existed between them had long since been broken. He could surely manage to be civil to him for a few minutes.

Reaching out, he grasped Doctor Carter's arm, guiding him to a chair on the far side of the room.

Now that they'd sat down together Doctor Carter seemed at a loss for words. He mopped his brow with his handkerchief, then sat wadding the damp material in his hand.

He had to say something to the man to break the silence, Michael told himself, equally at a loss. "I never knew you to take a medical journal," he managed finally.

Doctor Carter shook his head, barely glancing up at him. "Doctor Wilkins lent me his copy. You remember, he took the office across the street from mine. There's a report of a case he said might interest me."

Michael nodded, though he scarcely remembered the other doctor. Another moment of silence went by. "What did you think of our paper?" he asked at last.

Doctor Carter shook his head again. "I don't understand your reasoning. I don't see how you can conclude that animalcules too small to see could cause an affliction like cholera."

He paused, finally looking Michael full in the face again. "I didn't travel all this way to talk about a paper. Michael, you know I didn't come to—to put you in danger."

He supposed he hadn't, Michael admitted to himself. "Why did you come, Doctor Carter?" he asked quietly, waiting now to hear the man's answer.

The doctor hesitated a moment, seeming to grope for words. "All these years, I've blamed myself for causing you to run off like that. I couldn't imagine how you could take care of yourself without any trade ... When I read that letter— You told me once you wanted to become a doctor. I didn't see how it could be possible, but I had to find out for myself."

"It was a lot easier when I didn't have to turn all the money I sweated for over to you." He stopped short, remembering he meant to be polite to the old man.

Doctor Carter sighed. "David told me you could accomplish it if that's what you set out to do."

Michael smiled, relaxing a bit. "How is David? Has he become a lawyer?"

"He practices law after a fashion," Doctor Carter said shortly.

Michael thought of the lawyers he knew, men like Morris and Sumner—confident and self-possessed in front of a crowd. "I can't picture him arguing in a courtroom," he blurted.

"He hardly sets foot in a courtroom. If he draws up one or two leases or wills in a week, it satisfies him. He's never even attempted to make something of himself. He's not married, says he's content just earning enough for his share of our expenses. He still wastes half his time sketching everything he sees. Once in a while he paints backdrops for the Thespian Society."

"He always wanted to study art. He just took law to please you," Michael recollected.

"He does precious little to please me, Michael." Doctor Carter shook his head firmly, dismissing the subject.

"I still can't believe I'm sitting here talking to you, Michael. I've always hoped I'd find you again, but I never really expected it to come about."

"Did you?" Michael sat up straighter, looking at Carter intently, his anger renewing itself despite his efforts at self-control. "Is that what you were hoping when you sold me, Doctor Carter?"

Doctor Carter flushed. "I admit I acted too hastily, but you didn't leave me much choice, Michael. I simply couldn't handle you anymore. I didn't sell you South, you know. Armfield put it in writing that he'd find you a new master in Alexandria or thereabouts. He told me it was likely a smart boy like you would be bought by a craftsman of some sort, someone who'd train you in some kind of skilled work.

"I should have known you wouldn't see it that way, though. I've regretted for years that my haste caused you to run off."

Michael stared at Doctor Carter another moment. "I would have run off before long in any case. I was only trying to earn enough money to—to make it a little easier. Did you think I was content spending my life as your slave, Doctor Carter?"

"I couldn't have just turned you loose, Michael." Doctor Carter turned his palms up, his voice tinged with exasperation.

"I always intended to free you when you were ready for it. And you told me yourself you were saving to buy your freedom. Your friend Ned did, you know. He has a carpentry shop with his father over on Royal Street. Put some new siding on for me not too long ago, as a matter of fact."

"I'm glad to hear it. But I never had Ned's patience. How many years would it have taken till you thought I was ready for freedom, Doctor Carter?"

Doctor Carter looked at him with annoyance. "Michael, I can see that I was wrong about you. When I came in tonight and saw you reading that paper, I could hardly believe my eyes. But you couldn't have expected me to know it then."

Michael shrugged, turning at the sound of footsteps behind him. Isaac came up, speaking hesitantly. "Michael, it's getting late. They're waiting to lock up the room."

Isaac dropped his voice a little lower, his tone worried. "What do you want to do? Do you think he actually means to have you arrested?"

"No, I know he doesn't." Michael looked from one man to the other. "Isaac, this is Doctor Carter. Doctor Marks," he added to Carter.

Isaac glanced at Doctor Carter with curiosity as they shook hands. "Have you taken a hotel room, sir? Several of the doctors have carriages here if you're in need of transportation."

Doctor Carter nodded heavily, looking at Isaac awkwardly. He turned back to Michael. "When can I see you again?"

He didn't much want to see Carter again. What was there left to say to the man? "I don't see any need to meet again, sir. You've accomplished what you came for. You can see I'm all right."

Doctor Carter stared at him. "Michael, I traveled over three days to get here. I can't believe you don't intend to see me for more than fifteen minutes! I have a right to see you."

"You don't have any right to me, Doctor Carter!"

"I didn't mean— I should think you'd want to show me how you're doing now that you're a free man," Carter said finally. "You haven't said a word about your life here, not even whether or not you're married."

"Yes, I'm married. We have a son and a daughter," Michael added, anticipating Doctor Carter's next question. He thought with brief sorrow of Elizabeth, but there was no point in mentioning her now.

"I'd like to meet your family, Michael," Doctor Carter was saying.

He stood hesitating. Doctor Carter was right about one thing. Now that he was over his first shock at seeing him, he had to admit he was glad to have the chance to show Carter just how wrong he'd been in denying him any kind of opportunity when he was growing up. He was suddenly glad the doctor had been there when he presented the paper, even glad that Rachel had fussed so over his appearance.

It was out of the question to have Carter come to his house, though. He never knew when the Vigilance Committee would send him another fugitive in need of medical attention.

He could hardly say no either.

"I'll have to talk it over with my wife," he said at last. "She's expecting a child in a few months. I don't want anything to upset her."

"I wasn't intending to do anything to upset your family, Michael." Doctor Carter's voice was newly eager. "Do you live nearby?"

"I don't want you coming to my house, Doctor Carter," he said sharply. He sighed tiredly, seeing the older man's shoulders sag once more. "I can hardly walk in with you at ten at night, at any rate. Tell me where you're staying and I'll contact you there."

He stood watching as Doctor Carter followed Isaac from the building, then turned to walk home himself, his own shoulders sagging with weariness now.

He found Rachel waiting his return in bed, still easily tired from her pregnancy, her head nodding over the book she was reading.

He hadn't actually expected her to be upset by his news. He was wrong, he quickly realized.

She jerked upright, drawing her breath in sharply as Michael finished talking.

"Michael, you can't stay here now that he's found you! You've got to start for Canada tonight! Hurry and get dressed again, and we'll rouse Lewis Hayden to help you. The children and I can follow you in a week or so, just as soon as I get the house sold."

He tried to soothe her, surprised by the intensity of her fear. "Rachel, I don't need to go to Canada. He's not going to turn me in to the marshal. C'mon," Michael urged, pulling her down beside him. "I've got patients to see tomorrow. I'm not running off anywhere."

"How can you trust him, Michael?" Her voice was shaking. "I know he's your father, but you've said yourself that means nothing to him. It didn't stop him from selling you. How can you be so sure he won't betray you?"

"He's not that hard a man. Anyhow, he doesn't own me anymore. What reason could he have?"

She shook her head in disbelief, lying rigidly next to him now. Her hand crept under his nightshirt, her fingers tracing the thin ridges of scar tissue across his shoulder blades, and he felt her sudden hot tears on his neck. "I couldn't bear it if anything happened to you."

"It won't. Hush. It's not good for you to get so upset now," he added tenderly, placing his hands on her swelling abdomen to feel the child kick, then firmly stifling her protests with his lips.

Mornings were always rushed. He couldn't just tell the children about Doctor Carter as they hurried through their breakfast, he and Rachel agreed in the privacy of their bedroom. There'd be time that evening to sit down with them, and answer the questions they were sure to have.

Michael felt distracted throughout his rounds that day, grateful that none of the patients he saw were suffering from anything but minor illnesses.

He hurried home at the end of the day, agreeing with Rachel to eat early once again so they'd have time for a long talk with the youngsters before any patients might arrive.

Abigail had just finished setting the table as a knock

sounded at the front door. Michael headed down the hall-way, a little surprised. Patients and friends dropping by nor-mally waited till after suppertime, while any fugitives were usually brought to the less easily observed alley entrance.

The children had followed him he realized, as he opened the door. He drew his breath in with sudden annoyance at the sight of Doctor Carter.

Doctor Carter looked back with a trace of annoyance him-self. "I waited all day without hearing from you, so I looked up your address in the city directory."

"I've been seeing patients all day," Michael said sharply. "I asked you not to come here."

The older man shifted his position awkwardly. "Are you going to leave me standing here on the doorstep, Michael?"

He sighed tiredly. "Come in, Doctor Carter."

The children were listening wide-eyed now. "Daddy." Peter's voice was hesitant with disbelief at Michael's ear. "Who is he? He isn't the Doctor Carter you told us about that you ran away from, is he?"

Michael nodded. "Yes, it's him, Peter. He was at the meet-ing last night. Mama and I planned to tell you this evening."

Abigail clutched her father's hand as Doctor Carter stepped into the house. She was trembling, Michael suddenly realized. He was seeking words to reassure her when she dropped his hand, tears running down her cheeks as she rushed at Doc-tor Carter.

"Leave my daddy alone! I won't let you make my daddy a slave again!" Her sobs were coming too hard for her to speak now.

Stunned, Michael gathered her into his arms, holding her close, rocking her and trying to reassure her as the others clustered around them. "Hush, honey. He's not trying to cap-ture me." Peter tapped her shoulder. "Daddy's right, Abi-gail. He would have brought a policeman if he was."

215

After a moment, Doctor Carter knelt awkwardly alongside them. "Don't take on, child. I wouldn't do anything to hurt your daddy." He reached out, gingerly stroking her wet cheek. "I only came to visit your daddy, I give you my word."

Abigail subsided at last, still clutching her father. Doctor Carter stared angrily at Michael over her head. "For God's sake, Michael, what have you told them about me?"

Michael looked back at him furiously. "I haven't had a chance to tell them anything! Why in hell did you come to my house when I asked you not to?"

He felt Rachel's hand on his shoulder. "Don't swear, Michael." Her own fear was hidden now. "The fugitive slave law's put all of us in danger, Doctor Carter. You can't blame the children for being afraid. You did take us by surprise."

The old man looked back at her in silence a moment, then nodded with apparent embarrassment. "I didn't mean to frighten the child."

Another moment of silence passed before Rachel spoke again. "We were just about to eat. Will you have supper with us?"

She gently wiped Abigail's face with the corner of her apron. "Everything's all right now, Abigail. You go on and set another place for Doctor Carter."

Doctor Carter seemed to feel as awkward as the rest of them, Michael thought. It was hard to think of anything to say. "I don't suppose Aunt Sary's still alive?" he asked at last.

"No, she succumbed to pleurisy nearly ten years ago."

Michael nodded. He wondered if Cassie was free now. It was unlikely that Carter would know, though.

"Does Mister Hallowell still have a school in town?" he asked finally.

Doctor Carter nodded. "He's been very successful, had to move to larger quarters to accommodate all his students."

Michael smiled. "I'm glad to hear it."

"Hallowell's president of the Alexandria Water Company." Doctor Carter looked relieved to have found a topic of conversation. "They incorporated last year. He insists on serving without salary. His idea's to bring water from the Cameron Run over to Shuter's Hill, then let it flow through pipes into town by the force of gravity."

"We have water piped into Boston already." Peter spoke for the first time. "We went to the celebration when we were little. They had a parade with bands, and the water shot way up in the air when they turned it on."

Abigail looked up shyly. "There was a whole ship in the parade too, and we got to stay up late and watch the rockets go off." She managed a tremulous smile at Doctor Carter.

He smiled gratefully back at her.

The children still had lessons to do, Rachel reminded them, once they'd cleared the table. Doctor Carter stood watching with seeming fascination as Peter opened his arithmetic book to the multiplication tables. "He taught you, didn't he?" Carter asked suddenly.

Michael looked at him, startled.

"Benjamin Hallowell. He gave you lessons after all, didn't he?"

It couldn't hurt to reveal it now. Michael nodded. "I've always been grateful to him."

Doctor Carter nodded thoughtfully in turn. "I thought he must have done it."

Peter looked up. "My middle name is Benjamin, after him. Daddy told me how Mister Hallowell said it was wrong not to let colored people learn the same as whites, and he taught him all about numbers and natural philosophy. You wouldn't let him go to school at all, he said."

Doctor Carter looked uncomfortable returning Peter's gaze. "I couldn't have sent him to school, Peter."

Michael looked at him, suddenly feeling as resentful now

217

as he had as a boy. "You could have done anything you wanted to, Doctor Carter. You could have freed me and sent me up North to school. You didn't care about anything but keeping me your slave though, did you?"

"That's not true, Michael! I tried to do my best by you. You know I cared about your welfare."

I suppose when you said I deserved being cut with the rawhide for teaching Titus and Ned you had my welfare in mind, Michael thought with cold fury. He opened his mouth to speak, then caught Rachel's warning glance and nod at Abigail. His daughter's eyes were fixed on him, wide with worry again, her spelling book forgotten.

He took a deep breath. "You can't expect me to see things the same way you do, Doctor Carter, but there's no point in our arguing about it now. Anyway, we'd best talk in another room and let the children get their lessons done."

Doctor Carter wandered restlessly around the front room, once Michael had led the way there, reading the titles in the bookcase and staring a long time at Michael's framed medical diploma.

He stood finally in front of the mantel, studying the daguerreotype they'd had taken at the anti-slavery fair two-and-a-half years ago. Michael followed his gaze, studying the portrait again himself. The unsmiling faces of his family stared back at him, heads held stiffly in place by the daguerreotypist's neck braces. The older children gazed as solemnly as their parents—Peter's face a smaller, darker version of his own, Abigail's wide-set eyes and generous mouth a miniature of her mother's. Only Elizabeth's image was blurred, even Rachel's restraining arm unable to keep her still till the plate was fully exposed.

"We lost our baby girl to the cholera," he said, sensing Carter's unspoken question. "She would have been four now."

"I'm sorry, Michael." Doctor Carter spoke gently. "It's the

hardest thing in the world, losing a child."

Michael nodded mutely, watching the older man cross the room again and sink into a chair. He gave a last look at the portrait, then sat down next to him.

Carter sat motionless, eyes closed. Michael was wondering if he'd fallen asleep, when he spoke at last.

"In the '32 epidemic . . . " His voice trailed off a moment, then resumed, still so low he might have been talking to himself. "I heard at the apothecary shop that a Nigra boy'd died in the jail that morning. I ran all the way there. It wasn't till I saw with my own eyes that you were all right that my heart stopped pounding. I wanted to fall on my knees and thank God for sparing you."

Michael stared at him in silence, shaken by the man's unexpected emotion and by his own, vastly different, memories of that time.

Doctor Carter turned to look at Michael at last. "You don't believe me at all, do you?"

"I reckon I believe you," he said slowly, still remembering. "I would have traded places with that boy, though."

"Michael!" Doctor Carter's face seemed to crumple. "I can't believe I ever gave you cause to feel like that."

He shrugged. "I thought I'd never be able to escape from slavery after I went and got myself caught. It's what you wanted me to believe when you had me locked up, wasn't it? It just seemed to me back then I might as well be dead."

"What else could I have done? I'd just about lost control of you. You couldn't open your mouth without sassing me, and then you ran off without any cause. You couldn't have expected me to free you. I had to be hard on you to bring you to your senses."

Doctor Carter gazed around the room a minute before continuing. "Michael, I wish I could have raised you differently. I always knew you were a smart boy. But I couldn't imagine

219

any other kind of life for you. I can see now I was mistaken. I've already told you that. But I couldn't have known you would find any kind of opportunity up North."

"You never wanted to know, Doctor Carter!"

Doctor Carter looked at him angrily. "You haven't changed at all, have you? Every gesture I make toward you, you throw back in my face. I'd hoped for something different after all this time." He fell silent, his face seeming to sag with weariness.

Michael looked at him, sighing. He didn't mean to keep upsetting the old man. "You're right, sir. There's no point in our quarreling about things that happened twenty years ago.

"You said you came to see how I was doing as a free man. You've met my family now.

"Would you like to meet me tomorrow and see the Dispensary where I work? I could show you the microscope Isaac and I've been using too. In fact, I can show you all through Massachusetts General. There's nothing like it in Alexandria."

Showing Doctor Carter through Massachusetts General Hospital, it was easy enough to remain carefully polite. The facilities of the famed institution, especially the high domed surgical amphitheater, were impressive enough to command the elderly doctor's attention and he listened with interest to Michael's account of Morton's demonstration of ether there five years earlier.

Carter examined the microscope with interest as well, though managing to admit he was still more impressed by the fact that Michael had presented a paper to the medical society at all than he was by its contents.

It was harder to carry on polite conversation away from a medical setting. Doctor Carter's visit had stretched out to three days now. Despite Michael's intentions, Carter's presence seemed to revive all the resentment and bitterness he'd come to feel toward him as he was growing up, and avoiding the topics that lay between them was increasingly difficult.

To Michael's surprise, once Abigail had recovered from her initial fright she quickly made friends with Doctor Carter, chatting shyly with him about family and school. Peter was equally fascinated by the man, Michael saw, though his attitude toward him was noticeably more reserved.

Rachel was as uncomfortable as he was, Michael knew, though her feelings remained hidden by her courteous good manners. At her suggestion, Doctor Carter accompanied them to an evening lecture at the Adelphic Union Library Association. Michael noted with satisfaction Doctor Carter's evident surprise at the lively talk and the intelligent questions directed toward the speaker by the attentive colored audience.

He accepted their invitation to attend Sunday church services as well, awkwardly acknowledging Rachel's introductions to her family afterwards.

They had to invite Doctor Carter for Sunday dinner, of course. Michael sat with him while Rachel finished preparing the meal with Abigail's help, wondering just when Doctor Carter meant to end his visit and let them get on with their normal lives again.

He was still trying to think of a way to word the question without offending him when Doctor Carter brought the subject up of his own accord. "I'll need to start for Alexandria tomorrow. My practice isn't very large anymore, but I do have a few patients in need of attention."

Michael nodded with relief.

Doctor Carter continued before he could respond any further. "I'm at an age where I've been thinking of retiring from practice altogether and now that I've found you, I think the time has come. Doctor Wilkins is more than willing to take over my practice. I'd like to be able to manage a longer visit next time."

Michael stiffened, shocked out of his courtesy. It hadn't occurred to him that Carter would want to return for another visit. "You've surely satisfied your curiosity about me by now, Doctor Carter. Why do you need to come back?"

"It's not just curiosity, Michael. I want to see you again. And I'd like to get to know your family better." He hesitated a moment. "I never even knew your little Elizabeth. I'd like to watch Abigail and Peter growing up."

Michael stared at the man, at a loss. "You haven't even seen me for eighteen years. Why is it so important to you to visit us now?"

"Michael, we've lost too many years already." Carter spoke softly, as if hearing his own thoughts for the first time. "I'm—I'm a lonely man. I hadn't realized how alone I was till I saw you all here. I know I have my son's company, but days go by when David and I have nothing more to say to each other than 'please pass the butter'." He tried to smile. "Even James Harrison comes by mainly to see David, not me. And he's become angry and embittered since his wife died."

He always was, Michael thought. He always hated me, at any rate. He brought his mind back to Doctor Carter. "I'm sorry for you, sir," he said truthfully. "But there's nothing I can do to help you. There's nothing between us. My life doesn't have anything to do with you anymore, Doctor Carter. There's no reason for you to get to know my children better, or to see me either."

Doctor Carter winced. When he finally spoke, his words were barely audible. "Michael, don't make me beg you. You know there's—there's a bond between us."

Not one you've ever admitted, Michael thought, suddenly waiting tensely for the man's next words. He sat expectantly, but the older man had lapsed into silence. Another moment went by.

"What bond is that, Doctor Carter?" Michael's voice was

222

as soft as Carter's had been. There was no answer but a shake of his head as the older man looked down in silence, not meeting Michael's eyes. He should have known he wasn't about to admit to it now either, Michael thought bitterly.

"You never acknowledged any bond but that of slave and slave owner!"

Doctor Carter started to speak, cleared his throat, then started again. "Michael, I couldn't have done what you expected me to."

Why had he hoped for anything else, he asked himself. It certainly couldn't matter to him now, anyhow. He shrugged. "I never expected anything from you, Doctor Carter."

Doctor Carter shook his head, still staring down. "I know you did, Michael. You've always thrown it up to me—even here, in front of the medical society." There was a note of bitterness in his voice as he finally met Michael's eyes.

"But I couldn't have done anything differently. You've got to understand that."

"I'm sorry if I embarrassed you at the meeting, sir," Michael said slowly, "but you never cared to understand my feelings, either. I'm not talking about recognizing any bond. I don't give a damn about that."

He continued before Carter could respond, angrily determined to speak his mind after all. "You never cared anything for me except as your slave. You could have taught me if you wanted. You damn well know it. You knew how much I wanted to learn. I practically begged you, but you never wanted to give me a chance to escape from slavery, did you? The only thing that mattered to you was how much work you could get out of me."

Doctor Carter stared at him. "Michael, all those years you worked for me I taught you practically everything I knew about medicine. You told me just yesterday you were accepted into medical school on the strength of what you'd learned from

223

me. I never forced it on you, either. Why, from the time you were a child I couldn't keep you away from my office."

Michael shrugged. "I would have been working for you one way or another. Everything you taught me was just to make your own work easier. Outside of that, you did your best to keep me like a dumb animal. You wouldn't hear of letting Mister Hallowell teach me. You wouldn't even let me read, would you?"

"I never stopped you from reading." Doctor Carter's voice rose. "I even taught you how to use a pen properly. I suppose you've forgotten that!"

"After I'd learned to read and write on my own, behind your back. And that was so I could write out your labels for you."

"You know that wasn't my only reason!" Doctor Carter took a deep breath. "I'd never realized what you were capable of, you know. As you just said, you kept your learning behind my back.

"I was trying to do my best by you." He paused for a moment, shaking his head. "When I gave you that copybook, your face lit up like I'd given you a hundred dollars. I can't believe you were as unhappy as you claim. I can see you now when you were your son's age. You were so eager to help me. You always had a smile on your face and a dozen questions to ask."

Michael looked at him steadily. "I reckon I was happy enough at that age," he admitted. "You're right, I couldn't get enough of helping you and watching you doctor people. I was too young to worry about what was ahead of me then. Anyway, Mama told me reading and writing were a road to freedom. I guess I always hoped—" He shrugged. "I'm not sure now just what it was I hoped for. That you'd free me, I suppose.

"But you made sure to get any notions like that out of my

head, didn't you? I'll never forget how you had me thrown in jail like a thief for trying to get the freedom I had every right to. Or how glad you were to see the constable cut my back open just for reading a book with my friends! You remember how you told me it was just what I deserved?" His voice was still low, but he was trembling, hands clenched on the armrests of the chair.

"You completely misunderstood me if you thought I was glad then!" Doctor Carter ws shaking now too. "You hated me from that day, didn't you? Even now, after all these years."

Michael sat still, trying to calm down. "I don't hate you now, Doctor Carter. I'm sorry we got started fighting like this. You're an old man now. I didn't intend to hurt your feelings while you were here.

"But you can see it's too late for anything else between us. I don't want any more visits from you. You can't expect that much of me."

Doctor Carter sat motionless a minute. "Then I'd might as well take my leave of you right now."

"Aren't you going to stay for dinner, Doctor Carter? Mama made a pie." Abigail looked worriedly at them from the doorway. "She just sent me to call you to come and eat."

"I'll stay for dinner, child." Doctor Carter tried to smile at her, but continued sitting, making no move to rise.

Sighing, Michael rose himself, reaching out a hand to help the older man from his chair. "Let's not part with hard feelings, sir."

Ignoring his outstretched hand, Carter slowly pushed himself up from the chair, moving heavily down the hallway after Abigail.

When dinner was finally over, Doctor Carter seemed to have forgotten his hurry to leave. He settled himself at the kitchen table with Abigail, listening as she recited her spelling lesson and correcting her occasional mistakes.

Michael hesitated on his way out of the kitchen, unable to force his attention from the sight of Doctor Carter and Abigail bent over the speller together. It was still hard to believe that Doctor Carter had found him here after all these years, harder still to understand how Carter could expect to be welcomed into his life like a long-lost relative.

It was easy enough for Abigail to respond to the man's overtures. But Michael couldn't bring himself to share her feelings, despite Doctor Carter's conciliatory manner now.

He was sorry that he'd hurt the old man's feelings. He wasn't going to apologize for his words, though. He'd meant every one of them.

For a brief moment he wondered how things might have stood between them if Carter could have brought himself to treat him like another child in his household instead of his nigger slave. He imagined the man sitting with him, showing him his letters as he sat with Abigail now. He shook his head, wondering at himself. Why waste time now on fruitless fantasies? He turned finally, leaving the room.

None of their neighbors or relatives would drop by as long as Doctor Carter was still here, Michael knew. He might as well catch up on the journals that had been piling up on the front room table. He was halfway down the hall when a frantic pounding from the front door filled the house. He covered the remaining distance at a run, followed closely by the rest of the household.

The brawny colored man who burst through the door stood still a second, breathing heavily, his left hand steadying the heavy rolled tarpaulin he carried slung over his shoulder. Still gasping for breath, he laid the rolled canvas gently on the floor, carefully starting to unwrap the heavy cloth.

"Got a boy here hurt powerful bad, Doctor!"

Michael knelt at the boy's side as they freed him from the canvas, listening to the man's words with a portion of his mind

226

even as he examined the injured boy.

"Been hidin him since yesterday. I was helpin unload cotton off a schooner up from Charleston, when this here boy climbed out of the hold heading straight for the dock. Figgered him for a runaway right away. Seemed like he was gonna get clear away when the captain shot him down right there on the dock."

The man paused for breath a minute. "Only thing I could do was throw the bale I was toting right in the captain's face and grab this boy up while the cotton was still flying every which way. Got clean away with him with God's help, and through the back alleys to my room.

"Bleedin wasn't too bad by then so I bandaged him up good and got a slug of whiskey down him. He went right to sleep and I figgered he'd be all right, but his leg's been painin him something fierce today and he won't take no food though I don't reckon he found himself much to eat in that cargo hold." The man looked anxiously at Michael.

Michael nodded. "You did fine," he told him, wincing inwardly at the filthy cloth, stiff with dried blood now. "Let's get him on the examining table so I can take a better look."

Rachel had already hurried to light the lamps in the small middle room as Michael and the dockworker carried in the makeshift canvas stretcher. The boy moaned as Michael removed the bandage, his teeth clenched against the pain. He couldn't be more than fifteen, Michael thought. Sixteen at the most. "You'll be all right, son," he murmured, checking the pulse in one bony wrist as he spoke.

The bullet had left a ragged hole in the back of his right thigh. Through it Michael could see the youth's torn and mangled muscles. The bone was intact though, thank God. His leg needn't be lost.

There was no exit hole. Michael's probing fingers stopped as he felt the swelling flesh just above the kneecap. The spreading bruise was black with pooled blood against the brown skin.

"You'll feel better once the bullet's out." Michael reached into the cabinet of medical instruments, thankful that Doctor Bowditch had secured him a supply of ether for just such an emergency.

"Michael!" Doctor Carter caught his arm. "For God's sake, he belongs in a hospital. You showed me the surgical facilities at Massachusetts General yourself. How can you justify operating in your home with an institution like that so close at hand?"

"There's too much danger of his being turned over to the marshal there," Michael answered shortly, seeing the sudden comprehension in the man's eyes. He turned to his children, standing wide-eyed in the doorway. "I want you to stand watch at the front window, Peter, and you at the back, Abigail."

He turned back to Doctor Carter as the children hurried to their posts. "I could use your help if you're willing, sir."

Thank God for the ether Michael thought again, as he placed the neck of the inhaler between the boy's lips, breathing a sigh of relief as the boy slipped into unconsciousness. Ether was unpredictable in its effects, though. He passed the glass globe carefully to Doctor Carter. "Give him another breath of it if he shows any sign of waking."

Rachel handed him the newly filled water pitcher as he scrubbed his hands with extra care. The danger to the boy now lay not in the bullet wound but from the infection that was all too likely to follow.

His probe had revealed that the bullet was lodged too far inside the leg to remove without a new incision. The boy gave a faint moan as he drew the scalpel across his leg. Michael looked up quickly, but Doctor Carter was already thrusting the inhaler to his mouth.

Once the boy lay limp again, Michael held the edges of the incision slightly apart as he carefully inserted the forceps, slowly maneuvering the instrument till the bullet could be clamped in its jaws. Gently then, he withdrew the bullet from the boy's flesh.

The boy lay without stirring till his wound was cleaned and dressed. Michael let him waken then. "You'll be all right, son," he told him. "Your leg just needs time to heal now."

The boy's lips moved in a question. His voice was too weak to hear, but Michael knew what he wanted to know. "You're safe now. You're up in Boston. Nobody will let you be taken back into slavery from here. You can stay here with my family till you're feeling better, and then we'll see that you're carried safely to Canada."

The boy nodded in relief, falling into a fitful sleep again.

Michael looked at him a moment. Much as he hated to disturb his rest now, the boy would be far safer from discovery upstairs. Lifting the canvas stretcher with the dockworker once more, he maneuvered the youth up the two flights, laying him gently on Peter's bed.

Michael touched the man's shoulder as he left the house. "You'd best look for work other than on the docks for a while. You don't want to risk being recognized. The Vigilance Committee can help you if need be."

He stood watching the man hurry down the street a moment, then turned back inside. He could hear Rachel's voice from the kitchen as she and Abigail heated a kettle of broth to help the boy regain his strength.

Doctor Carter sat slumped in a chair in the front room, his head in his hands. He'd nearly forgotten him, Michael realized. He wanted to check his patient again before long, but for the moment he sank wearily down next to him.

The older man looked up at him. "Michael, what are you thinking of? You surely don't intend hiding him here."

229

Michael stared back. "What else can I do? He's far too weak to travel now. It would be risking his life to move him again till he's recovered."

"It's too much of a risk for you to keep him here, Michael." Doctor Carter shook his head as he spoke. "Don't you realize the penalties if you're caught aiding a fugitive? You've got to think of your own family first. How can you endanger their well-being like this?"

Peter turned from the window to face the two men. "We hide fugitives here a lot," he said proudly. There was a faint challenge in his eyes as he looked at Doctor Carter. "We even helped Shadrach and Ellen Craft escape."

"Never mind that now, son. I want you to run over to Uncle Jake's now and tell him about this boy. We'll have to arrange for transportation to Canada as soon as he's well enough to travel."

Michael turned back to Doctor Carter as Peter hurried to obey, looking at him in disbelief. "That boy could easily have been myself a few years back, Doctor Carter. Would you have me turn my back on him?"

"I'd have you show some common sense, Michael! The boy's known to be wounded. If a search is made for him, the authorities are bound to think of you. Surely someone else could shelter him with less risk to themselves."

"I don't need you to tell me what risks I should take, Doctor Carter! The boy's in need of medical attention. I've already told you I'm not turning my back on him. I'm a fugitive myself, in case you've forgotten!"

Michael stared at the shock on the man's face.

"I had nearly forgotten, seeing you living here like this." Carter looked around the room a moment. "You're in danger from the law yourself, aren't you?" He lowered his head into his hands again.

Several minutes passed till Carter looked up, his words halt-

230

ing, as if he thought them out as he spoke. "I've gotten back on my feet financially. Armfield and Franklin have sold their business to another trader, I understand, but I don't anticipate any problem arranging to purchase you back. I'd like to be able to free you legally. You'll accept that much from me, won't you?" he asked, his voice suddenly tart.

Michael nodded, too startled for speech for a moment.

"I'll send you papers of manumission." Carter rose, heading for the door. "I'll not intrude on your life anymore, Michael."

"Doctor Carter!" He caught up to the man, clasping his hand.

They stood silently a few seconds. Michael looked at Doctor Carter, knowing the older man stood waiting to be invited to return himself. Somehow, he still couldn't do it.

"Thank you, sir," he said finally.

Doctor Carter nodded stiffly, withdrawing his hand. "Goodbye, Michael. Please thank your wife for her hospitality." He walked silently out the door.

Chapter 15

1851

His home was a likely one for slave hunters to watch, Michael had to admit, but fortunately no search appeared underway for the wounded boy. The Boston papers made no mention of his escape, nor had the other members of the Vigilance Committee heard of any slave catchers hunting him.

Michael felt a sense of relief as the boy improved day by day. The incision he'd made was healing cleanly with no sign of sepsis around the sutures, and even the torn flesh of the bullet wound showed signs of mending, though Michael doubted he'd ever regain full use of his leg.

Rachel's nourishing cooking was helping the boy regain his strength, and he was able to talk with them a little now. His name was Joe, he told the Mabayas shyly, and he reckoned he'd turn sixteen sometime that summer.

"He hid by the docks down in Charleston two weeks till

he got a chance to get on a ship with no one seeing him, Daddy," Peter told him, "and then he was scared the whole time that it wouldn't carry him up North like he wanted." Peter was endlessly fascinated by the older boy and delighted to share his room with him.

"He couldn't read in the paper where they were going, you know. I'm starting to teach him to read. I've been showing him letters from the first speller."

Michael put his arm around his son's shoulders. "That's fine, Peter. Just don't wear him out. He needs his rest to recover now."

Joe continued to recover faster than Michael had dared to hope for. By the time a week had passed, he was able to hobble downstairs with Michael's assistance to take supper with the family. At this rate, he might be able to travel to Canada within another week, Michael told him.

"I wish he could stay here with us," Peter said later that evening.

Michael nodded. "I know, Peter. But he won't really be safe from recapture till he's reached Canada."

He wished they could take the boy in, Michael thought now. He hated to send him to a strange country alone at just fifteen years old, and probably lame to boot. He'd give him Ted and Lydia's address, he thought with sudden relief. They were barely settled themselves, but he knew they'd do what they could to help the boy. He'd had a brief note from Ted ten days ago. They were living in Montreal where he'd found work as a carpenter's helper.

There'd been no word from Doctor Carter in the week since his departure. He hadn't really expected to hear from him so soon, Michael told himself. For that matter, Doctor Carter could easily have changed his mind about purchasing him back and manumitting him.

Michael shrugged. It didn't really matter, one way or another. He wasn't in any real danger. It would hardly profit the slave trading company to attempt to recover him from Boston after nearly twenty years.

It was likely Doctor Carter just wanted to ease his conscience over selling him, Michael decided. He sighed, wishing they'd been able to part without bitterness between them.

There was nothing he could do about it now, though. He turned his thoughts elsewhere as he left the Dispensary and headed home.

Peter would miss Joe when he left, Michael mused. The two boys had formed a friendship in just the few days Joe had been with them. He was glad he'd have more time to spend with his son now that the presentation to the medical society was behind him.

Abigail would miss Joe too, he thought. Though she hadn't said it in so many words, he knew she was sorry Doctor Carter had left. He smiled then, thinking how pleased she'd be to help her mother care for the new baby. Rachel was due to deliver in less than three months from now.

"Doctor!"

Michael stopped, startled from his thoughts.

The other man stopped too, panting for breath, his face red with exertion. He looked at Michael with mixed distrust and appeal. "They told me at the clinic I'd be after finding a doctor if I hurried down the street. My wife's in a bad way, been having childbirth pains ever since yesterday morning. Midwife says there's nothing she can do for her because the wee one's after coming into the world feet first."

"The baby can likely still be turned," Michael said encouragingly. He reviewed his experience with breech deliveries with part of his mind as he followed the other man down the street into a long, winding alley.

The man stopped in front of an open doorway.

"Doctor Mabaya?"

Michael nodded automatically, then froze at the sight of the two policemen stepping toward him from the doorway. Surely nobody but other members of the Vigilance Committee knew about Joe. The children had been cautioned often enough not to give fugitives away.

"We'd like you to come with us and answer a few questions."

Even if they suspected him of harboring a fugitive, it hardly seemed reasonable to have staged this hoax and accosted him in this deserted alley. His address was known; it would be an easy enough matter for the police to apprehend a wounded boy, protected now only by Rachel and the children.

He stepped back in sudden, shocked comprehension, turning to flee. He felt his left arm grabbed by the nearer of the two police officers as the red-faced man stepped squarely into his path. Furiously, he swung his heavy medical kit at the man, driving him backwards.

He yanked at his arm, trying desperately to free himself. His free hand was drawn back to swing again as he started whirling back toward the two policemen. A heavy blow from a nightstick landed on his elbow, sending pain shooting through his arm.

He stood momentarily stunned as his kit smashed open on the ground and the second policeman grabbed his throbbing arm. The handcuffs snapped around his wrists as the policeman spoke.

"I have a warrant for your arrest as a fugitive, Doctor."

The police refused to tell him who had sworn out the affidavit naming him as a fugitive. He was hustled from the police wagon to a cell in the Courthouse with just the terse words that his master was on his way from Alexandria, Virginia to claim him.

It didn't matter. There was only one man it could be. Michael paced back and forth in the small cell, struggling with disbelief.

It was hard to believe Doctor Carter would take this revenge for his coolness to him, but what other explanation could there be? He'd obviously informed the slave traders where their missing property could be found and Michael had misjudged their willingness to pursue him. Or Carter had purchased him after all, but with a view to reenslaving him rather than freeing him.

Neither alternative bore contemplating.

He paced across the cell again, peering out the barred window and wondering numbly just how long it would take till fellow members of the Vigilance Committee learned of his plight.

He sank down on the narrow cot finally, his head in his hands. Rachel would worry, he knew, but he didn't think she'd be alarmed yet. He'd been kept late on emergency cases often enough.

An hour might have passed. A deputy marshal brought a plate of supper, but he couldn't bring himself to eat. He lowered his head into his hands again.

"Mabaya!"

United States Marshal Danvers stood just outside the cell, blocking Michael's view of the man standing alongside him.

"Your master's come to claim you, Mabaya."

Slowly Michael rose, then stood staring in silent shock at the silver-haired man who spoke to him next.

"You look surprised, boy. I reckon you were expecting to see your old master again. I'm afraid Doctor Carter has nothing to do with this. He'll be as surprised as you are to find out I own you.

"Franklin and Armfield were glad to sell you for a song. There's not much profit to be made from a nigger on the run. Big as their business was, it hardly paid them to beat the bushes looking for one runaway. Armfield was glad enough to write you off as a bad deal.

237

"I figured I'd be able to track you down, though I must say I never thought it would take eighteen years to make good on my investment."

Michael shook his head, still too numb to speak. Carter's brother-in-law had held a grudge against him since earliest childhood. He could scarcely take in the fact that James Harrison stood here now claiming him as his property.

His arrest couldn't be kept secret for long, of course. Robert Morris arrived before he'd even been brought breakfast the next morning, clasping his hands and assuring him that he was already at work with Charles Sumner preparing a defense.

Rachel was ushered in as soon as Morris had departed. They clung to each other a long moment before either could speak. Rachel's eyes were red from weeping, Michael saw, but she was dry-eyed now, calmly laying out a change of clothing for him and assuring him the children were doing their best to be brave.

Lewis Hayden had promised to take Joe out of Boston that evening, she added in a whisper. Michael nodded in relief, realizing he'd nearly forgotten the youth since his arrest. Rachel nodded quiet agreement to his suggestion now to send Joe on to the care of Ted and Lydia.

Other members of the Vigilance Committee were allowed in one or two at a time, the stream of visitors continuing through the afternoon. Word of his arrest had spread through the city, he knew. Angry shouts reached him from the street below. He looked through the bars again, startled to see police officers encircling the entire Courthouse with heavy chains, holding the growing crowd at bay beyond them.

It was nearly evening before Robert Morris returned. The young lawyer was as dapper as ever, but Michael saw his shoulders slump with momentary discouragement as he sank down next to him on the cot.

"Sumner's preparing a defense argument branding the Fugitive Slave Law itself as unconstitutional," Morris began. "There's little likelihood the commissioner will consider it, though."

Michael nodded soberly, knowing it was true.

"We still have a chance, though." Morris lowered his voice, though there was no one with them in the cell.

"I've been talking with your friend, Doctor Marks. He's willing to testify he's known you since boyhood."

For a second, Michael felt his eyes mist in gratitude. He shook his head reluctantly, then. "It won't work. Half the medical society must have heard me recognize Doctor Carter and admit to being a runaway."

Morris nodded. "Marks told me. We've got to make the attempt though. There's virtually no chance for a rescue. Marshal Danver's sworn in over a hundred additional deputies, and virtually every police officer in the city is on guard duty here. They're not taking any chances of an escape this time.

"We still have a chance with this tactic, though. I've talked to half a dozen of the doctors who were present, and most would be extremely reluctant to see you returned to slavery. There's understandable reluctance among them to give deliberately false testimony, of course, but at least two have indicated they may have trouble recalling your exact words." Morris smiled wryly. "And several others believed they could arrange for medical emergencies to call them out of town during the hearing.

"We've obtained a delay of two days to prepare our defense. I intend to contact the remaining doctors during that time.

"That still leaves the question of your recognition of Harrison. He has Danvers as his witness. Can you remember your exact words to him?"

Michael thought. "I was too surprised to say anything. I just stood there gaping like the village idiot."

"You're certain you said nothing that would indicate you knew him?"

"I'm sure. I didn't say a word to him."

"Thank God." Morris pressed Michael's shoulder briefly as he rose. "We still have a chance of winning your freedom then."

The crowd outside was even larger the following morning. Looking out the barred window, Michael felt a stirring of hope. It seemed impossible to believe that the people of Boston would allow him to be dragged back into slavery.

Despite the crowd of supporters though, many of Boston's prominent businessmen—dependent for their prosperity on Southern trade—argued that the property rights of slaveholders must be safeguarded, irrespective of the morality of slavery. Michael threw down the newspapers Morris had brought him with a sigh, walking back to the window again.

"You have another visitor, Mabaya."

He turned at the deputy's voice, wondering in dismay a second if Harrison had returned to trick him into an admission of recognition. But the deputy had already closed the cell door behind the visitor and taken his leave. Anyhow, he'd seen Harrison just two days ago and the man was aged now, his blond hair faded to silver.

He looked again, then managed a smile for the first time in two days.

"David!"

They clasped hands a moment. "I'm glad to see you again, Mike. I wish to hell it was in other circumstances, though."

Michael nodded in grim agreement. "I didn't realize you were here."

"Dad and I just arrived. He's terribly upset about what's happened. I wanted him to rest after the trip—he's all tuckered out—but he's gone to see Uncle James at his hotel in hopes he can persuade him to sell you back."

Michael slumped down onto the cot. "I still can't believe your uncle bought me after I ran off."

David spread his hands in puzzlement as he sat next to him. "I don't understand it either, Mike. He obviously expected to recapture you. God knows, most runaways don't get very far. But I don't know what he wanted with you. He always told Dad he'd ruined you as a slave by being too soft on you."

He always hated me, Michael thought. He stayed glumly silent as David continued.

"I never realized he could be so secretive. He never mentioned buying you in all these years. The evening Dad got back from Boston, Uncle James took supper with us. Dad couldn't stop talking about you." David smiled, shaking his head.

"He just went on all evening about how amazed he was to find you actually reading a paper in front of the medical society, and how you were married, with such a fine family, and what a fine doctor you'd become. He couldn't get over how you'd put yourself through medical school without anyone's help and made so much out of yourself." David's voice faltered a second. Michael looked at him startled, not knowing what to say. A moment went by before David managed a slight smile.

"So finally, Dad said he wouldn't rest easy till he'd bought you back and sent you papers freeing you legally. He said you didn't want to see him again, but he was sure you'd come around once he manumitted you."

Michael nodded slowly, wondering how he could have suspected Doctor Carter of trying to reenslave him.

"Anyhow, Uncle James just sat there listening without a word." David shook his head. "It wasn't till Dad spent half the next day over on Duke Street with the slave trader going through his old records that they found the bill of sale conveying you to Uncle James. He could hardly believe his eyes.

241

"In the meantime, Uncle James had already sent word up here to have you taken into custody. We wouldn't even have known about it if Bill McDougal—he's the telegraph operator—hadn't mentioned it to me when I stopped into Gadsby's Tavern for a glass of ale.

"Nobody seems to be talking about anything else up here, though. It took me half an hour to get through that crowd into the Courthouse."

Michael sat silently a moment, thinking over David's words.

"Do you think your uncle will agree to sell me?"

"I don't know what he intends, Mike. I always thought we were close, but I don't understand him at all now. But it stands to reason if he was willing to sell you to Dad, he would have offered to do so back home instead of putting everyone through all this.

"I intend to see him when I leave here. But I don't know how much good it will do." David sighed, crossing his legs and then straightening them out again. After a minute, he pulled a folded envelope from his breast pocket, absently starting to sketch the cell on its back with the stub of a pencil.

Michael watched him a moment, then looked up as a deputy briefly opened the cell door to admit Robert Morris. David shoved the sketch out of sight as Michael introduced the two men. "It's safe to speak in front of him, Robert," he added quickly, seeing the lawyer's concern as he identified David.

David spoke quietly as Morris hesitated. "You can trust me. Mike and I are— We grew up together."

Slowly Morris nodded, quickly reviewing his preparations for Michael's defense. He looked steadily at David as he finished. "If Harrison knows your father is in Boston he'll surely have him called as a witness. You realize we have no chance at all if he testifies against Michael."

David nodded. "I understand. Dad traveled up here to see what he could do for Mike, of course, but I can't speak for

242

him as to what he'll be willing to swear to on the witness stand."

"I'd like to speak with your father before the hearing tomorrow," Morris said quietly.

Michael watched as David and Morris left the cell together, almost afraid to hope.

Doctor Carter would do his best to keep him from being returned to slavery, he knew now. But whether Carter would be willing to tell less than the truth on the witness stand was another question. He'd never known the doctor to refuse to acquiesce to society's rules.

Michael took a deep breath as he was led into the courtroom, hoping his fear was well hidden. Rachel had brought his good suit and he'd dressed with extra care, walking with his head held high now between the heavily armed deputies.

The packed courtroom grew hushed as he moved slowly toward the prisoner's bench, his footsteps hampered by ankle fetters and chain. Despite additional guards posted at each door and window, his ankles were manacled to the heavy bench. Ted's warning that the next fugitive taken would be guarded well sounded futilely in his ears as he sat down.

He turned his head a moment, meeting Rachel's eyes in the crowded courtroom, swallowing hard as he saw the children at her side. Peter sat dry-eyed and erect, his hand on his mother's arm. Abigail's eyes were filled with fear, Michael saw. She leaned slightly against her grandfather, Jacob Gardner, his right arm held protectively around her shoulders.

Michael listened grimly as Harrison's attorney presented his evidence of ownership to the commissioner: a notarized copy of the bill of sale, dated the first day of January, 1834, transferring all rights to Michael from Armfield and Franklin to Harrison, for the sum of one hundred twenty-five dollars.

Only Harrison's sworn affidavit was needed in addition to establish the validity of his claim. He looked calmly at Michael before giving his oath that there was no doubt in his mind that the runaway slave was "one and the same with this Nigra man here, who calls himself Michael C. Mayaba."

The law wouldn't allow him to testify in his own behalf, Michael knew. He could only listen passively, hoping that the defense prepared by Sumner and Morris would be sufficient to convince the Federal commissioner to rule in his favor.

Sumner presented his plea first, his eloquent voice ringing through the courtroom. "The Constitution of this great Union, established to secure the blessings of liberty to our forefathers and ourselves, nowhere countenances the reduction of a man to a thing, an article of commerce between traders. This fugitive slave bill is plainly and simply unconstitutional, and as such, must and shall be declared void and unenforceable.

"I ask that the righteousness of this court stand like the flaming sword of the cherubim between this citizen of Massachusetts and the bottomless abyss of slavery."

Michael listened to Sumner's words with little hope. If the cause of justice had been rejected by the Congress of the United States it was hardly likely to sway the commissioner now.

His only hope was for Isaac's testimony to be believed. He held his breath as Morris told the Court that in addition to the unquenchable moral force of Sumner's argument, he would now submit evidence demonstrating that the accused prisoner was not in fact the same man as that sought by the plaintiff as a runaway.

If Isaac was nervous in front of the crowded courtroom, his discomfiture was well hidden as Morris called him to the stand. His voice was calm and convincing as he testified to having met Michael in Portland, Maine, "in January or February of 1833"—nearly a year before the defendant had supposedly escaped from slavery, Morris pointed out.

Michael listened with amazed gratitude as Isaac added that he'd seen Michael several times prior to 1833, while visiting the office of Portland physician, Levi Smith. "He was working as a serving boy for the doctor then. I never actually spoke with him though, till after I started my medical apprenticeship with Doctor Smith."

The doctor had been impressed by Michael's quickness, Isaac explained, taking him on as an additional apprentice about the same time, and later encouraging him to enter the Medical School of Maine. "We both entered the school in February of 1836, and settled in Boston at the end of our studies." Morris entered the two men's medical diplomas into evidence as Isaac left the stand.

Michael glanced quickly at Harrison as Isaac concluded. He was leaning over whispering to his lawyer. After a moment, the attorney rose to ask a day's recess for the purpose of calling additional witnesses. His request was quickly granted.

Michael could scarcely sleep for worrying over the testimony of Harrison's witnesses. Isaac's story would be difficult to challenge directly. His mentor, Doctor Smith, was long deceased, and Michael felt sure Professor Cleaveland of the medical school would never come forward to betray him.

It was obvious, though, that Harrison was aware of his encounter with Doctor Carter at the medical society, and intended to call the witnesses to their meeting to the stand. Whether they would be willing to protect him by their silence was still open to question.

Harrison's lawyer had managed to produce just half of the physicians who'd witnessed his meeting with Doctor Carter by the following day. Michael surveyed the half dozen men anxiously, trying to predict their words. His heart fell as he saw Doctor Holmes among the group, remembering how the doctor had signed the letter of public support for Webster's speech urging passage of the Fugitive Slave Law.

At least he could rely on Doctor Bowditch. The man's staunch anti-slavery principles would give him no qualms about bending the truth in order to save him from bondage, Michael knew.

Bowditch didn't disappoint him as he testified that he'd observed no sign of recognition between Doctor Carter and Michael. Their conversation was concerned only with the issues raised by the cholera research.

The two succeeding witnesses quickly stated that they'd been unable to hear anything that had passed between Michael and Carter. Michael breathed a little easier, though he knew there was no chance that the next witness, Doctor Potts, would hesitate to testify against him.

Michael winced nevertheless as the portly physician repeated word for word the angry accusations he'd hurled at Doctor Carter, looking straight at the commissioner as he added, "I'm not in the habit of eavesdropping on private conversations, but I had no trouble overhearing Doctor Mabaya under the circumstances."

Potts paused as he stepped down, startling Michael as he spoke, his voice a blend of belligerence and apology. "You can't expect me to perjure myself for you, Mabaya."

He'd known Potts wouldn't, of course, but his spirits sank further as the next witness corroborated Potts' testimony.

Michael hoped his nervousness didn't show as Doctor Holmes took the witness stand. The words of the well-known physician were bound to be weighed heavily by the commissioner.

Doctor Holmes' normally goodhumored expression was grave as the lawyer asked for his testimony. He sat silent and abstracted. The attorney repeated his question.

"I beg pardon. I confess, sir, my thoughts tend to fasten on a topic like the wheels of a railroad engine on its track. At the time you ask about my mind was preoccupied with the possible uses of the findings presented by Doctor Marks and Mabaya. I'm afraid I was too rapt in consideration of their paper to take notice of any conversation around me."

He gave a barely perceptible nod in Michael's direction as he returned to his seat.

Michael felt limp with relief.

Doctor Carter's testimony could still condemn him to bondage, though. He sat scarcely able to breathe as the doctor was called on to testify.

Doctor Carter walked slowly to the witness stand without glancing at Michael. He did look exhausted, Michael thought, seeing the tremor in the elderly doctor's hands.

Carter's voice was firm though as he answered the attorney's questions. Yes, he had traveled to Boston at least partially in search of a former slave, he admitted.

Harrison's attorney looked squarely at him. "Will you look at the prisoner, sir, and tell the court if this is not one and the same man."

Michael sat without stirring as Doctor Carter turned in his direction. For a long moment they looked each other in the eyes before Doctor Carter turned back to the lawyer, shaking his head.

"Why no, this isn't the same man at all," he said mildly. "The similarity in names had led me to hope he might be the same, but as soon as I saw this man at the medical society I knew I was mistaken. The runaway I was looking for was a common Nigra boy, and I assure you he never had a day of schooling in his life.

"I heard your prisoner here deliver a scientific paper and I spoke with him afterwards. He's obviously an educated man, and, I'm told, a fine doctor. How could he possibly be the same man?"

The words were scarcely out of Carter's mouth before Harrison jumped to his feet, shaking with fury. "That's an outright lie! I had it from your own lips—"

The commissioner's gavel thumped down, cutting him off. "Your comments are out of order and uncalled for, Mister Harrison. There's no need for further testimony. I have all the information I need to make my ruling."

Michael could hear the shouts of the crowd outside, but the courtroom was still as he was led back in and shackled to the bench to await the commissioner's ruling. The recess had been a brief one, but the moments of waiting seemed endless. He sat trying to calm himself, glancing around once more at the tense faces of his friends and family.

It was more than he could bear to see the barely hidden fear on the faces of Rachel and the children. He pulled his gaze away, trying to draw reassurance from the silent support of the massed members of the Vigilance Committee.

He glanced at Doctor Carter. The man sat silent and erect, but Michael could see his hands still shaking as he pulled out his handkerchief. David sat next to him, apparently sketching again, Michael saw, startled. For a moment he laid his hand over his father's, then abruptly returned to his sketchbook.

There was a low murmur as Commissioner Curtis entered the courtroom. Michael couldn't bring himself to believe the Federal official would condemn him to slavery, but he felt his hands grow clammy. He gripped the edge of the bench tightly.

The courtroom grew hushed again as the United States commissioner began his statement. He dealt quickly with Sumner's opening argument. Any question as to the constitutionality of the Fugitive Slave Law lay outside the province

248

of his judicial powers.

It was what Michael had expected. He swallowed hard, waiting for the commissioner to rule on the rest of the testimony.

The Federal official wouldn't look in his direction Michael realized, his heart sinking. He squeezed his eyes shut a second. He couldn't shut out the man's words, though, as he announced in a hurried monotone that despite the attempts to subvert the law by obviously perjured testimony, the prisoner was beyond reasonable doubt a fugitive and would be remanded immediately to the custody of his rightful owner.

Michael sat stunned, barely hearing as the courtroom erupted with cheers from Southern sympathizers, quickly drowned out by angry shouts and cries of "Shame!" Echoing shouts came from the street outside as the news spread to the waiting crowd.

Additional guards moved to surround the prisoner's bench, though the chain that fettered him was surely far too strong to break. He heard Rachel's imploring voice through the melee. The guards parted a second and his family rushed to his side.

"He mustn't give up hope," Rachel whispered through her tears. Reverend Snowden had already begun to raise funds to ransom him from slavery. He nodded helplessly. "Don't you give up either," he managed to whisper finally.

Peter was crying silently too, as he promised to look after his mother and sister till his father could come home again.

Abigail was beyond words. She clung to him, shaking with uncontrollable sobs. He sat, numb with pain, stroking her hair with his shackled hands and trying to murmur consolation, till the guards finally pulled her away.

The police left him manacled even after they'd locked him back in the cell again. He wasn't allowed any visitors now. Night had fallen before Robert Morris was admitted briefly.

"I asked Commissioner Curtis to delay your return to Virginia, in order to give us time to negotiate your sale with Harrison," he reported grimly. "He refused. He says the law requires that you be returned South, that a free state can't countenance the business of buying and selling men." Morris smiled bitterly a second.

"Bowditch and Snowden have made a good start at raising money to buy your freedom, and Doctor Bowditch has already made preparations to travel to Alexandria. Don't despair, Michael. You've got to trust in God's mercy now."

Michael caught a sudden glint of tears as Morris turned away at the guard's signal.

It was still night when the guards took him from the cell. He caught a brief glimpse of Courthouse Square as he was led outside, then the police escort surrounded him.

Even at this predawn hour the streets were lined with protesting crowds. Michael glimpsed them briefly through the raised nightsticks of the law officers. He moved numbly as the force of two hundred Boston police started him on the forced march to the government ship that would carry him back to slavery.

He still wrestled with disbelief as he walked, his head held high, but his fettered feet seeming to move through no volition of his own. It couldn't be true that he was being dragged from the Commonwealth of Massachusetts back to a life of bondage.

His foot slipped on a loose cobblestone, jarring him back to reality. One of the law officers caught his arm, keeping him from stumbling. He turned his head, nodding his thanks. The young policeman looked quickly away, unable to meet his eyes.

He looked back up the street then, straining to see over the tophats of the policemen. American flags, draped in black bunting, flew upside down from the upper stories of half a dozen State Street shops.

He couldn't find it in himself to be heartened by the show of support. Ted was right, he thought bleakly. He didn't have a country anymore.

The crowd knelt in prayer as they reached Long Wharf, their voices rising in a hymn as he was led aboard the revenue cutter.

The sounds died away as he was hustled below deck. His manacles were fastened to a berth, and he was left alone with his thoughts.

Chapter 16

1851

There was a crowd waiting on the Alexandria dock as well. The jeers of thirty or forty rough looking whites assaulted Michael's ears as he was brought up to the deck. Their taunts followed him to the Courthouse, where the accompanying United States deputy marshals formally relinquished custody.

He was almost too tired to care. He stood wearily, exhausted from the sleepless nights chained to the hard berth. His wrists and ankles were chafed raw from the handcuffs and fetters, and he bit back an exclamation of pain as Harrison approached.

Michael hadn't seen the man since the hearing, and he straightened up stiffly as Harrison took formal possession of him.

Harrison looked at him, smiling coolly, taking in his bedraggled clothes and bloodshot eyes. "Didn't you have a good trip, Michael?"

It was still impossible that this man could call himself his owner. Michael looked back at him, determined not to show weakness. "You don't really think you can keep me as your slave, do you?"

Harrison smiled again. "So you have a tongue after all, boy. No, I don't reckon I would keep you long if I gave you the run of the town like your old master did. But you needn't worry. I've reserved you a stout cell in the jail till I can make further arrangements for you."

It was the only thing the man could do, Michael thought numbly. It couldn't be more than another day or two till a representative from the Vigilance Committee arrived with the funds to ransom him, he comforted himself. He breathed deeply of the fresh, damp air as he was herded off to prison once again.

The old jail on the corner of the market square had been replaced by a larger building a few streets away. Michael caught a quick glimpse of the gable roofed brick structure as he was marched up Princess to Saint Asaph Street. The heavy steel door slammed shut as he was led inside.

There were four cells opening off the narrow passageway on the second floor. The jailer led him to the last one along the corridor, fitting his key into the heavy padlock on the cell bars. "You just see you behave now, boy, and you won't have any trouble here."

Michael glanced around the cell as the jailer spoke. The bars of the cell fronted on the passageway; the three interior walls, broken only by a small rear grate for ventilation, enclosed a space perhaps four feet by ten. In addition to the narrow bench that served as a bed, the cell held only a chamberpot and water bucket. He sank onto the bench, absently rubbing his chafed wrists.

The jailer looked at him a minute. "I don't reckon there's need to keep you in those irons, if your master'll agree to taking them off. Ain't no bustin out of this jailhouse."

Michael nodded gratefully, looking around the cell again as the man departed. He was right, he thought. The cell walls looked to be a good foot thick, and the bars solid steel. The entrance to the passageway was guarded by another steel barred door, and the corridor window—through which he could catch a mere glimpse of tree branches outside—was also heavily barred.

The minutes went by slowly. An hour must have passed since the jailer left, Michael guessed. Doubtless Harrison had refused to agree to removing the manacles.

He heard the passageway door open and slam shut then, as footsteps sounded approaching his cell. The jailer entered, accompanied by a second, well-armed guard who Michael guessed might be a town constable.

"Your master was none too pleased bout taking these off," the jailer informed him, unlocking the heavy manacles. "Fact is, he prob'ly wouldn't of agreed at all if I hadn't pointed out how these sores from them rubbing was gonna lower your value to him when he goes to sell you." He paused, apparently waiting for Michael to respond.

Michael stared back at the man, still barely able to believe he was once again a slave, whom other men spoke of buying or selling as they would a plow horse or a load of cotton. He could see the jailer meant well, though. "Thank you," he managed, weakly.

The jailer nodded, gratified. "I told him I didn't look for no trouble from you. Now, the doctor here's been askin to see you since they brung you in. Your master was dead set against it, but he's agreed to allow him up for just a minute so's he can put some salve on your sores."

Michael looked up, suddenly realizing that Doctor Carter stood just outside the bars, half hidden by the hefty constable. The man had aged in just the few days since he'd seen him last, Michael thought, shocked at the growing tremor in his hands.

"I never meant this to happen, Michael." Doctor Carter's voice shook as well, as he sank down by him.

It never would have if only he hadn't gone in search of him, Michael thought a second. He looked at the older man's hunched shoulders, hoping he hadn't read the thought in his face. "I know you didn't, sir," he answered.

He hesitated a second before adding softly, "I'm—I'm grateful to you for not giving me away at the hearing, Doctor Carter. I know it wasn't easy for you to give false testimony."

"I just wish it had been of help to you, Michael." Carter's voice faltered. He laid his hand on Michael's a moment, then slowly began applying the ointment he'd brought.

"All I accomplished, though, was to enrage James. I can't forgive myself for leading him to you like I did. But I had no idea, Michael, I never dreamed ...

"I begged him to sell you back to me, but he just laughed in my face." He paused a moment. "I'm sure he'll come to his senses before long, though, Michael."

Michael nodded. The man couldn't keep him a prisoner forever. He'd have to agree to sell him to the Vigilance Committee. He laid his hand on Doctor Carter's a second. "I'm sure he'll see reason, sir."

Sleep overcame him as soon as he stretched out, limp with exhaustion, bringing welcome dreams of home. The reality of his situation came flooding back as he awoke.

He used the chamberpot and ate the breakfast the jailer pushed through the slot in the bars, then sat down on the bench to wait. There was nothing else to do.

The corridor door clanged again at noontime. Michael looked up eagerly as the jailer unlocked his cell, but no one accompanied him except for the stony-faced constable.

"The doctor came by hopin to see you again, but your master left word he's not to be let in. Doctor left these here for you." The jailer looked at him curiously as he handed Michael a washbasin containing a folded blanket and bar of soap. "What's he so int'rested in you for, anyhow?"

He looked back at the man a moment. "He used to own me before I escaped from slavery."

The jailer nodded. "Reckon you're sorry now for running off from such a good master."

He slept poorly that night, despite the comfort of the warm blanket. Day was a repetition of the one before, the hours seeming to drag on endlessly.

His spirits sank as afternoon drew to a close with no word from the Vigilance Committee. He hardly bothered looking up as the passageway door opened. Footsteps came down the short corridor, stopping in front of his cell. He glanced up, then sprang to his feet.

"Isaac! Thank God!"

Michael clasped his friend's hand as the jailer admitted him to the cell. "I can't ever thank you enough for testifying for me." He pressed Isaac's hands a moment longer. "I didn't expect to see you here."

Isaac looked around the cell, distress showing plain on his face. "Doctor Bowditch asked me to come in his stead. Another fugitive's been taken—a boy of just seventeen years. He thought as a member of the Vigilance Committee, he'd be of more use staying in Boston."

Michael nodded, his heart sinking a second at the thought of yet another fugitive taken, and still a boy at that.

"We've raised over eighteen hundred dollars to free you," Isaac continued. "Reverend Snowden and Bowditch have gotten contributions from all over Boston—even from some of your patients at the Dispensary. I'm sure there's more than enough for your ransom. But I had to see you first and make sure you're all right."

"I'm all right, Isaac. Have you seen my family? Do you know how they're doing?"

"Sarah went to see Rachel the day before I left. Your mother-in-law is staying with her, but Sarah thought Rachel was of more consolation to her than the other way around. She's not despairing at all, Sarah says, and she's managed to keep the children's spirits up as well."

"Thank God for that!"

"You'll be back with them yourself in just a few more days, Michael. I'm sure Harrison will want to conclude a sale as quickly as possible."

Isaac glanced around the cell again. "You must have felt completely abandoned, locked up like this. But there's tremendous support for you at home. Churches have been offering prayers for your deliverance, and our rabbi did the same at Shabbes services. Even the newspapers have been sympathetic. Not the Courier, of course. But the Evening Transcript reprinted this drawing from the Liberator on their editorial page."

Michael stared, shaken, as Isaac handed him the paper. Captioned "A Family Farewell in the Land of the Free," the sketch captured his family's agony in just a few stark strokes of pen and ink, Abigail clutching him in desperation as he sat chained and helpless to comfort her.

He blinked a second, then looked at the sketch again. It was David's, he thought wonderingly.

"I brought you the rest of the papers," Isaac was saying, "and Rachel sent you clean clothes to travel home in. There's a note from her folded inside them.

"I'd best be going now. The sooner I can arrange to meet with Harrison, the sooner we can get you out of here."

He'd read Rachel's loving words a dozen times the evening before, but Michael read through the note once again as he sat finishing his breakfast. He folded it on top of the newspapers finally, trying not to be too impatient as he calculated how long it might take Isaac to come to terms with Harrison.

He sat still another minute, then rose to dress, though he knew it would surely be hours till he could leave. Stripping off his soiled shirt, he poured water from the bucket into his washbasin, grateful for the clean change of clothing. He scrubbed himself happily, rinsing off with additional water from the bucket. He was reaching for his clean shirt as the cell door opened behind him.

"Just wait a minute before getting dressed, boy! I want a better look at you. And I want to know what you done to catch those stripes for. When I buy merchandise, I like to make damn sure I know just what I'm getting."

Michael whirled, staring incredulously at the sandy haired man the jailer had just let into the cell. "Like hell I will! Who the hell are you, mister?" He thrust his arms furiously into his sleeves as he spoke, shoving the shirt tails down into his pants.

The white man spat a stream of tobacco juice on the floor by Michael's foot. "I'm in town to buy up a load of niggers for shipment to South Carolina. That's all you need to know, boy. Excepting you'd better keep a civil tongue in your head if you're hoping to be sold to a good master!"

Michael stared at the slave trader another minute. "I'm not about to call any man 'master.' And you're not buying me. My friends have already collected enough money to regain my freedom."

The man spat again. "So you're the runaway, are you? Well, you've got yourself caught now, haven't you? Where in hell'd you take off for, anyway?"

"Boston."

"Hell of a long way off, nigger. How far'd you get?"

"I ran away eighteen years ago, and I've been living in Boston most of that time," Michael said evenly.

The slave trader stared incredulously in turn. "Eighteen years! Chrissake! What in hell'd you do up there?"

"Practice medicine. I'm a doctor."

"A nigger doctor! For Chrissake!" The man shook his head, glancing around, his eyes lighting on the thin stack of newspapers. "What in hell you doing with these? You know how to read?"

"Yes, of course I do."

"Christ. I wouldn't touch you with a ten foot pole, boy. Not if your master was to offer you to me free for the taking. Put you in with a lot of good niggers and you'd ruin the whole bunch, faster than a rotten apple'll spoil a barrel."

Michael sat, angered and shaken, after the slave trader's departure, his brief happiness vanished. It would be only a few more hours till he could leave slavery behind for good, he reminded himself. His mood remained sober nevertheless.

He leaped up eagerly though at Isaac's return—then stopped, shocked at the misery on his friend's face.

"Harrison refuses to sell you."

Michael stared in disbelief as Isaac sank onto the bench, his head falling into his hands. A minute went by before he turned to Michael again.

"I must have talked to him for close to two hours. He wouldn't budge from his position. He absolutely refuses to make a deal with anyone from the Vigilance Committee.

"I thought at first he was just holding out for a better offer. I told him I thought we could raise just about any amount he named, but he insists it's not a matter of money." Isaac spread his hands helplessly. "All he would say is that he's not about to let any of your nigger loving friends from Boston get their hands on you. I'm sorry, Michael."

"Did he give any reason?" Michael's mouth felt so dry he could barely get the words out.

"None at all. But he's furious at me because of my testimony. We should have thought to send someone down who hadn't offended him. But the Vigilance Committee members were in an uproar over this new arrest, and of course none of your colored friends could travel down here to a slave state. It just seemed like something I could do . . . No one suspected he'd refuse to sell you."

Michael nodded, numbly. "He can't go on keeping me locked up forever."

"He said I should tell you he has his own plans for you." Isaac looked at him miserably.

For a second, thoughts of the slave trader filled Michael's mind. He pushed them aside, as Isaac continued.

"I tried everything I could to change his mind, believe me, Michael." Isaac raked his fingers through his hair, knocking his yarmulke to the floor. He crushed it absently in his hands before clapping it back on his head. "I told him how much good you do as a doctor, about your family . . . I might as well have been talking to the wall.

"I talked with David Carter afterwards, though." Isaac brightened a little. "He thinks he can influence his uncle to see reason. He's promised to speak with him this evening."

When David finally visited Michael the next day, though, his news was grim.

"Uncle James threw me out of his house last night when I tried to plead your case. He told me I'm dishonoring the memory of my mother." David shook his head bitterly. "He doesn't care at all what this is doing to Dad. I don't know what's come over him."

Michael's heart sank. "Are you sure you can't get him to change his mind? He's always been so fond of you."

"He's furious on account of the drawing I did of you holding your little girl in court." David looked momentarily embarrassed. "It was printed in *The National Era* the other day, and someone's shown him a copy. He won't speak to me at all now.

"There's still a strategy we can use, though. I've advised Doctor Marks to request George Kephart or one of the other slave traders to buy you. Marks can offer them an immediate profit reselling you. Dad and I have some money we can contribute if the funds he's brought aren't sufficient. It'll probably take a few days to arrange, though."

David sighed. "I wish I had better news for you, Mike, but there's nothing else I can do."

He nodded, thinking of how anxiously Rachel and the children must be awaiting word of him. "Do you have a pen and paper I can write a letter home with?"

David smiled ruefully, fishing a few sheets of folded foolscap and a lead pencil from his pocket. "That's one thing I can help you with."

Michael sat with the pencil in his hand for long minutes after David's departure, groping for words to reassure Rachel and his children when he had no reassurance himself. The clanging of the corridor door reminded him painfully of his imprisonment.

"What do you think you're doing, boy?!" James Harrison stood glaring angrily through the bars.

He looked up at him bitterly. "Writing my wife."

"Who let you have writing supplies? I never gave you permission to have them. You give them here."

Michael set the unfinished letter carefully on the bench, anger pushing caution aside as he walked slowly toward the bars.

"You'll have to come in here after them if you intend taking them from me, Mister Harrison." He felt his hands clench into fists as he stared back at the older man.

Their eyes locked. They stood rigidly a long moment, held apart by the steel bars. Michael felt a sense of grim satisfaction as Harrison broke their gaze first.

"That's all right, boy." Harrison gave him a slight smile. "Write what you want. It'll never get you up North again. Did you think I went to all the trouble of bringing you back from Boston just to send up there again?

"The only place I'll sell you is to a Southern trader."

It took four days before Isaac was able to report good news. Kephart was definitely interested in arranging a deal. He'd promised the slave trader a profit of five hundred dollars over whatever he paid Harrison for Michael, Isaac added.

"He was very cordial—insisted on showing me all around his place of business." Isaac shuddered. "He has dozens of people locked up there, sleeping in the cellar like animals. Women and children too. Some of them were no older than our own children, Michael, yet he's selling them away from their parents.

"I didn't dare voice my feelings, though. Our arrangement with him is our only hope of freeing you."

Michael sat lost in thought for hours after Isaac had left. Memories of Sammy's face, as his friend was dragged off to be sold South, rose unbidden in his mind as he struggled to keep up his hopes.

He rose, pacing the few steps from one end of the cell to the other, forcing himself finally to compose his mind enough to pen a note of hope to Rachel and the children.

There was nothing else to do then but wait.

By morning he'd managed to regain his optimism. Kephart had sent word that he'd arranged an appointment with Harrison and expected to come to terms with him shortly, Isaac reported. "He asked that I have the funds in readiness to consummate our agreement as soon as he's taken possession of you."

He could barely contain his impatience through the rest of the day, leaping to his feet eagerly whenever the corridor bars clanged. Isaac returned that afternoon, but with nothing further to report.

Kephart would surely strike a bargain with Harrison by the end of the next day, Michael told himself that night, trying in vain to find a comfortable position on the bench. Sleep eluded him till an hour or two before dawn. He slept heavily then, dreaming he lay holding Rachel in the tender moments after lovemaking.

It was nearly noon before Isaac reappeared. Michael didn't need to ask him for news. One look at his friend's face told him that this attempt, too, had failed.

"Harrison's managed to learn of our agreement," Isaac said bleakly. "He told Kephart he'd sell you only on condition that a clause be included in the bill of sale prohibiting your resale to anyone intending to grant you freedom."

With the deal with Kephart called off, Isaac spent the next days making discreet calls on slave dealers up and down Duke Street. His efforts were in vain. All had been forewarned. Harrison refused to sell Michael to any purchaser who would not agree in writing not to resell him to the Carters, Isaac, or anyone else who might be acting on behalf of the Vigilance Committee in their efforts to regain Michael's freedom.

He couldn't stay away from home any longer, Isaac told Michael miserably. He had to get back to his practice, and to Sarah and his daughters.

Michael nodded, wondering bleakly if he himself would ever practice medicine again. "You've done as much to help as anyone could do," he said gently.

"We'll still find a way to free you, Michael." Isaac's voice trembled. "The people of Boston aren't going to forget your plight. Harrison can't hold out for long against public demands for justice."

Michael nodded again, praying it was true. There was no counting on it, though.

"Isaac, Rachel's due to have the baby in two months. I—I don't want some midwife delivering her."

Isaac looked as stricken as he felt himself, Michael thought. "You'll surely be home by then."

"We can't be sure. If I'm not ... "

"I'll take care of her, Michael. I promise you."

He embraced Isaac quickly, feeling his last link to home severed now.

With Isaac gone, Michael found it harder to forget Harrison's threat to sell him South. During the next few days, the jailer brought a steady stream of traveling slave traders to view him in his cell. After a few questions though, all left in disgust, echoing the sentiments of the first trader that he'd been ruined for slavery.

None of the established Alexandria companies were interested in him either, David assured him. He could offer Michael little other encouragement, though. Isaac had entrusted him with the funds raised to purchase Michael's freedom, but his uncle had broken off relations with him, David admitted.

"We'll just have to wait him out, Mike," David said finally, looking up from his sketchbook. "He's stalemated now. He won't sell you to Dad or me, or to the Vigilance Committee, but no slave trader will touch you, either. He's not going to want you on his hands indefinitely. He's bound to see reason before long."

It was easy enough for David to counsel patience. He wasn't locked in a cell, powerless to control his fate.

Michael had never felt so helpless, waking each day to concrete walls and prison bars. With no hope of immediate release he felt stifled by the closeness of the walls, restlessly pacing the half dozen steps up and down the cell. Even the low ceiling—a scant foot above his head—pressed down on him.

It was as hard to occupy his mind as his body. It took but a few minutes a day to read through the copies of the Alexandria Gazette that David brought. David brought him the latest novels from the Alexandria Library Company as well, but he couldn't bring himself to concentrate on them.

Despite Isaac's reassurances, it was hard not to feel abandoned to his fate. Even the Boston papers Isaac had left him carried but a few words about his plight. The excitement of the latest fugitive case filled the better part of their news columns.

Michael read through them again, bleakly wondering if he had been forgotten even by his friends on the Vigilance Committee. He reproached himself then. How could he resent the efforts made to aid a seventeen year old boy?

The Committee's efforts were of no more use to the boy—Thomas Sims—than they had been to Michael himself. Grimly he read the Gazette's account a week later of Sim's return to Georgia slavery, wincing at the editorial column's sarcastic denunciation of Boston abolitionists for failing to follow through on their pledge not to allow a fugitive slave to be taken from their midst.

"They do not even 'interpose their bodies,' or appear in the streets, when the time comes for fulfilling their loud threats. All the courage excited at anti-slave-law meetings vanishes."

The final blow was the Gazette's approving quote from the Boston Courier that the abolitionists "have not the power to delude one in a hundred of our population into the mad design of obstructing by force a law of the United States ... Boston is sound to the heart's core in her attachment to the Union and the Constitution."

Michael threw down the paper in despair.

Michael looked up as the jailer unlocked his cell. He'd had no visitors other than David since Isaac had left for home.

266

Doctor Carter had tried to see him a number of times, he knew, but the jailer had always followed Harrison's instructions to turn him away.

The soberly dressed man whose thick locks of hair were combed back from a high, balding forehead looked familiar, Michael thought. The visitor's face lit up with a gentle smile.

"Michael, I was distressed to learn thee had been taken like this."

Michael felt his own face light up at the sight of Benjamin Hallowell.

He was sorry not to have visited sooner, the educator was saying, but the strain of overwork had left him in poor health for some months. He was not without standing in the community, he added in his straightforward way, and would try to mediate for Michael as best he could.

After a few more minutes discussion of Michael's plight, Hallowell gently shifted the conversation to other matters, describing the compound microscope he'd recently obtained for his students' use and questioning Michael with interest about the research he'd done on microorganisms.

Michael responded eagerly. For the brief span of an hour's visit, he was able to forget his imprisonment and feel his mind come alive again. He managed to maintain some sense of hope even after Hallowell had bid him goodbye.

David brought another bit of encouragement the following day, along with a letter from Rachel, sent in care of the Carters. Several ministers serving on the Vigilance Committee—including its founder, Unitarian minister Theodore Parker—were organizing efforts to focus the conscience of the public on his plight, a brief note from Robert Morris informed him.

He was posting two sketches of Michael in his cell to the Liberator, David said. An additional drawing had been printed a few days before in the Washington city anti-slavery paper,

The National Era, and its editor had requested further sketches from him, David added, almost shyly.

Michael nodded. "The more papers that print them, the better. They show the injustice of the Fugitive Slave Law so clearly, they're bound to convince people to bring pressure to bear on your uncle."

"I hope so." David smiled wryly. "It's all I know to do."

Benjamin Hallowell's efforts to reason with Harrison were of no avail, but his acquaintance with the publisher of the *Gazette* was of more use. Michael was astonished to open the Alexandria paper the first week in May to an editorial urging Harrison to relent in his position.

"Recent events in Boston naturally tend to clothe any clearly established claim upon a fugitive slave with deep interest to the people of every city and state in the Union. None support more staunchly than ourselves the right of a property owner, under the law of the land, to demand the arrest and return of a runaway.

"James Harrison, a respected gentleman and member of our community, has every legal right to the services of the returned fugitive, Michael Carter, or Mabaya, as we are told he now terms himself. We applauded the willingness of Mr. Harrison to journey to Boston to recover his runaway negro, and to assert his own rights, and the rights of all Southerners similarly situated.

"Having clearly asserted his legal rights, however, we would urge Mr. Harrison to relent in his stated determination to refuse all offers to purchase the recovered fugitive by abolitionists or their agents. It is clear from reports we have received from interested and respectable persons that Mabaya is a most uncommon negro indeed. It was with no little amazement that we learned that during his years at large, he has not only succeeded in passing a course of medical studies, but in becoming a recognized medical practitioner in the city of Boston.

"In point of fact, this negro man serves as the exception that proves the rule, to such an extent that he is no longer fitted for a return to service. It is a fact implicitly acknowledged by his master by his continued jailing of the negro, as well as by the disinclination of knowledgeable dealers in slaves to evidence the slightest interest in purchasing him.

"Under the circumstances, we aver that the proper course now is to temper 'justice with mercy.' We urge Mr. Harrison to accept the funds raised by the abolitionists for the purchase of his negro, and thus release Mabaya to return to his home and family."

Michael read the editorial through twice, praying that Harrison would be moved by its appeal.

He didn't have to wait long to learn Harrison's response. It came in the form of an irate letter printed in the *Gazette* two days later. He saw no reason to set an unfortunate precedent, Harrison wrote, by rewarding a fugitive negro for anything he might have done while unlawfully evading service. In any event, what he chose to do with his own property was none of the newspaper's concern.

There was no reason to let his disappointment deepen into despondency, Michael told himself. The campaign to enlist public support was gaining strength. Harrison would have to give in before long.

The *Gazette* editorial and Harrison's letter had been reprinted in the columns of *The National Era,* and within a few days were widely reprinted in Northern newspapers, along with open letters of appeal to Harrison penned by Michael's family as well as by the clergymen serving on the Vigilance Committee. Michael felt his eyes fill with tears as he read the pleading words of his wife and children.

"Our own pastor took Uncle James to task after church

last Sunday," David reported. He sighed. "I just pray it puts an end to his stubbornness. You don't know how hard this has been on Dad. I'm afraid for his health. I know he's not sleeping; I hear him walking around half the night.

"There's nothing I can say to him to raise his spirits. He just says he can't stop blaming himself for having put you in this position."

A petition drive, spearheaded by the *Liberator,* collected thousands of signatures within the span of the next few days, asking Harrison to reconsider.

It seemed impossible that Harrison could continue ignoring such strong appeals to conscience.

Michael's hopes were quickly dashed. Harrison's one response was to address another letter to the *Gazette.* He had no intention of changing his mind, he informed the editor, "whether ten or ten thousand abolitionist dupes attempt to force my hand into disposing of my property against my will."

The *Liberator* two days later ran David's drawing of Michael soberly penning a letter to his family, above the caption, "Is He a Man or a Thing?"

An accompanying appeal by Unitarian minister, Theodore Parker, called on men and women of conscience to shame Harrison out of his insistence on holding a man as property. Force the kidnapper into accepting a ransom of blood money, he urged, with a deluge of banknotes—dipped into blood, as a symbol that all mankind is of one blood, united in brotherhood under our Creator.

Michael read his words with little hope. If earnest appeals and petitions had no effect on Harrison, it seemed unlikely that Parker's scheme would. It was beginning to seem that nothing could change Harrison's mind.

Parker's plea appealed to the imagination of the public, though. To Michael's amazement, David reported that envelopes containing bloodstained one dollar bills were arriving

270

daily—addressed to James Harrison, in care of the town hall of Alexandria, Virginia.

Within a few days, the flow of "blood money" had increased from tens to hundreds of bills a day. The *Gazette* ran another editorial, urging Harrison more strongly to negotiate Michael's return North.

The city of Alexandria, and indeed the South as a whole, faced embarrassment through Harrison's obstinacy, the editorial writer stated. "Indeed, we fear that through his misplaced zeal, James Harrison has provided better fodder for the abolitionist extremists than any they could have provided on their own account."

Michael read the editorial carefully, praying that perhaps the Southern paper's words would reach Harrison this time. He read through it once more, ignoring the slam of the corridor door.

"Don't be too quick to gloat over that paper, boy. It's not about to get you out of here!"

Michael sprang up, staring back at Harrison. The silver haired man was smiling mockingly at him. Michael was filled with helpless rage, as he thought how the law of the United States gave this man absolute power over his life.

He hated to bring himself to plead with the man, but he couldn't afford letting any chance to change his mind pass by. "Mister Harrison, I have two little children, and my wife's about to have another baby. What gain is it to you to keep me like this? For God's sake, please take the money and let me go home!"

"So you miss your wife and children, do you? Well let me tell you, boy, you're not the only one to lose someone you love!" Michael stared in bewilderment as Harrison spoke, his voice losing its tone of cool mockery and filling with increasing rage.

"My sister might well be alive today if not for you! Your

abolitionist friends choose to send me 'blood money.' Well, my sister's blood is on your head, boy!"

Michael stared, dumbfounded. The man had gone crazy, he thought numbly. He could barely find his voice.

"Do you mean David's mother, sir? I was an infant when she died. How can you blame her death on me?"

"Yes, I mean David's mother, boy. My sister, Anne." For a second, Harrison's voice softened. "She raised me from the time our mother died, till she threw herself away on Carter. I tried telling her he wasn't half good enough for her, but she was too infatuated to listen.

"It didn't take her long to regret it, though." Harrison's voice roughened with anger again. "She suffered the pangs of childbirth to give him a son, and while she was still too weak to rise from her sickbed, Carter was fornicating with your mother in her own home.

"You think my sister didn't know how he was carrying on! She never regained her will to live, boy. And no wonder! How could she have lived down the shame of her husband's nigger bastard born and brought up under her own roof?

"He never even kept you in your place. He always took up for you when he should have given you a taste of the rawhide. Well, he can't protect you now, boy. You'll stay here till I find a purchaser who's not too squeamish to enjoy breaking a stubborn nigger."

Chapter 17

1851

David had good news, he told Michael a few hours later. The town council agreed with the Gazette's assessment of the situation. "They've just voted to refuse to rent space in the jail to Uncle James after the end of the week. That means he'll have to negotiate your release, Mike. There's nowhere else he could lock you up except one of the slave pens, and none of the dealers will agree to put you in with his negroes."

Michael shook his head, still numb from the confrontation with Harrison. "He's not in his right mind, David. He'll find some other way."

David remained unconvinced, he saw, despite his repetition of Harrison's words, but Michael lay sleepless that night, filled with anxiety over Harrison's threat. The man was out of his mind. No wonder he hadn't responded to any reasonable appeal. He was too bent on his senseless revenge.

He must have slept at last, he thought groggily the next morning. He came awake to the sound of the jailer's cheerful voice as he pushed his breakfast through the slot.

"Reckon you're glad to be gettin out of here, boy."

Michael looked at him in silent inquiry.

"Your master came first thing this mornin," the man continued. "He's made arrangements to ship you on a brig sailing for Savannah tomorrow. Says he reckons he'll sell you easier down there, away from all these ab'litionist doings." The jailer paused a second. "Reckon you'll be right glad to get out from behind bars and get yourself a new master."

He couldn't eat the breakfast. He sat slumped on the bench with his head in his hands, numb with helpless misery.

He could see that David was beginning to appreciate his plight, when he visited again a few hours later. David shook his head silently when Michael had finally ended his desperate flow of words.

"I've heard talk around town this morning that he means to take you down South. I wish to God there were something I could do, Mike."

"Can't you stop him? You're a lawyer. There must be something you can do!"

"I'm not much of a lawyer, Mike. I suppose Dad's already told you that." David smiled humorlessly. "But there's nothing I could do in any case. He hasn't done a thing that's unlawful. You know that."

He did know it. "I'm grasping at straws," Michael admitted. "But can't you at least talk to him?!"

David shook his head. "Don't you think I've tried, Mike? He won't speak to me anymore. I'm as helpless as you are."

Michael sat motionless after David had gone, too miserable to move. He thought bleakly for a moment of ending his life. But there was no means at hand, even if he could bring himself to such a deed.

He lowered his head into his hands again, trying to shut out the harsh sights and sounds of the prison, trying to escape even his own thoughts.

"Michael, here, take these!"

He stood, automatically reaching for the plate of biscuits the colored man outside the bars was pushing through the slot. He took another look at the tall, mahogany skinned man then.

"Ned!" Michael clasped his old friend's hand through the bars, managing a smile, "I'm glad to see you. Doctor Carter told me you'd bought your freedom."

Ned nodded. "Me and Marnetta and our young uns, we're all free now, thank the Lord. My daddy and me got our own shop over on Royal, and my oldest boy's already near as good a carpenter as me." He paused a second. "You were right about readin and figurin, Michael. I ain't never regretted learnin.

"That ain't why I come to see you, though." Ned lowered his voice. "I told the jailer Doctor Carter sent me with these here biscuits. Truth is, I was too feared of gettin into trouble to visit you fore now. But I been hearin talk around town that Mister Harrison's gettin ready to carry you down South to sell you.

"I been thinkin on it all mornin. Daddy and me done worked on this jailhouse when it was first put up." Ned lowered his voice even further.

"These here walls is solid, but that ceiling over your head ain't nothin but plaster laid over the subfloorin. Wouldn't take much to chisel through it and pull yourself up into the attic. They's two windows up there big enough to climb through. Get yourself some kinda rope, you could let yourself down to the street easy."

Michael thought frantically as Ned finished speaking, suddenly alive with hope. He'd need someone to help him make his way from the jail unseen, once he'd reached the street. He couldn't ask Ned to take any more chances helping him.

"I can't ever thank you enough, Ned!" He lowered his voice, too. "I'll need help in getting away. Could you find David and tell him I need to see him?" There was no one else he could ask.

Ned nodded. "I'll find Mister David just as soon as I leave here." He took Michael's hand once again. "I'll be prayin the Lord be with you, Michael."

Thank God night had finally come! Michael had thought the hours of waiting would never pass.

To his relief, David had quickly agreed to help him. A British ship would be sailing from Alexandria to Barbados in two days, David told him. Once Michael had broken out of jail, he was certain he could arrange his passage safely out of the country.

Michael nodded thankfully, whispering to David that he thought Benjamin Hallowell might be willing to give him refuge till then.

His task now, though, was to get himself out of this cell. Taking the penknife David had slipped him out of his pocket, Michael climbed onto the bench, putting himself in easy reach of the low ceiling. He jabbed the point of the knife into the plaster.

A shower of plaster dust fell in his face. He choked back a cough. He couldn't afford any unnecessary noise! He paused briefly to tie his handkerchief over his nose and mouth, then swiftly returned to work on the ceiling.

He quickly settled into a rhythm. Jab with the point of the knife. Scrape the loose chunks of plaster with the edge of his spoon. Jab with his right hand, scrape with his left. Jab and scrape. Jab and scrape.

An hour passed. The hole in the ceiling looked wide enough

to admit his shoulders. He stopped, examining the planks of the subflooring above his head.

Cautiously, Michael pushed up against the boards, testing each in turn. Rapping softly with his knuckles, he located the cross beam just above his head. Even more carefully then, he pried gingerly at the adjoining boards.

None of the boards gave way. He felt a quick rush of panic. Calm down, he admonished himself.

He pried once again at the plank closest to the cross beam, working the point of the penknife up and down the narrow crack. The board resisted another moment, then suddenly gave way.

Michael breathed with relief.

Working methodically then, he pried up one board after another, till the gap in the boards was wide enough to admit him. Piling the loose boards quietly to one side, he tested his weight on the beam a moment. It held him easily.

He slipped the penknife back in his pocket, then thrust his blanket through the hole in the ceiling, quickly pulling himself up after it. He wriggled cautiously along the beam, before pausing to catch his breath.

The attic was quiet except for the faint skittering of frightened mice disturbed in their nests. Moonlight entered faintly through the dusty windows. He reached for the blanket, brushing cobwebs off his hand.

Cutting the blanket at its edge made it easier to tear into strips. Michael tied them together, forcing himself to take the time to check each knot.

Making sure to keep his weight on the main beams then, he crawled carefully toward the nearest window. He pushed up on the sash. The window stuck, resisting his efforts.

Bracing himself, he pushed up on the window again. He winced at the noise as it gave way.

He heard no sound of alarm from the street below, though.

He sighed with relief once again.

Tying one end of his makeshift rope firmly to a rafter, he looked out the window. David would be waiting with a rented buggy under sheltering trees down the street, out of sight of the patrolling night watchman.

No one was in sight. Looking once more up and down Saint Asaph Street, Michael waved his handkerchief out the window in their prearranged signal. He waited for the buggy to start toward him before moving again, knowing David would wait till the time for the hourly patrol had passed.

Watching intently, he caught his first sight of the buggy as it started slowly toward the jail. Quickly, Michael pulled himself to the window sill, holding tightly to the rope with one hand. He hesitated a brief second, looking down at the sidewalk thirty feet below, then grasped the rope with both hands and lowered himself from the sill.

For a second he dangled precariously in space, then he brought his knees together in a tight grip on the rope. It was easy enough then to let himself down slowly, hand over hand. David had stepped from the buggy, draping the reins over the dashboard. He stood alongside the waiting horse, anxiously watching Michael's descent. Michael grinned at him with relief as he reached the ground.

"Stop right there, nigger!" A shot exploded overhead simultaneously with the shout. Michael gasped in disbelief as two nightwatchmen rounded the corner from Princess, a handcuffed prisoner in tow.

He couldn't be taken! He whirled, tensing his muscles to spring for the buggy. A second shot sounded, closer by. The horse bolted, racing up the street.

David was frozen with shock, Michael realized in horror. He yelled at him frantically to jump out of the way of the careening buggy.

It was too late. The front wheel smashed into David as the

horse continued its headlong flight. He fell backwards, striking his head heavily on the cobblestones. He lay still, unconscious.

Michael heard angry shouts drawing closer as he knelt by David, trying desperately to determine the extent of his injury. He breathed a small sigh of relief as he felt his pulse.

Thank God he was still alive!

Rough hands grabbed Michael then. He tried to shake them off. "Let me examine him! I'm a doctor!"

The policemen paid no attention to his plea as they dragged him into the jail.

The jailer looked at him bitterly as he locked him into manacles again. "Thought I could count on you to behave yourself. Look at the mess you made of this cell!" The man spat in disgust. "You gone crazy, boy? I'll be right s'prised if your master don't ask the constable to give you a good whipping when he comes tomorrow."

Michael tried not to think about the man's words. "Where is David? What have you done with him?"

The jailer stared at him in silence.

"Mister Carter. Where is he?"

"Downstairs in a cell, where he belongs. He oughta be shamed, helpin you bust out like this."

Michael shook his head despairingly. "He's hurt! He needs to be under the care of a doctor."

The jailer gave him another look. "I already sent for the doctor."

He couldn't calm down. He shuffled up and down the cell, the fetters heavy on his ankles.

The thick walls kept out sounds from the cells below. There was no way to tell how David was faring. The moments seemed endless to Michael as he paced, the memory of David's still body on the cobblestones vivid before his eyes.

He'd been so sure he'd found a way out of his plight at last!

The only result was to leave David wounded or worse. He closed his eyes, trying to pray.

The sound of the corridor door opening at last brought him rushing to the bars, gripping them tightly as his eyes searched the passageway.

The jailer unlocked his cell. The constable with him had his gun drawn and at the ready.

"The doctor claims his son is hurt bad, needs some kinda op'ration if he's gonna live. Says his hands're shakin too bad to do it himself. He says I should bring you to help him."

The jailer gave him a look of angry suspicion. "Don't think you're gonna get away with another trick, hear! The officer here's gonna have his gun right on you."

Michael nodded quickly, trying to control his impatience as the jailer freed him from the fetters, his heart pounding as he followed him downstairs.

The cell was identical to his own. David lay motionless on the bench, his father kneeling at his side.

Doctor Carter's voice shook. "His skull's fractured. He has no chance at all if the pressure on his brain isn't relieved. I can't hold a scalpel steady anymore. But you've become a better doctor than me, anyhow."

Michael couldn't take time to talk. He knelt at Doctor Carter's side, his fingers smoothing David's hair away from the depressed bone at the back of his head.

He turned quickly to the jailer. "I'll need as good a lamp as you have, and a stool to set it on. And clean water and soap to wash with."

The jailer gave him an aggrieved look, but left abruptly, returning with the items a few minutes later.

Doctor Carter was fumbling with the latch of his surgical kit. Michael touched his hand a second, before moving to open the kit. "He hasn't been unconscious long. He has a good chance of recovering."

280

The sooner the fractured section of bone could be removed, the better his chances would be.

Michael quickly clipped the hair away from the injured area with a pair of surgical scissors. Using the scalpel then, he cut through the skin of David's scalp around three sides of the fracture, wiping away the seeping blood with a clean cloth. He set the scalpel down, picking up the trephine saw, as Doctor Carter shakily held the flap of cut skin back from his son's skull.

He heard the jailer's quick, indrawn breath behind him, then he blocked out everything but the task at hand.

Centering the small round saw over the cracked section of cranium, he pressed steadily till the sharp serrated edges penetrated the bone. Slowly and steadily, he rotated the instrument.

Thirty minutes passed as he continued sawing steadily through the bone. He slowed the trephine's rotation as the teeth dug farther into David's skull, painfully aware of the danger of accidentally cutting into the membrane that protected the brain.

The circle of bone loosened slightly. Michael slowly started withdrawing the saw, pressing gently against the bony disk to loosen it further. He set the saw aside then, pressing lightly with his fingertips at one edge of the bone. The edge lifted slightly. With infinite care, he removed the plug of bone.

He breathed a sigh of relief as he saw the membrane, swollen but intact. Doctor Carter's fingers trembled as he released his hold on the cut skin. Working quickly again, Michael sutured the flap of skin back into place.

There was nothing else to do but wait and pray.

The jailer and constable had retreated to the corridor outside the cell. The jailer looked pale and shaken as he took a step toward Michael. "You done op'ratin?"

Michael looked up. "I'm not leaving him."

"Reckon you might as well stay here then." The jailer hurriedly padlocked the cell, leaving them alone.

Michael felt David's pulse repeatedly during the next few hours, taking heart each time he found it strong and steady. David's breathing was even as well, though he'd showed no signs yet of regaining consciousness.

He'd be all right, Michael told himself. The pressure on his brain was relieved; infection was the only danger now. He bowed his head, praying for David's recovery.

Doctor Carter sat hunched on the stool next to his son. An occasional tremor shook his body.

Michael looked at him with pity. "His vital signs are strong. It's bound to be a while till he recovers consciousness," he said gently.

The older man looked up. He was weeping silently, Michael saw. "I pray to God you're right, Michael."

He paused, his voice trembling. "I always let him know he was a disappointment to me. I never even told him I love him."

"I'm sure he knows you do, sir." Michael let his hand rest gently on Doctor Carter's shoulder a moment. "But you can tell him now, when he wakes."

Doctor Carter shook his head. "I just pray the Lord doesn't take my son from me." His voice broke. "All those years, run out—like blood into the bleeding basin."

Michael pressed his shoulder again. "There's still years ahead."

David stirred. His eyes opened. He looked around, dazedly. "Dad? What—?" His whispered words broke off.

He had no memory of the accident, Michael saw. "You hit your head on the cobblestones, but you're going to be all right. How do you feel?"

"My head . . . It hurts— I'm— I'm sick—" Michael held

his head as he vomited abruptly.

It seemed to relieve him. He closed his eyes, sinking into unconsciousness again.

It was dawn before he woke. The nausea had abated. Michael felt a deep sense of relief as David took a few sips of water. He lay back again, holding his father's hand as he drifted off to sleep.

Michael brushed back stray strands of David's hair—matted with dried blood from the scalp incision—to check the sutures, then listened carefully to David's deep, even breathing. He took his pulse once again, then rested wearily on the floor, suddenly and thankfully certin that David's recovery would be complete.

The jail door slammed. Michael started, brought back to renewed awareness of their plight.

He could hear the jailer's worried voice over the sounds of rapidly approaching footsteps. The key turned in the lock and the cell door opened.

James Harrison pushed his way in ahead of the jailer. He froze, staring at the scene, then his words burst forth, shrill with anguish. "David! Oh, my God! You've killed him!"

Michael stared in surprise as he scrambled to his feet. "He's not—"

Harrison struck him across the face, cutting off his words. His head rocked back with the force of the blow as he struggled to keep his balance.

"You've killed him, you damn nigger bastard!"

Shaken, Michael glanced behind him at David's still form. He lay deeply asleep, his quiet breathing nearly imperceptible.

Michael breathed deeply himself, as he started to face Harrison again. Without warning, the man's arm caught him across the windpipe, cutting off his breath. He gasped, half choking, struggling to bring his own arm up to free himself.

"Don't make a move, boy!"

283

Michael froze, feeling the barrel of Harrison's revolver shoved firmly against his temple. The sound of the gun being cocked filled his ears.

"You'd better say your prayers, boy, before I shoot you."

There was no question that he meant it. Michael stood motionless, weak with fear.

Sounds seemed to reach him from afar. He was vaguely aware of the jailer's voice from the passageway. "Hey, you can't just shoot him, even if he ain't nothin but a nigger."

Harrison ignored the man. "You saying your prayers, boy?"

Michael forced his panic down, trying to talk to the man. "You're wrong. I didn't—"

The gun barrel slammed against the side of his face. He fell silent, ill with pain and fear.

He heard Doctor Carter's pleading voice. "James, for heaven's sake, David would have died if he didn't operate. He's not—"

"Shut your mouth, George!" Harrison's half-crazed voice drowned out the rest of Carter's words. The man was beyond reason, Michael realized numbly.

The gun was at Michael's head again as Harrison continued. "You can't help him now, George. You should've rid yourself of him the day he was born. It didn't matter to you at all that Anne died on his account, did it?"

"James! Come to your senses!" Doctor Carter's voice was shaking almost too much to understand. "It's me your grievance is with, not him. He's done nothing to wrong you."

Harrison's voice was even. "He killed your son, George."

"They're both my sons! For God's sake, James, they're both my sons!" Doctor Carter was shaking with sobs, unable to continue.

"Your son! Your bastard, you mean." Harrison laughed shortly. "You always thought of him as your son, didn't you? You were even so damn proud to discover he'd followed in your foorsteps. Well, it's not going to save him, George."

Michael tensed, still sick with terror. Harrison's arm pressed harder against his windpipe, choking off his feeble attempts at struggle. He felt the gun move against his temple. Harrison's finger was on the trigger now, he knew. He closed his eyes in desperation, praying for God's mercy.

"Uncle James!" David's voice was so weak, Michael couldn't be sure he'd heard it. He could feel Harrison loosen his grip on him, though, his eyes swinging to David.

"For God's sake, Uncle James, drop the gun!"

Harrison stared another second, releasing Michael abruptly. The gun slipped from his fingers, falling loudly to the floor.

Michael stood still, too limp with relief to move, watching dazedly as Harrison dropped to his knees beside his nephew.

"Michael!" He turned at Doctor Carter's cry. The man was still shaking with sobs. He was on the verge of collapse, Michael saw.

He moved quickly to catch him in his arms. He held him close then, rocking him gently like one of his children. He felt his father's arms encircle him in turn, clutching him as he wept.

They stood holding each other a long moment. The elderly man's sobs finally eased a bit. Michael held him another moment, then helped him to a seat on the stool.

David was talking to his uncle, his words inaudible to Michael. Harrison nodded slowly, fishing paper and pencil from David's jacket and starting to write at his nephew's direction.

"Dad." David's whisper was weak but insistent. "Give him a dollar."

Michael stared, bewildered. Sudden understanding filled him with grateful relief then as Doctor Carter pulled a banknote from his pocket with trembling fingers, shakily signing his name to the bill of sale.

David lay back, smiling faintly, as the constable and jailer affixed their signatures witnessing the transaction. There'd be no charges brought under the circumstances, the constable quickly assured him. He'd see he had assistance carrying his son home, he added to Doctor Carter.

The doctor nodded thankfully. "I'd be grateful for your signatures witnessing a deed of manumission as well. I'm long overdue in granting my other son his freedom."

Epilogue

1851

He'd sent the good news to Rachel over the telegraph wires. If he left now, he could catch the afternoon train from Washington city for the first leg of his journey home. His old friends—Ned, Marnetta, Cassie an their families—were waiting to accompany him to the ferry.

Michael looked around once more. It was strange to return as a son and brother to the house where he'd spent his childhood as a slave. There wasn't time to dwell on it now, though.

David was resting comfortably in bed, his improvement continuing as Michael bid him goodbye, examining him for the last time.

"You've got to see that no dirt gets into his sutures," he cautioned Doctor Carter.

The older man nodded impatiently. "I'm not totally

ignorant, Michael."

He smiled. "I know you're not, sir."

Doctor Carter embraced him quickly. "Michael, will I see you again, son?"

"I'm sure you will." Michael returned his embrace, hesitating a moment before speaking again. "Come for a longer visit when David's recovered. I'd like my children to get to know their other grandfather."